# A SMALL DARK QUIET

# About the Author

Miranda Gold is a writer based in London. Her first novel, *Starlings*, published by Karnac in December 2016, reaches back through three generations to explore how the impact of untold stories about the Holocaust ricochets down the years. Before turning her focus to fiction, Miranda took the Soho Theatre Course for young writers, where her play, *Lucky Deck*, was selected for development and performance. *A Small Dark Quiet* is her second novel.

# A SMALL DARK QUIET

MIRANDA GOLD

This edition first published in 2018

Unbound

6th Floor Mutual House, 70 Conduit Street, London W1S 2GF

www.unbound.com



ISBN (eBook): 978-1-912618-83-5

ISBN (Paperback): 978-1-912618-82-8

Design by Mecob

Printed in Great Britain by Clays Ltd, Elcograf S.p.A.

*For my father*

Dear Reader,

The book you are holding came about in a rather different way to most others. It was funded directly by readers through a new website: Unbound.

Unbound is the creation of three writers. We started the company because we believed there had to be a better deal for both writers and readers. On the Unbound website, authors share the ideas for the books they want to write directly with readers. If enough of you support the book by pledging for it in advance, we produce a beautifully bound special subscribers' edition and distribute a regular edition and e-book wherever books are sold, in shops and online.

This new way of publishing is actually a very old idea (Samuel Johnson funded his dictionary this way). We're just using the internet to build each writer a network of patrons. Here, at the back of this book, you'll find the names of all the people who made it happen.

Publishing in this way means readers are no longer just passive consumers of the books they buy, and authors are free to write the books they really want. They get a much fairer return too – half the profits their books generate, rather than a tiny percentage of the cover price.

If you're not yet a subscriber, we hope that you'll want to join our publishing revolution and have your name listed in one of our books in the future. To get you started, here is a £5 discount on your first pledge. Just visit unbound.com, make your pledge and type SMALLDARK18 in the promo code box when you check out.

Thank you for your support,

Dan, Justin and John

Founders, Unbound

# Super Patrons

Ros Abramsky
Francesca Alberry
Gunilla Assmundson
Michelle Austen-Marriott
David Baillie
Joanne Baird
David Baker
Harvey Bard
Jeremy Baum
Melissa Beck
Julian Birch
Stephanie Bretherton
Arvid Brobeck
Anthony Brown
Kate Catch
Anne Cater
Tony Chan
Frank W Chapman
David Clifford
John Cohen
Simon Cohen
Henry Cohn
Vera Coleman
Joe Collman
Jeffrey Collman
Tamsen Courtenay
Ian Critchley
Flora Crowder
Annabelle Daiches
Rachael de Moravia
Jessica Duchen
Rosie Eleanor Canning

Paul Elster
Anisa Fakhro
Angela Fakhro
Fatima Fatima
Karen Featherstone
Charles Fernyhough
Gail Flesch
Susie Foottit
Miranda France
Evelyn Friedlander
Ariel Friedlander
Angela Gabriela Horne
Ally Gipps
Matt Gold
Rozalind Gold
Willow & Sidney Gold
Mel Goldberg
Alec Goldin
Howard Goldsobel
Anthony Goldstein
Anita Goveas
Anthony Gover
Lucille Grant
Steve Haines
Matthew Harragin
Anna Hart
stuart Hazeldine
David Hebblethwaite
Denise Hooker
Chris Howe
Jennifer Jankel
Alice Jolly
Sarah Jones
Ellie Jones
Michael Joseph
Ann Keable

Richard Kelsey
Dan Kieran
Maddy Klein
Anders Krag
Gogo Lamb
Sally Ann Law
Sara Levy
Caroline Levy
Frances Levy
Julia Levy
Kenneth Levy
Roger Lewis
Leslie Lipert
Nikki Livingstone-Rothwell
Jacqui Lofthouse
Pana McGee
Carole McIntosh
Catherine McNamara
Jennifer McVeigh
Jonathan Metliss
John Mitchinson
Martine Montgomery
Indu Muralidharan
Lisa Murphy
Sebastian Murray
Adrian Naftalin
Robert Nash
Carlo Navato
V R B Neat
David Neill
Jill Nicholls
Jason 1
Charles Palliser
Lev Parikian
Harry Patel
Anna Payne

Poppy Peacock
Kate Pemberton
Hugo Perks
Erica Phillips
Sushi Phillips
Justin Pollard
Alex Preston
Sylvia Pryor Nicol
Montserrat Robinson
Jeremy Robson
Carole Robson
Manuela Robson
Gordon Rustin
Adrian Sacco
Dinah Senior
Rachel Shirley
Natalie Silver
Adam Simmonds
Michael Simon
Seth Sinclair
Jeffrey Sloneem
Jeremy Solnick
Tony Stalbow
Katarzyna Stawarz
Ronald Stern
Margaret Stone
Edward Stonehill
Matt Storey
Dorian Stuber
Bart Terblanche
Robert Turner
Kerstin Twachtmann
Vlad Vexler
Sara Walden
Edgar Wallner
Richard Watson

Charlotte Weatherley
Valerie Webb
Valerie West
Trudy White
Laura Wilkinson
Daniel Williams
Hyman Wolanski
Meike Ziervogel

With grateful thanks to Edgar Wallner who helped to make this book happen.

# Part One

Had both of the twins made it out of the womb alive there wouldn't have been a name and a life going spare. The name was Arthur and the life waiting to be filled had been made in the shape of a proper little English man – a proper little English man and a proper little soldier.

*March 1945*

Harry looked different in Mrs Cohen's arms – he looked how a baby was meant to look. Sylvie's eyes turned from the tiny puckered face that had absorbed Mrs Cohen's gaze, listening to the shush dusting the silence it kept. Just Harry's breath starting to slow now, slowing Sylvie's with it, an invisible cord winding her back to him again for the first time since he'd been born. She'd carried twin heartbeats, twin boys, but it was only Harry who came screaming his rude health into the world, slick with her loss. Harry and Arthur, tucked round each other, named the day Mrs Cohen cracked the first egg of the year into the pan and proclaimed a double yolk was a sign.

As Sylvie fell back onto the bed, two cold buds, one in her pelvis, one in her heart, tightened against the spring. The winter hadn't been as fierce this year, but, just as London's bones seemed to be beginning to thaw, Sylvie felt a second frost take hold.

*Good boy,* she mouthed in time with Mrs Cohen, *such a good boy,* finding a stillness in repetition until a gulp of air shook the rhythm and Sylvie flinched back into her own skin. Mrs Cohen's gentleness settling Harry filled the room, unlocking Sylvie's throat, hands, hips, letting her rock forward –

*Such a good –*

Her closing eyes opened at once by the pressure against the empty swell of her abdomen.

'Let's put this little mite down now, shall we?' Mrs Cohen said. Sylvie bent her head, sight glazed over her knees, the nod that was meant for Mrs Cohen slipping unseen towards the floor. She pulled her chin in to her throat, sliding it hard across her clavicles as Harry's cry began its crescendo – stop, it had to stop, before that cry unleashed her own.

*When the bough breaks –*

Sylvie followed Mrs Cohen –

*The cradle will –*

Hearing herself aloud stopped her – was that her? It had been five days since her voice had been made to carry words. Five days that had left Sylvie behind in the body just split to the absence of Arthur, Harry's collection of sticky limbs slapped against her, his chest fluttering with new breath and rich blood, but alien-cold without –

*Arthur,* she'd called out, *where are you taking my –*

Then bringing Harry home, passing the gashed city by – it was as though a mask had been dropped over her face, the air enough to choke her. She'd just wanted to get them into the house, cough London out of her lungs and breathe Harry in, breathe in whatever of Arthur might still be held in Harry's skin – but, soon as she got inside, Harry's head nuzzling between her neck and her shoulder, her throat closed. Couldn't answer the door that evening, Mrs Cohen's knock –

*Go away, couldn't she just go away?*

She'd sat with Mrs Cohen most evenings from the day Gerald was called up till the day she'd gone into labour. Mrs Cohen was always getting little extras for Sylvie; she'd known she was expecting before Sylvie did, reading Sylvie's squeezed eyes and hands as fear that Gerald wouldn't come back, rather than the fear that he would: the man who arrived home on leave never seemed to know her any more than she knew him – a little less of him returned each time, blotting out who each of them had been. She could almost hear Gerald's voice in his first letters home, reminding her of the jugglers and tricksters that had sprung up in the dark that night they'd been caught in the crowd. The gathering roar of the city had seemed to melt under the sound of a flute rising and the voice of a flower girl calling –

*Violets. Lovely sweet violets –*

The flower girl had wished them luck, her hand tight round the florin Gerald had given her, and Sylvie had looked back but Gerald was already moving into the gauzy light streaming through an arch, beckoning for Sylvie to follow, their silhouettes thrown by a lantern swinging in the alley, those backstreets empty but for the boys playing marbles and a night porter's step – yes, of course – then what? Swallowed back up by the throng again, making it to the theatre just before the curtain went up and Sylvie humming the tune of the last song all the way to the river. They'd soon be having their walks by the river again, Gerald had said – she hadn't forgotten, had she, that evening over London Bridge? No, she hadn't forgotten – and for a moment the thought was enough to staunch the dread that crept up to the bedside each morning. But whatever echo of her husband she heard on the page was lost as soon as he came through the door: his eyes reaching past her, his few words, sharp and sudden, equal to silence. Somehow the odd tumbler knocked off the table or the box of records they'd collected kicked across the floor let her breathe, drawing the gasp that was just enough to cut the air thick with what was left unsaid. Gerald's mother had counselled Sylvie not to ask questions, to be attentive but not intrusive, bright but not loud. Articles snipped from magazines advised how best to placate the returning soldier – but Sylvie, just watching the clock tick until his leave was up, found herself bargaining with a God she'd never believed in to get her through each night without waking to the urgent burn of Gerald inside her.

'You're quite sure they're his?' Gerald's mother had asked, not waiting for a response. 'Well as long as they come out white.'

Sylvie wasn't sure she wanted them to come out at all – until one didn't and then the want opened, widened, until it was all she was. Sleeplessness had made the days bleed into each other – it was only Mrs Cohen's knock that struck an interval. Three times a day that knock, each hatching the same thought from collapsed time: if she slipped out just as Mrs Cohen came in, left Harry there, found Arthur…

*Good boy, such a –*

'Sylvie dear!'

Mrs Cohen, blurred by Sylvie's eyes, had taken her hand, insisting its warmth be accepted, careful not to sound anything but practical, crisp. Only to bring a bite, she'd said, quite sure Sylvie was managing just splendidly. But Mrs Cohen couldn't do crisp, gliding down the hall, swiftly unpacking her string bag in the kitchen before going up to Harry, smiling as she lifted him from his cot.

'Precious little…'

*Precious little –*

Not without Arthur. She had to send Harry back into her body, find his brother, so that she could know them both. They'd taken her Arthur away before she'd held him but, dead or alive, her arms cradled the shape he might have taken.

Should count y'self lucky, the midwife had said when Sylvie asked where they'd taken her Arthur, you've still got the one, war's taken all my boys.

Lucky Sylvie. Well it could take her too. Let it have her. Be best for Harry if it took him as well. And Gerald. What had it all been for? Rushing for cover under a molten sky, the frantic hands of strangers dragging her down into the shelter, all only to wait for the same again. There was, of course, no interest in what would have been freely given. Aunt Cynthia had been right, should never have come to London –

*London eats girls like you alive –*

Others it might, Sylvie had thought, kissing Aunt Cynthia goodbye, but not her.

If only it had, swallowed her whole before she'd met Gerald and brought children into a world that wasn't made for children – is that what Arthur had understood? When the war had made a hell out of the skies and a pot-luck limbo out of the earth, the only heaven was underground.

Sylvie reached for her shoes, stretching them before she forced her feet in, Mrs Cohen whispering as Sylvie got up –

'Are you alright, dear? Where are you going? Sylvie dear –'

Harry's cry, gathering force, was only steps away, but it felt distant, as though it was coming through the wireless. Mrs Cohen was calling after her now – her coat, where had she put – never mind that, she'd do without it, only be a minute or two –

'Sylvie dear, the baby—'

Mrs Cohen's voice only quickened Sylvie's step, legs taking her on: up Llanvanor, on to the Finchley Road and into the park, not stopping until she reached the bandstand. She went a little further, paused by a branch of white buds nodding in the wind. She picked off a handful and scattered them, kneeled and pressed a cheek into the ground until a child's shout shook her into the cooling light. She didn't feel the rain begin to spit, only saw the first spots bleed into the petals that hadn't been turned and carried by the wind. That child's shout again. How long since she'd heard it? Weeks, maybe even months – certainly not since – but listen, yes – a laugh in it now too – a flurry of notes, high and light and clear. The wet petals seemed to be dissolving into the grass. *Wait for me!* the child called out, running, tripping, his hand on his tin hat. The image, unchanged, had become as familiar to her as the rhythm of the twins' kicks, appearing every time she felt her boys' insistent fists and feet. Queuing up at the grocer's the first time, digging around in her bag for the green ration book she'd been given. Never liked to get the book out, the way eyes would glance from the book to her belly pushing against the buttons of her coat, and then the comments, the advice, a look, distaste or concern or envy. Pregnancy had divested her of discretion and identity: a body to be prodded and measured by visiting midwives; an exhibit to be appraised and critiqued by the bored, the impatient, the wise. A woman in the queue had commented that Sylvie was *doing her bit* and gave her a wink. *One in the eye for Hitler,* she'd said. It must have been the closest she'd felt to patriotism – but it wasn't patriotism. She'd given an inward wink to each of the boys: *two in the eye,* she'd thought. No, that wasn't patriotism, it was her own dazzled sense of herself carrying two grand boys, inhabiting the body that had felt obscene and foreign moments before, making her native to the tiny world she was – and there, in that instant outside time, the only space was the shelter she gave and the shelter she took – but, just as she allowed herself to sink and settle, she found herself displaced: *not this world, it wasn't a world made for children.*

Remembering now how the boy in the tin hat had seemed to rush up to her and tug at her sleeve just as she felt Arthur test a foot inside her. *Be patient, Arthur!* she'd said, looking round to answer the tug, only to feel instead the relay of glances along the queue. *No telling with some,* came a mutter that encouraged others. Eyes down till she reached the counter, trying to make sense of the tug, verifying the identity of a foetal clench of fingers.

It had only ever been the one boy she'd seen, never two – and it was the same in that dream she had: pushing the pram up to the bandstand, the baby's face cut from glass shattered in a raid, the skin shredded and the face just a crying wound. Couldn't go back to sleep after that, just stood outside the room that would be for the boys, the blacked out windows not letting her know how long it would be before the morning came to dim the fear of what she'd seen. She'd find a reason why she needed to go over to Mrs Cohen's, always wishing she'd tidied herself up a bit. She'd spend as long as she could pretending to absorb herself in the patterns Mrs Cohen had swapped, eyes caught by the needles crossing and clicking.

'You mustn't fret, Sylvie. A worried brow won't do the babies any good. Remember what Lord Woolton says?'

Lord Woolton's cheery lines on the wireless, parroted by everyone, never leave her head now:

*Welcome Little Stranger.*

Sylvie didn't mind it so much when Mrs Cohen said it, but the click and cross of the needles kept catching her – no, no she would never do that – and it was only the blasts and the brawls and the throng of useless songs meant to drown out the sound of wasted lives – only that, not her. She'd known a girl who'd done it – only fifteen, could understand now how desperate she must have felt, how trapped. Everyone found out, whispering what a whore she was, some not even bothering to whisper at all. Terrible thing was it didn't even work. Local prophets cast the all-seeing eye: a girl born to a tart like that would come to no good. Aunt Cynthia had said they should pray for her. She was hidden away somewhere, which was probably for the best, some home for unmarried mothers. People didn't talk here like they did in Maldon, but they talked all the same. The little one must be six or seven by now. No, she wouldn't dare do it herself – she couldn't bring herself to. The girl seemed almost courageous to her in that moment. Was cowardice all that was stopping her? It was too late anyway.

Unbearable to think now that she might have wanted to get rid of them – how the sight of the needles had slid straight into the image of herself holding them between her legs, not even a breath as she stabbed – the violence of it so detached, so sudden. Thought so tangible it might be as brutal as the act itself – couldn't have been enough to take her Arthur, no of course not, ridiculous, smacked of the whispering gossipers back in Maldon. Yet the boys did seem to anticipate her fear before she felt it – their turning more restless, restless but weak – and she seemed to hear their jagged pulses –

*Welcome little –*

Would it have been love to have welcomed them into this? Into an ashen world that had to keep hoping because hope was all that was left.

Sylvie tried to pick the flecks of white still visible against the green, barely able to feel the grass beneath her – and there, for an instant, she felt as though she might have caught the flight of those high, clear notes. The sound drew her eyes up but the image of the boy in the tin hat wouldn't hold, his outlines dissolving, making him as far and unreal as he was – Arthur's laughing shadow. She looked over towards the gates and, securing a point of reference, saw again the automated steps she must have taken here – it was as though her legs had walked her away from the house. The sequence, returning to her in disordered fragments, resisted continuity until she could grasp how each action had given way to the next – leaving Harry in Mrs Cohen's arms, down the stairs, out the door and straight to the park, no intention or direction necessary –

*No not this world, this wasn't a world made for –*

Cheek pressed against the ground again and closed eyes that wouldn't cry made her retrace her steps from Llanvanor –

*Sylvie dear, you've left the door – Sylvie the –*

Harry, she'd left –

Mrs Cohen was lulling him as Sylvie came in, rocking from one foot to another, stopping as her eyes met Sylvie's, teeth pulling in her lip, 'Oh Sylvie, your face,' fingertips touching the cheek Sylvie had pressed into the ground.

'Gerald's mother will be round soon,' Sylvie said, turning, 'I need to get started on the washing.'

'I'm right here if you need anything.' Mrs Cohen's hand opened towards Sylvie, a falling leaf for an instant suspended. 'Do take care, Sylvie dear, do.'

Sylvie dug her knuckles into her eyes, slapped her face, and went to the window to see Mrs Cohen standing at the end of her front lawn, back to waiting for the post that would never come. Only the letters and parcels sent back. There must be some confusion, she used to tell Sylvie, the War Office mixed things up all the time. She'd waved the telegram at Sylvie three years after it was dated and asked her how they could make mistakes like this. Mrs Cohen's husband had been taken from her before the war had even begun; the Lord, Mrs Cohen was sure, would never let her son be taken from her as well. Her hand would float over the mantelpiece and she'd be wondering aloud how she would tell her boy what had happened to his father. She'd never have to now.

Sylvie closed the curtains and watched Harry's face scrunch and redden, touching it for traces of Arthur.

*

People would come to speak of two Londons: one gutted and one singing. Sylvie had found herself in each, straddled them, yet she struggled now to recall either. Dimly aware of the bodies trapped under rubble and talking to a woman, holding her hand until the stretcher came; of the jitterbug that had danced round her one night – yes, the ladies in the shelter had taught her, packed in as they were, and drafted her into their world. A gentleman had warned them not to excite a lady in her *condition.* The ladies' cheeks had pinched, laughter held in check until the gentleman's back was turned. Sylvie couldn't resist mimicking him, to hell if he heard, she'd said as the ladies covered their mouths and snuck glances in his direction, the ageless glee of midsummer fairies flushing their faces. *Oh you should be an actress,* one said. *No chance of that now,* another said, her eyes, mellowing, on Sylvie's belly – she had squeezed her hand then, holding it for a moment longer, pressing warmth into her palm as though it might be something Sylvie could carry with her.

But then, from Harry's birth to Arthur's death the arc of life was crossed at once. Empty cradle had been twinned with empty grave and took all sense from the body she'd have to live in, from the city she was meant to call home.

The last all clear wouldn't sound for another week and, while infant heads and hands and feet were blown from tiny bodies rendered nameless, Sylvie forged a tiny corpse of her own. Binding sticks and twigs, lined with moss and stuffed with stones, she wove her Arthur into deathless life and laid him in the ground, piling the warmth of the earth over him, planting him in a second womb. We'll visit, she promised, every Thursday.

## *June 1947*

Sylvie crouched and turned up the sleeves of the boy's coat to find his hands and took one between both of hers. The boy lifted the face he'd buried into his chest just enough for her to see that it was all creases and caverns. It seemed to contain more lives than a single face could hold, as many as the journeys he'd taken. Sylvie clasped the hand in hers a little tighter as though it might still the tremor that crossed his eyelids – the twitch of a moth's wings unable to close. His biography was studded with gaps and conjectures, linked by the gates he'd been bundled through, the arms that had carried him, the shifting borders he'd crossed, the wheels that had halted over a patchwork of wastelands peopled by spectres emerging to speak for the dead. Two years since he'd been delivered from an underworld that was cant to have no exit, two years of strange eyes and new voices.

'I'm to be your Ma,' she told him. The boy dipped his face again but let her keep his hand, his black eyes on her knees until, crouching too, they found their way up to hers. 'And you,' she said, 'are to be Arthur.'

'He's a bit small,' Gerald said, 'a bit small and a bit dark – he'll never match up with Harry.'

Quiet too, Sylvie thought. No, he never would match up. All there seemed to be to make the boy and Harry a pair was the age they shared. Not a day apart. It wasn't possible, Sylvie had said, the pen she'd been given to sign with falling out of her hand, the sharp black marks numbering the date on the form seeming to move again. She reminded herself it must have been estimated, maybe even just filled in at the last minute, one day might be as good as any other. Numbers had been rounded off, ages approximated. Even that morning, taking out a second set of sheets and towels, the child that had begun to take shape in Sylvie's mind remained a composite: the faces of toddlers snapped for the *Sunday Pictorial*, clutching stuffed bears, sitting cross-legged in a circle round the matron playing the harmonica – the constriction Sylvie had felt in her throat though, undeniable, that moment when Gerald's mother had unfolded the paper and laid it in front of Sylvie, urging her to turn to the next page –

*This is a story about children, anybody's children.*

Over a year since she'd seen the caption, but the imprint it left was visceral, while the report written to sponsors appealing for funds and all those whispers, relayed from committee members to Gerald's mother to Sylvie, had barely touched her, too carefully varnished in Gerald's mother's voice. Sylvie recalled that Tuesday morning she'd sat opposite the child welfare officer, her head clamouring with the instructions from Gerald's mother – and yet still the boy hardly seemed to take life beyond the latest scrap of knowledge she'd managed to assimilate – just that he was one of a possible thousand orphans to be granted entry into Britain.

The child welfare officer, blinking behind her wire-rimmed spectacles, had licked a finger and flicked through the file on the table, saying it wasn't only the youngest whose names and birthdays had been allotted, some of the ones old enough to speak might be too frightened to say, others couldn't remember. *Of course, of course,* Sylvie had murmured, trying to hold the child welfare officer's eye. It was as though their histories had been erased, Sylvie had said to Gerald later, her arms suddenly weak as she lifted Harry from his bath. *Tabulae rasae,* Gerald had said. He'd started walking away then – *records had been scattered*, he reminded her, *destroyed, blanks left pending* –

Too small. Too dark. Too quiet.

Yet the less the boy matched up to Harry the more he seemed, at least to Sylvie, to fit the life that had died inside her, that she had felt shrivel while Harry grew and grew.

Still, Gerald promised Sylvie, he'd make a proper little Englishman out of him: a proper little Englishman, a proper little soldier and a proper little Arthur.

Sylvie had prepared herself to assume the role of mother – nothing more. A role she would play with the same indifference as she played wife. But then, the boy in front of her, seeing him take in his new world inch by inch, his eyes beginning to chart the ground just beyond his feet – this tiny act of courage, small and quiet as the boy himself – drew Sylvie to take his hand, and the veil of indifference had shown itself to be threadbare. Gerald's eye checked her: *What was best for proper little soldiers?*

Sylvie's fingers straightened, a hardened palm across her belly: proper little soldiers needed efficiency, a firm hand and firm tone, and being pulled under by the touch of him, the quiet of him, wasn't going to make a proper little soldier out of anyone – least of all her. And she had to be. No one was getting out of the army now.

Gerald glanced Sylvie over with a casual efficiency that peeled back her tone: 'Bath, dinner, bed.' The boy's head disappeared between his knees, his arms wrapped round them, a prickle-skinned ball as Sylvie's hand reached to touch his shoulder.

'Maybe he's deaf,' Gerald suggested.

'I think he's tired,' Sylvie said, standing back. 'We should try and get him upstairs.'

Gerald picked Arthur up and laid him on the mattress next to Harry's bed. It seemed as though he handled the child with the same vague irritation that accompanied the mechanical duty with which he wielded garden tools. But he had lifted his hand to the back of the boy's neck then, holding it there as he sighed and closed his eyes, opening them as soon as Sylvie reached to touch his arm. He straightened, nodded, saying he'd leave Sylvie to it, that he had things to do.

'Gerald—'

'Not now, Sylvie.'

And not later. Again she'd seen the instant before the General gave way to the man – and Gerald couldn't forgive her for seeing that.

Sylvie bent over the curled child, lowering a hand that didn't yet dare touch his cheek. A single glint in the half-darkness of the room told Sylvie he'd never sleep and the open eye sewed itself shut. Sylvie looked over at Harry, splayed on his back, open-mouthed, the surviving half of a double yolk. She'd walked him down to the swings that morning, telling him he was getting a new brother to play with. 'Swings?' Harry had asked, pulling his hand out of hers and running ahead. 'Harry! Harold!' She'd started to run after him and then just stopped, barely able to tell him apart from the other children, lost in delighted shrieks. She shook herself and rushed towards the huddle of nannies burdened with bags and coats, watching him prance and stumble. *We're getting you a new brother,* she said to herself. *Arthur – can you say Arthur, Harry?*

As far as Sylvie would remember it, the boy's silence would not break for another week, the instant snatching her back to the howl she'd once felt but never heard. A second cry was meant to rise up and join Harry's that spring but, without a living voice to carry it, the silenced wail of primal need was trapped in the womb that had failed it. More animal than human, it dissolved Harry's cries to little more than background noise. That same soundless howl pitched its helpless terror again – but this time it found a voice in the boy's cry: embodied, it filled her grieving womb with her dead child, lending flesh to the twig baby she'd planted and fresh hope to the white buds she'd scattered, melding the two Arthurs to one. The cry pulled her up and told her, if only for that night and the days that followed, that this small dark quiet they'd named Arthur was *her* Arthur – and her Arthur had gone.

'Go back to sleep, Sylvie,' Gerald groaned.

'He's not there. He was crying out.'

'How can he have gone if he was crying out?'

'You've got to get up.'

'I've got to sleep. Go to sleep, Sylvie, go to sleep.'

'He was screaming.'

'The only one screaming is you. You'll wake Harry.'

'I'm not screaming.'

When Sylvie found him, blanket-wrapped in the airing cupboard, she hovered her palm just close enough to his head to feel the fine crown of black hair beneath it. 'It's alright,' she said, 'you can stay here if you like.' So she sat on the floor beside the open cupboard and told Arthur stories about another little Arthur just like him who was also very small, and also very quiet, but no one in the whole wide world had ever seen him, no one knew why he'd gone or where he'd gone – no one but her – but if Arthur was very very good she would take him one day and show him this other little Arthur. She'd show him where she'd planted him. Every day he grows a little bit bigger, she told him, a little bit bigger and a little bit stronger and when he's big enough and strong enough it would be time to pull him up and out of the ground for the whole wide world to see.

Sylvie stroked the boy's head and he looked up at her, one of his hands gripping the blanket. Feeling him shiver, she unfolded another and laid it over him, telling him to close his eyes, 'that's it,' she whispered, 'just close your eyes.' He'd settle now, she told herself, hearing again the end of the story she'd just told, seeing the wish it held take root, *yes, just close your eyes.*

*March 1965*

Arthur still couldn't get his tie straight. The mirror insulted him with his fourth attempt. He stared at the bulk in the centre of his collar and took little solace in the fact that it was of no consequence: there had not been one occasion when Professor Epstein had quite managed to lift his eyes from his desk while displaying his *cause for concern* – all that would address Arthur this morning was the back of a yellow-nailed hand while he strained again to hear a lamentation in memoriam of Arthur's *unmet potential*, no louder and no less irritable than the pen scratching over the page. This was, of course, all assuming he could get out the door.

'Arthur! Is that you?' Gerald's voice halted Arthur at the bottom of the stairs, sinking his chin to meet the failure that was the knot of his tie, and hauled him into the kitchen.

'And where do you think you're off to?' Gerald asked, peering up from the headlines he'd been shaking his head at. Sylvie was standing at the open fridge. 'Milk,' she said, 'there's no milk.'

'I've got to see the professor, I thought I said—'

'Not so fast, your mother wouldn't hear of you entering such a formal engagement on an empty stomach.'

'There's no milk,' Sylvie said a little louder.

'I'll get it,' Arthur said, looking past her before those half-closed eyes caught his.

'You'll sit down is what you'll do,' Gerald said.

'I'm late.'

'I'm paying your fees.'

'What fees?' Trying to get the upper hand was never a wise tactic, particularly if it involved the truth.

'Even worse,' Gerald said, 'wasting the state's money instead. You let me worry about punctuality. Sit down.'

'Morning all,' Harry chirped, kissing Sylvie's cheek. Her hand slid from her face onto his before it fell. 'No milk,' she said.

'I'll get it,' Harry said, stripping a banana and munching it in two bites, swinging the empty skin before he dropped it in front of Arthur and went to the front door. He was incapable of shutting doors (he could only slam them), always sending a shudder through Sylvie. Arthur slid his hands under his thighs before they caught the vibrations of her fright.

'Milk!' Harry held the two bottles up, hands round their necks, and set them down in front of Sylvie. He stopped, lightly tapped his knuckles against his forehead and lowered a stiff hand towards Sylvie's shoulder. 'I – I got your milk, Ma,' he said, beam receding as he looked up towards Arthur and then over towards Gerald, waiting for his father's nod.

'I've got to go, I've got an appointment,' Arthur said.

'You hear that, Harry? Your brother's got an appointment. Our college man has an appointment.'

'Scrambled please, Ma,' Harry said, his indefatigable glow, restored, pouring over the table.

'I asked you what you made of our college man.'

Harry's head dropped a little to one side. 'I think he needs to sort his tie out,' he said, finger and thumb coming towards his own, unable to read the accuracy of his conclusion in Gerald's face.

'I should say he does. You want to look the part, Arthur.'

'He wants a hat,' Harry suggested.

'Well then he must have a hat!'

'I do not want a hat!' Arthur exploded.

'Yes you do – Harry, get Arthur my hat.'

Arthur's eyes, attempting assertion, set themselves on his father, 'Now,' he said, his fingers forming tense bridges on the table as though he was at the ready for the starter's gun before a race. Trying to keep his eyes on Gerald was making him blink – he shifted them to the table... *Now* – Gerald and Harry were exchanging raised brows and smiles. Arthur bit down a little too hard on his lip and watched his fingers splay as they slid down – *no, he would not let them play dress-up with him like that.*

'Nice case, though,' Harry said, smoothing fingers over the satchel he had passed on to Arthur. Arthur kept meaning to buy another, but asking Gerald for a bit of spare cash – *you after pocket money again, old boy?* – meant being handed the coins one by one as Gerald counted, taking out a note, putting it back.

'It *is* a nice case,' Gerald agreed. 'I wouldn't mind a case like that myself. You know what a case like that tells me, Harry?'

'What, Dad?'

'A case like that tells me this young man is going somewhere – this young man is on his way up. *This* young man is someone we shall wonder how we ever did without.'

'It's a satchel,' Arthur muttered, picking it up. '*Your* satchel.'

'Because, you see now, the point is to be *indispensable.* Do you understand me, Harry?'

'I think so, Dad.' Harry shifted in his chair, 'In-dis-*pens*—'

'Indispensable. Good. Now, tell me, what do you think a college man would carry about in a case like that?'

'It's not a case!' Arthur tried, but Harry was holding the satchel up, shaking it for clues.

'I don't know, Dad,' Harry said, a pretence in cheeriness lightly bruised. 'A college man's case is a conundrum.'

Arthur rolled his eyes – Harry was trying on this voice for size again, stretching out each syllable, growing hoarse as he strained for a pitch that wasn't his own.

Gerald's chuckle started and stopped just as suddenly – what had he said about trying to be funny? If this was going to be anyone's joke it would be his. He gauged Arthur, Harry and Sylvie in turn.

'Sylvie!' Gerald's voice jerked her round.

'Breakfast,' she said, a plate with Harry's eggs in her hands.

'Breakfast will have to wait,' Gerald said, 'we're in the middle of a game.'

'Guess what's in the case,' Harry said, cheeriness recovered.

'But it will go cold,' Sylvie said.

'All be the same in his guts – now: Guess. What's. In. The. Case.'

'I don't know,' she said. Arthur looked up, caught her eyes, and looked away.

'Well try!' Gerald insisted.

'I—'

'Yes?'

'I said I—' Her hands mimicked her stutter. Arthur shut his eyes before he had to see the plate slip, lumps of rubbery egg at Sylvie's feet.

'Is this because you mixed up your pills again? Sylvie? What have I said about doing the pills yourself?'

Arthur knew he shouldn't look up – those half-closed eyes again, her hand coming over her throat, 'Sorry, I don't know what—' she stopped, kneeling to pick up a piece of china, a bit of egg.

'Oh love,' Gerald sighed, kneading an eye with the heel of his hand.

Harry scanned the table for direction. Finding none, he looked down, scratching his neck, eyes roaming over his breakfast's fate.

'Never mind, Ma,' he tried, attempting to offer his chuckle only to find it checked by Gerald's instructive hand – they watched it rise and bang down on the table. 'Well don't just leave your mother with all that,' Gerald hissed, sending Harry for a cloth. Arthur drew his satchel into his lap, his head dropping towards it.

Gerald suggested Arthur's exit with a nod towards the door, 'Your *appointment*...'

Arthur peeled himself up, assessing whether he was being offered a rare mercy or just being shooed away before Gerald set about reprimanding Sylvie. He watched Harry scurrying with the cloth until he glanced up – *Go on,* Harry's eyes said. Arthur would have given anything to get away – but leaving was one thing, being exiled another.

'Come here love,' Gerald said to Sylvie, his words coming through a sigh. Hearing the endearment made Arthur pause – it was as though the acid had been drained from Gerald's voice, but Arthur couldn't be sure whether it was gentleness or just a tone too worn for exasperation, let alone mockery. He put his satchel over his shoulder, tightening his grip of the strap, wanting to shield Sylvie from the verbal whip that would surely follow. But Gerald went over to her instead, his voice just audible – *oh love*, he was saying, *what are we going to do, eh? What are we going to do?* – taking long, slow steps, careful as he put his arms round her, bringing her up – and, just in that moment, Arthur might have been watching someone else's father. 'It'll come right,' Gerald said, his lips touching her forehead, 'it'll come right.'

Arthur stood outside, folding his key in the palm of his hand. *It'll come right.*

The later it got the more Arthur slackened – he'd never make it now, old Epstein would just spread his hands over his desk, bark for Arthur to enter, raise his flattened skull and bark again before shaking his head at the closed door. Epstein couldn't abide knocking – Arthur had learned, a little too late, that any unanticipated sight or sound derailed Epstein's fragile train of thought, and a barely repressed screech, torn pages and thrown books were the result. Gerald wasn't unlike him in that way, it was just that instead of pages and books it would be the china and Arthur. But the bark from old Epstein never came. Arthur sat on one of the chairs outside, yanked his tie loose and pulled his satchel a little closer – the strap was breaking, which, in that moment, was evidence enough that he should renounce all future efforts and tell Epstein what he could do with his *concern.*

A swirling mop and an anxious mutter came towards Arthur. 'Wet, wet,' the caretaker warned, his hand flying up as though Arthur had any intention of moving, 'much care, please,' he said, a second hand flying, leaving the mop and the pocket dictionary that had been tucked into the caretaker's sleeve to land in front of Arthur. Arthur's eyes darted for Epstein's door, the caretaker's for his dictionary. 'No injury,' he said, opening it, patting the photograph taped on the inside of the cover.

'It's alright, he won't have heard a damn thing – certainly never hears anything I say,' Arthur said, bypassing the cause of the caretaker's relief to align it with his own, picturing Epstein digging out ear wax, insensible to anything but the ancient truths he'd be reciting from the scroll before him. Even so, Arthur had to check the door again in case Epstein, transformed, bounced, unimaginably lithe, over the threshold and pounced on Arthur to inform him that, on the contrary, he heard everything. Arthur took a thankful breath – Epstein was no more lithe than a crippled ox; the man couldn't move, he'd be wedged into his chair, finger in ear, sermonising through his teeth. Arthur gave the caretaker a conspiratorial nod – and it was then that the caretaker's half-moon eyes lit to take him in. Arthur tried to pull his gaze away, his hand reaching for his satchel and fumbling with the strap, fastening his eyes where the dictionary had fallen, waiting for the caretaker to move himself, his dictionary and his mop along. Arthur sent his first hopeful glance at Epstein's door.

'Perhaps a moment I sit,' the caretaker said. 'Words I must to find.' He ran his finger down a column, turning the pages, 'moment a moment,' he said, getting up, mop in hand, 'Aha! Yes, now you see,' he said, turning to the inside cover and holding the taped photograph beside Arthur's face – 'Look! You must to look! Here is me, and here my friend.'

The picture was too blotched and creased for Arthur to recognise the caretaker as one of the two men. 'In Poland, all before,' he said, 'yes, you see.' He held the picture up again, smiling – 'how you look… twenty years' – his words breaking as he raised his hand – 'no' – and began counting off his fingers – 'twenty-one, twenty-two, twenty…' He waved his hand softly and let it drop, his mouth wilting and tightening before it gave him away.

*See what?*

The caretaker brought a hand to his face and then towards Arthur, making him dodge as though the cautious hand were taloned, lunging for prey.

'Too sorry,' the caretaker said, his sudden shift aside mirroring Arthur's dodge, each of them unable to comprehend how they could be perceived as a threat to the other. 'So long I search – asking, asking, everyone I ask, check every list…' The rush of insistent words seemed less for Arthur than for the two faces in the photograph, as though they held an accusation and demanded an explanation. The caretaker's defence trailed to a stop, his eyes softening as they rested on the photograph, a finger held just above it. He nodded and looked up again, 'but to see – so like...'

Arthur gauged him for a moment, he seemed to be about to say something else, but he just turned his hands over, drew in his lips and began walking away. 'All before,' Arthur heard him say as he went. He stopped, tucked the dictionary back up his sleeve and stretched his arm to check it was safe. 'Too luck.'

'Lucky,' Arthur said to his satchel. *Lucky.* He might have said so, a small thing it would have been, just to say. But you couldn't go encouraging types like that, Gerald would have said the caretaker wasn't right in the head – that was what he used to say about Mrs Cohen. The caretaker's hand – it wasn't quite steady, it wanted something without saying what. 'Hey,' Arthur shouted down the hall, but the caretaker had gone.

'What's all this noise about?' Hands raised on either side of his head, Epstein had been dislodged from behind his desk. 'Shouldn't you be in a seminar?'

'You asked to see me.'

'I most certainly did not.'

'You did,' Arthur said, getting up.

'I haven't the foggiest what you're talking about.'

Arthur, having no inclination to illuminate him, busied himself with his satchel, gave his apologies and, making his way towards the seminar, found the stairs and the front door more compelling. He stopped just as he got outside – Pete would be giving his presentation in a few minutes, shuffling his papers at first, clearing his throat before he looked up, eyes seeming to take in a full congregation rather than the sleepy cluster of students in a dusty seminar room at the rabbinical college. He'd been going over it in the Old Bull last week, Sammy pitching in, Pete gliding on then halting to take a gulp of ale and check if either of the boys had anything to add. Arthur had looked up, Sammy and Pete waiting for him, Pete nodding as Arthur opened his mouth and closed it, shaking his head, saying it didn't matter, a minor grammatical point. Sammy had given his shoulder a light squeeze, called him a pedant – *my favourite pedant, mind* – and told him to get in the next round. Arthur had put his hands on the bar, looking back over his shoulder at Sammy and Pete – Pete scribbling, Sammy laughing and catching Arthur's eye, raising his empty glass.

Wondered now how he'd managed to slip so far behind, how distant the seminar room at the end of the corridor was from the world he'd glimpsed sitting with the Rabbi that Wednesday afternoon he'd knocked on his door. Almost a decade ago – he'd just passed his eleventh birthday and still believed what the Rabbi had said was true: we cannot chase the answers – answers don't like to be chased.

*Just keep coming back to the questions – hold your question up to the light… turn it over again and again, question the question –*

So he went, every Wednesday afternoon from March to September until the Rabbi said it would be time to join the others, time to start thinking about his Bar Mitzvah. The Rabbi's wife had come in then and set a tray of tea on the table, reminding the Rabbi he'd promised Rachel he'd help her with her piece. Rachel was their daughter, a head taller and three years older than Arthur. He'd hear her begin practising the cello in the room next door towards the end of each of his afternoons with the Rabbi, the same bar over and over, and Arthur would lose what the Rabbi had just said, caught between the tug of the notes and the tug of the Rabbi's voice. The Rabbi would pause and smile, drawing Arthur back to the page.

'You will give her a few minutes later,' the Rabbi's wife said.

'A few minutes, a few minutes,' the Rabbi said absently.

The Rabbi's wife had shaken her head, leaning down to Arthur as she gestured towards the shelves behind him, 'he has every single one of these books in his head but I sometimes wonder if he remembers his own name.'

'My name?' the Rabbi asked with a gentle wink, and Arthur would find himself mesmerised by the crinkles gathering round the Rabbi's eyes.

'Oh you are a…' The Rabbi's wife waved her hand, laughing as she went out.

Arthur rubbed his knee, hand tight round the pencil, wanting to fold himself up, to disappear without having to leave. But he'd have to, before the Rabbi started talking about his Bar Mitzvah again. 'But my dad,' he'd mumbled before the Rabbi had said another word, 'I don't think I'm allowed.' The Rabbi poured tea into each of the cups. 'Allowed?' the Rabbi had asked, taking a sip. Arthur rubbed his knees again and put his pencil away, saying he was sorry but he had to go, scurrying out and having to rush back in to grab the kitbag he'd left under the table, 'sorry, thanks,' and the Rabbi saying that if there was anything he might need help with, anything Arthur might like to talk about – 'No, thanks, but –'

He hadn't knocked on the Rabbi's door since – used to see Rachel quite a bit though, carrying her cello to the bus stop, always trying to gather the *hi* he wanted to say as he walked past, promising himself he'd say it next time, yes, and that the next Wednesday he'd go and see the Rabbi. Took until he was fourteen or fifteen for him to give up on both but then, years later, trudging through the summer weeks after he scraped through his A-levels – weeks that everyone else seemed to be dancing through – he was pinched by an urgency to find his way back and it was becoming all too clear that sitting in Gerald's office filling out accident and sickness insurance claims wasn't going to provide it. He'd spent one of the long evenings circling the park until it closed – people were rolling up blankets, packing up picnic baskets, others were stretching out their last minutes in the sun, leaning back or flopped on their bellies, opening another bottle. He'd pictured himself walking up as far as the corner of the Rabbi's street, thinking how he'd begin, what he'd say, how he'd be unsure where to look in those minutes when the Rabbi would have to find the thread that connected the eleven-year-old boy who'd come to him on a Wednesday afternoon to the young man blundering up to his door on a summer evening with no way of explaining the time between. Arthur tried to recall the sound of Rachel's cello – how did it begin? No, he couldn't go back, not now – *Karnovski,* he'd say, *Arthur Karnovski* – and the Rabbi would look at him just a little more closely, as though he were stumbling upon marginalia he'd once pencilled. Arthur had felt his stomach twist and sink – well of course he couldn't go back – what was he even thinking? He'd be filling out those forms for Gerald and getting the sandwiches indefinitely – he'd turned back round the corner then and stopped – the chatter about universities and applications and interviews coming back to him, filtered through the twilight, conversations he hadn't been a part of, couldn't have been a part of. He'd barely allowed himself to consider it – not after the subject was raised and dropped with such immediacy, but standing there, on the corner of the Rabbi's street, studying at the Rabbinical college or at UC began to feel plausible – not just plausible but necessary – take the academic route, of course, no question about that, anchor himself in the rigour of it.

He'd told himself he'd broach it with Gerald the next day – just get his thoughts in order first – but that was all, no use putting it off. Knew Gerald would laugh of course – well let him, no doubt there'd be a threat to follow for good measure, ask him if he hadn't told him his whole life not to go mixing with *that lot.* But there would be months of tutorials in Biblical Hebrew if he wanted any hope of getting in, cramming till a fog crept over his forehead, mouth drying with the fear he'd be groping his way through the same fog as soon as the paper was set in front of him. Gerald had said he wouldn't pass but that had spurred him, driven him through the struggle to parse until the sense, coming into focus, began to glow through the leaves, recovering the texture he used to hear in the Rabbi's voice – the layers and weight of generations, each opening another door, offering their own commentary, interpreting anew, in that moment – 'Not *God is the giver of the Torah,'* the Rabbi had told Arthur once, 'but *God is giving.* Not just once, but over and over, for all time.' But just weeks into the first term the script was closed to him again – strange shapes and dots, a code or secret he couldn't share. Sammy and Pete had tried to help him out, of course. Still felt as though he'd been blindfolded and spun, hands grasping at the air – and what for? Arthur heard the question again in Gerald's voice just as the strap of his satchel broke. He dropped it and kicked it before hauling it up. *What for?* The feeling behind the answer was palpable but he couldn't articulate it and when he tried, even to himself, it not only seemed reduced by the labour to find words but laughable – Arthur, who had only ever attended a service a handful of times, who had never taken his Bar Mitzvah, who –

And yet somehow that hadn't even mattered, the offering was held in that second chair the Rabbi brought up to his desk for Arthur just as much as it was held in the teaching of the Torah – offered without condition, without question – regardless of the fact his face would barely be known to the other congregants, he was never a guest or a stranger, there was always a place and the Rabbi's door, on a Wednesday at four-thirty, would always be left ajar.

*

'Hey, Arthur!' Sammy was running towards him, tucking his shirt back in as he came to a stop. 'Where you going? We're late, come on!'

Arthur nodded and looked back over his shoulder, holding up a hand to make his explanation for him.

'Seminar's already started,' Sammy said, 'Pete's doing his presentation today.'

'Yeah, I know but—'

'You alright, Arthur?' Sammy gave Arthur a moment before he ran on, calling behind him that they'd catch up with him later, 'join us for a pint, eh? You hardly ever come for a drink these days.'

He'd gone for a drink the other night hadn't he? Sliding in once he'd given up on his efforts to translate that passage from the Book of Jeremiah – three hours sitting over the same lines, the possibilities multiplying and competing, each evading his grasp. He'd stood outside the library, still trying to catch hold of the lines that had eluded him, not realising he was muttering them aloud until a stifled snigger ricocheted through a band of students on their way in. Finding Sammy and Pete at their usual table in the Old Bull had seemed a haven after that, the three of them suspended in the smoke and the voices melting into each other. Sammy was always the one to draw Arthur in, the light punch on the arm, getting him to diagnose Epstein – and it was Sammy who had come up to Arthur, bumbling lost on the first day, and introduced himself, telling Arthur he'd already had a second tour and he still hadn't a clue where he was going.

Sylvie was standing at the open door when he'd got back that day – a faint sketch of the Sylvie who had waited for Arthur and Harry when they started senior school. She'd straightened their collars and paused before she followed them inside, Arthur looking back to see Sylvie lifting the lid from the little brown pot on the ledge in the hall. *For the buds, Ma,* he'd said, when he gave it to her – brought it back for her – when was it? Last summer of junior school, perhaps. No, it would have been before – long before, soon after Gerald had thrown the blue china pot against the wall – white petals and glazed shards of brilliant sky all over the hall carpet. Coming back to him now – how he'd slunk off when Harry and his chums were making a den from bricks on a bombsite and he'd found the brown pot in an old pram filled with junk and rubbish, the speed of his heart as he'd run home with it – not just the speed but the force – and Sylvie asking where Harry was and Arthur just holding the pot out towards her –

*For the buds, Ma, for the buds –*

It was a few moments before she took it, rubbing away at the dust and the dirt as soon as it was in her hands, running her fingers over the flowers engraved –

*For the buds, Ma –*

She'd tilted her head towards her shoulder, mouthing *for the buds, yes, the buds –*

Never would be, though – the brown pot was left empty for years until Gerald dropped the spare key inside it.

Arthur seemed to hear again that smash against the wall, Gerald's steps back down the hall and the buds, like giant snowflakes –

*What's wrong, Ma?*

*Nothing, darling,* she'd said, turning with a quick sharp smile.

Harry had almost gone without Arthur that morning, telling Arthur to get a wiggle on when he went upstairs again – *just got to check something,* Arthur had said, intercepted by Gerald before he stalled on the landing again, *Playing for time, eh chum?* He'd just wanted to give Sylvie another minute – she might want to come and say goodbye, make sure they were neat and tidy, that they hadn't forgotten anything, first day of senior school and everything – she'd want to, Arthur was sure she would. Of course Gerald would have said they were too old for all that fuss.

Sylvie was already receding then but on that first day after he'd started at the college she didn't seem to see him until he spoke. Wasn't she cold like that, with the door open? he'd asked and she shook her head, eyes meeting his, holding her hand out towards him. 'It was good, Ma,' he'd said, smiling at her smile, hesitating before he took her arm and tried to guide her inside. What would he say to her now? Couldn't always be sure of what she took in, which words lost sense between being spoken and being heard.

*

Arthur made his way to the bench Sylvie used to sit him and Harry on when she took them for their Thursdays at the park. No – he'd never go back – not to Epstein, not to the caretaker –

*See what?*

Arthur felt as though that hand was coming towards him again. Whatever the caretaker saw was nothing Arthur needed to know – not any more than he needed Epstein's *concern. Concern, yes,* Arthur had mumbled, brow scrunching at the word that would morph into a euphemism before the term was out. Well Epstein could keep his *concern.* Arthur pictured him sinking deeper into his chair, hands and eyes locked, slave to a sermon Arthur would never have to hear – no, he would never have to hear that sermon or another word from Epstein again. The thought was exhilarating, gifting him with a speed and certainty that marched him back to Llanvanor, galvanised by a succession of absolutes surging as he went: *never again would he have to hear Epstein, never again stumble over semantic hurdles or trip up on trick questions, never feel his throat clogging with strained prayer, hinged on that eternal seesaw of faith and doubt…* Arthur cursed the 113 as it went past – no, he was alright, he'd still be home before Gerald and Harry, no chance of them interrogating him between knocking back their fistfuls of nuts. Straight back, yes, get a fire going quick as he could and set light to every last scrap from the college.

Only Sylvie's eyes waiting for him at the top of the stairs curbed his rush to get inside the front door. He turned his toes towards each other in the hallway; distance from both the college and Llanvanor had leant him a hypnotic self-assurance, but now inside the house, his broken momentum mocked him. Gerald didn't need to be there for Arthur to feel an elbow, feigning play, jab him in the side – *Appointment went well then, eh chum? Your mother will be so proud.* She wasn't at the top of the stairs, though – yet the expectation of her waiting eyes made her presence irreducible. She was in her room, of course, which meant the house was as good as empty.

Still a good couple of hours before the working men loosened their ties and dropped the last file on the secretary's desk. Harry and his father always referred to the secretary as *the girl* and Arthur probably wouldn't have known her name if he hadn't asked her. Jenny. She was alright. Arthur had met her when he was in the office for a few days last summer on a 'trial' he had every intention of failing. Harry spent the mornings pacing round, giving Jenny dictation, the keys of the typewriter clipping the seconds of the hour while Arthur resisted letting his head fall on the desk. It was twelve on the dot on Arthur's first day when Jenny said she was going out to get the sandwiches. A screen had been erected behind Gerald's desk to give the impression of a division between chairman and employee. He appeared immediately, as though the line about the sandwiches was just what he'd been waiting for.

'As you were,' Gerald told Jenny, lowering his hand without looking at her, 'Arthur will get those. Petty cash in the top drawer, Arthur – and don't forget the post.'

Arthur had wanted to say something to Jenny but she had her shoulders up so tight and kept smashing her glasses back up over the bridge of the nose. Thought she'd do herself or the glasses an injury. Arthur counted the petty cash a few times while he worked out whether it would be better to say he liked her glasses or ask her if she wanted a cup of tea. He went for the latter, feeling unusually optimistic about his choice. She shook her head and lowered it sharply so that her hair curtained her face, the sudden drop of her head making her shoulders absurdly high.

'Get the sandwiches,' Gerald instructed as he came round again. 'You can do the tea when you get back.'

Questions might have been the last thing he wanted as he went up the stairs at Llanvanor, but the thought that Sylvie wouldn't even hear his footsteps made him pause just beyond her door. It would be almost pitch dark in her room – once she'd even been alert enough to make a crack about how making blackout blinds had been good practice. *Put that light out!* Her voice pantomime deep before Gerald chuckled something about *his old girl.* He'd had his arm round her and patted her hand and Arthur had waited for Gerald's face to turn, for his tone to sour. It didn't though, not just then – *I always told the lads you could do all the voices,* he'd said. But she'd winced, mouth tight as she lowered her chin, breaking the spell. She'd raised her head when Gerald got up, forcing a smile, looking up at Arthur before her eyes followed Gerald's steps to the door. It was that evening she started making dinner again – an answer to Gerald's suggestion that she *thought about making more of an effort.* 'Unless I need to get the doctor round again – do I? Unless there's something *wrong* with you?'

She'd sat at the table, staring ahead while she was peeling the carrots, and cut herself. Arthur grabbed the knife out of her hand and tipped the carrots into the sink. Only a few were smeared, but Arthur rinsed them urgently, as though they were covered in blood. They were clean but he kept the water running over them, stunned by himself as much as Sylvie, not wanting to turn back round and be the witness that might make her conscious. 'I think I should put something on this,' she'd said vaguely, gaze set over the thin red train running down her finger. 'I'll do the potatoes in a minute.' Arthur picked one up – he'd do them himself. Except that would make it worse. Say that she wasn't capable, a nuisance, redundant – confirm Gerald's suspicion that they needed to get something signed once and for all – 'How many specialists are we supposed to get through before we call it a day?' he'd asked more than once.

Arthur had tried not to watch her when she came back down and started again, holding the knife so hard it made her hand shake. 'Don't look at me like that, Arthur. You make me nervous.'

She'd wanted to go upstairs as soon as everyone was sitting at the table, but Gerald said she was staying put, observing the pinched crown of the plaster she couldn't get to stick neatly round her thumb, the cut drying on her index finger. A potato rolled onto the floor. Gerald made a point of observing that too, commenting on both by saying they were sitting together like a normal family for once and no one was getting up until their plates were empty. The five minutes past the seven-thirty start hadn't helped but a few mouthfuls settled him.

Arthur tightened his grip round his fork, watching the mince slide back onto his plate, his eyes darting to Sylvie as Gerald scraped his cutlery against the china. There were still days, sometimes weeks, when a little of Sylvie would return to them, her face easing just enough to let an unstrained smile through, the staccato rhythm of her step and voice halting a little less. But that night, hearing the ghost in Sylvie's short breath, she seemed barely able to hold herself up, a husk that might crack under a glance. Arthur felt the time Sylvie had been lost to them gather and bear down over them – months unbroken, chained under the same sky. Especially these last few years – years that rarely saw Gerald home before midnight, staying as late as he could at the office, picking out of the fridge when he got back, apparently unaware of Arthur leaning against the counter, of Harry sobering up over his takeaway, slurping noodles out of a cardboard container.

It wasn't incapability so much as an unspoken understanding that they couldn't sit at the table, let alone sit together, while Sylvie's continued absence pricked the moments between Gerald and Harry's efforts to dissect Arthur. And it would have been an effort: winding Arthur up could stop being amusing horribly quickly when he kept looking up at the kitchen door between mashing his mince into his potato, lifting and lowering his fork without taking a bite, leaving Gerald to sigh and mutter that they were all trying to test his nerve, Harry objecting, Gerald raising his hand to ensure silence.

Gerald laid his cutlery down, pushed his plate away and leaned back, casting his eyes over Sylvie before he turned his attention to Arthur.

'Now what I want to know,' Gerald said, drumming his fingers on the table, 'is how our Arthur here got all these *pretensions* into his head, eh?'

'Pretensions?' Arthur's bafflement was only too sincere.

'Yes, chum – pretensions!'

Sylvie looked down at her potatoes and then at her fork, as if acknowledging the two would need to be coordinated.

'Is this about studying at the college?' she asked, eyes coming up.

'Hah! Funny the times the cat lets you have your tongue back!' Gerald said, stabbing a carrot. 'This,' he said, holding it up, 'is raw.'

'I think Arthur should go to the college if he likes,' Sylvie said. Her voice was still faint but it was more familiar than it had been, no gaps between the words. She lifted her fork and pressed it into the potato, the lump crumbling before it reached her mouth.

'And you'd know about being a college man, would you? Is that your subject Sylvie, your *specialism?*' He brought up a forkful and pointed it at Arthur, 'speaking of *specialisms,* I wonder if Arthur would like to tell us a little more about this *course* of his.'

'I just think Arthur should go if he wants to, that's all.'

'And I think my carrots are raw. Are your carrots raw, Harry?'

'Erm, a bit raw.'

'Well I do know a thing or two about college men,' Gerald said. 'They're lazy buggers who turn into vegetables.'

Even Harry seemed to be struggling to work through this logic – he looked at Arthur, his brow uncharacteristically blighted by horizontal trenches.

'My father was a college man and look what happened to him.' Gerald said. 'A. Vegetable.'

'He was wonderful!' Sylvie said – and just then she slipped back into a woman neither Arthur nor Harry had met. Eyes open, clear, voice rounded almost, yes there was a fullness in it, in her.

'Wonderful?' Gerald spluttered. 'I'd like to hear how you define *wonderful.* In case you hadn't noticed –'

'I noticed,' Sylvie said, voice beginning to taper again, 'days when he… There were days, Gerald, I saw him, even your mother said –'

'Said what?'

'He came back. If you could have just sat with him a little longer – seen what happened when he sang – you'd have seen –'

'I saw quite enough, thank you –'

'Just before the fire went out –'

They waited for her to say something else, even Gerald was waiting, but her chest caved and she was sinking under an invisible weight again.

'I saw what happened when he sang – and not only in that bloody Polish of his. Leyning and wailing at dawn in the language of dead men, my God,' he stopped and looked at Arthur. 'Because that's what Biblical Hebrew is – a language that makes a man fit for nothing but the asylum and the grave.' He closed his eyes, taking a breath as he lifted his hand from the table. Arthur waited for it to slam down, but it fell slowly, landing silently. 'Useless bugger,' he muttered, letting out a raspy laugh, 'after all that, eh? After all… go on then, good luck to you.'

Less than twenty minutes into his first seminar and the knotted script he was meant to unravel tightened, revealing nothing but the truth of Gerald's warning: useless – he was utterly useless. At least a vegetable wouldn't have had to suffer awareness of the fact – but it had all made absolute sense when he enrolled. There were languages that would sound themselves inside him – but they were just traces and vibrations of an underworld without image, a time and place without root – barks, a song that seemed to arise without a singer – he'd sense the meaning but couldn't have explained it any more than he could have silenced it. Hebrew had drawn him, though, right from that first time he'd found his way to the synagogue, pulling him through a limping search towards it, as though a language could itself be a place, somewhere you arrived at, could settle. It was Mrs Cohen who had told him what a Semite was; she might have gone on to explain that there were Jews – and then there were *Jews*. It was Gerald who cleared that one up, refining his point by stating that he and Arthur were not the same kind. What kind was he? The kind, Gerald informed him, that set the rot in. Arthur had looked down then, reaching his hand up the sleeve of his coat and scratching his arm. *You and your questions, chum.* Gerald had folded his arms, releasing them to place a hand on Arthur's shoulder. Look here, he said, lowering his voice, I'm just trying to keep you out of harm's way, there's a funny lot that bring their shtetl life and their shtetl ways, there's the danger, Arthur, do you understand? It's the ones that go advertising themselves, drawing attention – it's asking for trouble. The more they let in the worse it gets for the rest of us.

Sylvie wasn't Jewish, Arthur knew that – Mutti had said so. Mutti was what was they had to call Gerald's mother. Sylvie didn't have a mother – she'd gone away to where all the dead people go. 'Is that very far?' Arthur had asked. It was a little while before she answered and she kept pressing her ear against her shoulder, 'No,' she said, looking up, 'it's not so very far.'

'Further than that other little Arthur?'

She blinked and looked away, *the brittle heart of her Thursday nightmare twitching behind her eyes. Feeling a crack in her ribcage, she heard the snap of twigs and held out her hand to catch the buds before they dissolved against the ground –*

'Ma?'

'Not now, Arthur. Not now.'

Arthur edged back, tracking the course of Sylvie's eyes as they followed his feet. She looked up and he stopped, watching her press her hands against the floor, his own hands clenching –

*Ma* –

Arthur and Harry had to stay with Mutti sometimes because Sylvie kept getting very sleepy and falling over. Mutti asked them if they kept the commandments and said their prayers. Arthur and Harry had looked at each other and then at Mutti.

'Well?' she'd asked, adjusting her brooch, flashing as it caught the light.

Harry kicked Arthur under the table and nodded, sucking in his lips before he said yes, he said his prayers every single night and knew all about the baby Jesus, he'd learned in school and was in this play and they sang this song –

Both her hands came up then, juddering as she spoke. 'Your forebears will be turning in their graves,' Next she took Arthur by the wrist, her eyes hard and red and small, opening her mouth to speak but letting Arthur go without a word.

'There's a boy at school,' Harry whispered, 'who says the Jews killed the baby Jesus.'

'That boy,' Mutti had said, 'is a liar!'

Arthur had clasped his hands under the table and squeezed his eyes but then Mutti said she had something very special to teach them and Arthur looked up to see Mutti's thin lips smiling, her hands patting her hair and face. They had candles that night and a sip of wine each and Mutti had torn a piece of bread for them – soft and sweet; bread kept hidden under a silky cloth. She'd piled their plates higher and higher and tucked napkins into their collars, telling them to *eat, eat,* her eyes moving from Harry to Arthur and back. Arthur found it hard to swallow and had to keep chewing, unsure the next mouthful would go down.

'Not too much trouble were you, boys?' Gerald had asked when he picked them up the following morning.

'No trouble at all,' Mutti had said.

'We had candles and wine!' Harry burst out.

Gerald had put his hand on Harry's shoulder, 'I see,' he said and clicked his tongue. 'Wait in the car, boys.'

Gerald had been caught up in the riots after the Battle of Cable Street and had been on guard for Mosely's descendants ever since – they'd find their opening, he used to say, and rally a fresh breed of Blackshirts. He'd taken the boys down to where it had happened, stopping at the point where his aunt had chucked a swill of piss and shit over an officer.

Still in short trousers when he went to Synagogue the first time. It wasn't far – he'd get there in time for the start of the service and be back by lunch. Just wanted to see for himself what Gerald meant –

*There were Jews – and then there were Jews –*

See what kind he was –

*The kind that set the rot in –*

But if he could just see – see the difference between the good and the rotten, then maybe he could learn how to be good.

Saturdays were Gerald's gardening days and Sylvie wasn't coming down until the afternoons then so Arthur could get out easily enough. Only Harry noticed him going –'you'll get in trouble,' Harry said, 'where are you going anyway?'

'Nowhere.'

'Liar.'

It was a few weeks before he went inside though, going back home almost as soon as he arrived, wondering what he'd do about getting the little hat you were meant to wear and the scarf with the tassels. In the end he took his school cap and stripy scarf and hoped it would do. 'You'll be wanting one of these,' the warden said, handing him a kippah. Arthur held it for a moment before he put it on, touching the back of his head to check it wouldn't fall.

'I don't think I've seen you before,' the warden said, lowering his voice and head. Arthur's eyes fell down to his shoes, his toes curled tight, only looking up as he felt the warden's light hand on his head. 'We normally just lend these,' he said, patting his own kippah, 'but you hang onto it if you like – just don't tell anyone.'

Arthur nodded and touched his scarf – he needed a scarf with the tassels, didn't he?

'Oh don't you worry about a tallit – they're not for young chaps like you. Wait till you're a bit bigger.'

Another man came in then and shook the warden's hand, putting his head back round the door to call after his wife. Arthur shifted back as the woman kissed each of the warden's cheeks, asking whose boy that was as though Arthur couldn't hear. Maybe he shouldn't have come – just give the kippah back and go home –

'On you go,' the warden said, 'just up one flight.'

People were murmuring greetings as they sat down, hugging and kissing, others waving and mouthing across the rows, someone trying to get their baby to quiet down, standing up and rocking side to side. Where was the gallery he'd seen in a picture? There was one in the drawing Mrs Cohen had shown him – one by her son, she said, showing him the desk where the Rabbi read the Torah and the Eternal Light and the Ark. Mrs Cohen said her son would take Arthur to synagogue when he got back from being a soldier in the war, he'd be like a big brother. Would Arthur like that? Maybe – maybe it would be like that dream he had sometimes, following an older boy round a garden as big as a field – sometimes there were lots of boys and girls, all of them in a circle and a lady with a harmonica. If Arthur could just have that dream every night he'd never be afraid of going to sleep and close his eyes just like Sylvie said.

The woman next to him gave him her prayer book – he hadn't known then that she was the Rabbi's wife. 'Didn't Peter give you one?' she asked. Arthur shook his head – who was Peter? It was only when the organ started playing that the voices fell to mutters and whispers, a ripple of heads turning to look at the woman rocking her baby until she slipped outside. Arthur listened to her *Shhhh* until it disappeared, braving glances up, meeting a new pair of eyes each time, a new smile, sometimes a nod too. He wasn't sure about smiling back yet. The woman leaned over his prayer book and turned it the other way round, her stubby red nailed fingers flicking though the pages until she pointed a nail beneath a line and squeezed his arm. He'd wanted to keep the book closed. It was better to just listen, that way he could sometimes join in, but the black marks crossed and clashed and wouldn't let him in. Arthur scratched his legs and screwed his eyes up, it was starting to feel as though his head was underwater and making himself tight as he could made his head and his legs and the chair solid. He felt his arm being squeezed again – *Look,* the woman mouthed, turning towards the velvet curtains being opened. That must have been it – it was – it was the Torah being taken out of its own little house in the wall – the Ark like Mrs Cohen had said – dressed in cloth and silver, being walked round the congregation like a child-king, the men reaching to touch it with their tallits. Arthur's eyes were fixed on its journey and wouldn't leave it until it had been put back inside its house in the wall again.

When the mutters and whispers rose into laughing and chattering again the woman kissed him on both cheeks.

'Shabbat shalom,' she said, spitting on a tissue and rubbing her sticky lipstick kisses off his cheeks. 'And now you say Shabbat shalom back.' She kept smiling even while she shook her head at Arthur sucking in his lips, waiting for her to go so that he could rub the kisses off himself. *Shabbat shalom* – it wasn't hard to say it in his head, he'd practise on his way back. Lots of hands on his shoulder then, voices bending down to his ear too, people nudging past him gently. They didn't seem to mind him being here though – maybe they couldn't see that he was rotten. The Rabbi stopped him when he got to the end of the row and Arthur screwed his eyes up again, head down – *he was rotten, the Rabbi could see, the Rabbi knew – and now the Rabbi was going to ask how he got in, make him give back the kippah –*

'Shabbat shalom,' the Rabbi's voice was softer than everyone else's had been – it had a funny accent like some of the others that made the words sound coated and clagged. His big warm hands had taken one of Arthur's hands lightly between his.

'Shabbat shalom,' Arthur said – but his mouth was fixed where the end of the last word had brought his lips together and wouldn't let him smile back. 'Um, thanks for having me,' he added, mouth giving way unexpectedly, eyes not sure where they should go. The Rabbi gave a feathery laugh. Maybe that wasn't the right thing to say. Arthur pulled his hand away.

'There is no need to thank,' the Rabbi said. 'You are very welcome, everyone is very welcome.'

'Do I have to believe in God?'

'I will tell you a secret,' the Rabbi said, looking about him before he bent his head. 'I don't always believe in God, but that is OK. He doesn't need us to believe in him always, he just wants us to try always to believe in Man.'

'I have to go,' Arthur said, already sliding away and down the stairs.

'Aren't you going to stay for kiddish?' the warden asked as he was going out.

Arthur didn't know what kiddish was but it was better to just shake his head. 'Can I really keep this?' he asked, holding his kippah against his head.

The warden didn't say anything and looked away slightly so that Arthur understood. Arthur would take the best care of it. Maybe the warden didn't think he was bad. Or the Rabbi. Maybe he could come back.

'Shabbat shalom,' Arthur said. He wasn't going to say thank you for having me again.

'Shabbat shalom.'

Harry was swinging a racket outside Llanvanor. 'Where've you been? What's that?'

Arthur took the kippah off and put his hand behind his back. 'Nowhere.'

'Dad! Arthur's been stealing things!'

'No I haven't – I haven't.'

'What is going on out here? Your mother's not well – what have you got there?' Arthur held his hand out, his mouth tight, eyes on the ground. Gerald snatched the kippah, 'Well now,' he said quietly, 'I can't think where you might have got this.' Arthur shook his head at his feet.

'I can't hear you,' Gerald said, bending down. Arthur swallowed and opened his mouth to speak, specks moving in front of his eyes. He tried to blink them away. Gerald lifted Arthur's chin with a finger, the kippah disappearing into his folded arms. 'Get upstairs, you can forget lunch. I'll deal with you later.'

It was getting dark by the time Gerald came to get him. 'You know what we're going to do, chum? You and me? We're going to make a fire. Every good little soldier needs to know how to make a fire.

'I don't want to.'

'And I don't want a boy that goes behind my back—' Gerald stopped, sighing as he put a hand on Arthur's shoulder, 'Don't you get it, chum?'

'I'm sorry, Dad—'

'You will be,' Gerald said, his raised hand falling back to his side. He looked behind him for a moment before he turned back to Arthur, holding his eyes as he crouched down. 'I'm trying to keep you from meeting a nasty end – you want to know what sort of bother I got as a boy?' Gerald straightened and Arthur looked up, mouth parted, nodding then shaking his head, taking his cue from Gerald's silent tread to the end of the garden.

Arthur kept his eyes on the circle of lawn Gerald had cleared, its green hem visible under Gerald's roving torch. Gerald hadn't shouted like Arthur thought he would, but he did this sometimes – pretending to be nice just before he picked Arthur up off the ground and barked into his ear. Eyes screwed up again, waiting. Arthur heard Gerald stamping round, scrunching up paper, breaking twigs, the thud of chunks of wood, the graze of branches. A match struck and the hiss and pop opened his eyes. Smoke seeped between skeleton twigs and the flames fed, fattened and bred more, licking up and up in liquid yellow tongues.

'Here you are,' Gerald said, handing him the kippah.

Arthur shook his head. It was from the warden. He couldn't. No.

'It's for your own good.' Gerald pressed his hand down on Arthur's shoulder, 'You get rid of all this or I'll get rid of you. I won't have you putting us in danger, Arthur. None of us know how many Hitlers are queuing up. They're lurking, they're waiting for you.'

*

Arthur felt the same twist and spasm in his gut now as he had then. Somehow dared to go to the synagogue again after that. But when? He'd have been out of short trousers certainly, started at St. Paul's. The years between were hard to tell apart now, just watching Sylvie losing substance as they passed. The room to her door closed more often. The housekeepers employed and sacked, Gerald furious with the way they moved things about, tossing Arthur's school report back at him. He'd had to copy it out himself: *Karnovski did not get off to an auspicious start*... tempted to give an alternative assessment. Yes, he'd gone back to the synagogue by then – spent months debating when to chance it, clocking Gerald's patterns step by step. He couldn't risk a Saturday morning again but Gerald was already starting to work late then and the Friday nights they'd never marked were newly lit by his absence, his return delayed until after the boys were supposed to be in bed. Arthur would hear him get back and open his eyes in the dark, tracing the light edging the door frame, counting the stairs as Gerald came up. If it was a night when Sylvie had come downstairs she'd have asked Harry and Arthur to set the table, taking the lid from the pot the housekeeper had left on the stove, holding the spoon over it, saying they should wait, going to and from the front door before asking Arthur to serve –

*Not too much for me, darling –*

Her hand resting on the counter a few moments longer before she sat down. Arthur would hear the beginnings and ends of the prayers he'd heard Mutti saying that Friday night he and Harry had stayed with her. He'd watched her lips moving and tried to catch the sounds, his eyes back down on the tablecloth as soon as Mutti looked up, her voice falling to a mutter until she stretched out the last phrase. It was only when he was sitting with Harry, looking up at Sylvie, listening for Gerald to come through the door, that the snatches of the prayers he'd managed to keep burrowed their way out, even without the wine and the candles to bless, the words sinking back, burying themselves deep again as Sylvie nodded to the boys to start – she'd get up then, a glance brushing her untouched plate, saying she needed to lie down –

*Make sure you wash up – and get on with your prep, no leaving it till the last minute, remember what your father says –*

Arthur, spooning up a mouthful, eyes up at the door as Sylvie left, would picture the congregation going down the stone staircase, their protracted goodbyes, goodnights, Shabbat shaloms, cheeks kissed and hands taken and then, seeing how he could fit himself amongst them, adapting the picture week by week until the Friday afternoon he let himself fall behind Harry and the others kicking the football between them on their way to the park. Turning back as he reached the entrance, he tried to place when Sylvie had last taken them – she'd made them stop by a blossom tree that had flowered early, saying how sad it was, so sad the wind would blow it away so soon.

Arthur made a seat for himself on a low brick wall halfway to the synagogue, wondering which of the people that walked past might be having Friday night candles and challah that evening, which of the men would be wearing a kippah later. Arthur jumped down and saw a figure outside the shop at the end of the street. There was a bundle at his side and a cap at his feet, the sound of his harmonica drawing Arthur towards him. Arthur dug in his pockets – he had a penny and a stick of liquorice and put them in the cap, slowing his steps before the corner to keep the sound of the harmonica just a little longer.

Arthur held back once he reached the synagogue, waiting until he could shuffle past the early arrivals. First came two elderly couples, greeting the warden. Arthur had kept his hand tight in his pocket as though protecting the hope he might weave through unseen – but the warden touched Arthur's forearm, lowered his chin and pointed him towards the prayer books. Arthur stuttered the apologies he'd been holding on to for three years – there'd been an accident, a mistake, he'd meant – and he'd touched the back of his head, swallowing the next sorry –

'Good to see you, young chap,' the warden had said, glancing towards where the spare kippahs had been left –

What would Gerald have said to all of that? Arthur was thrilled to think now of the gall he'd had –

Kisses on both cheeks again from the Rabbi's wife (as sticky as last time with less opportunity to rub them off) clasping his hands after the service, saying she was sure she remembered his face.

'I never forget a face, dear. Tell me, now, what is your name?'

'Karnovski. Arthur Karnovski.'

She'd kept hold of his hands, nodding, 'We thought you Karnovskis had all but disappeared,' she'd said, urging him towards the Rabbi as the last members trickled away.

'I have a Karnovski here for you, Leo,' she told the Rabbi.

The Rabbi held out his hand and put the other round Arthur's as he took it. 'Shabbat shalom. Have you far to walk?'

'Llanvanor Road.'

The Rabbi's wife went ahead, arm linked with her daughter's, the Rabbi at Arthur's side. 'I think I taught your father his Bar Mitzvah portion,' the Rabbi said.

'Oh no – no I don't think so,' Arthur said.

'Ezra – certainly I taught an Ezra, Ezra Karnovski – and a Gerald –'

Arthur scrunched his nose – 'No,' he said flatly, 'my dad doesn't like synagogue.'

The Rabbi smiled, 'Perhaps that is why we haven't seen him for some time. Would you like to join us for kiddish?'

Arthur saw the Rabbi's wife and daughter going through the gate a few houses along – no, he had to get home – he shook his head, mumbled his thanks and goodbye, his voice returning without warning as the question he didn't know how to ask tumbled out –

'How many types of Jews are there?'

The Rabbi paused before he said that there were as many types of Jews as there are Jews. Arthur repeated the answer to himself and looked up at the Rabbi.

'You have many questions?' the Rabbi said, 'It is very good to ask questions, it is the most important thing. We cannot always find answers but still we must keep asking.' Each week Arthur asked another and each week the Rabbi invited Arthur to join them for kiddish. Arthur would take his sip of wine and look up, eyes pulled towards the door, leaving before they started dinner just in case it might be an evening when Sylvie came down or Gerald came back. But it was only ever Harry in the living room, eyes an inch from a comic, a half-eaten marmalade sandwich on the sofa, the lid not yet lifted from the pot on the stove.

The Rabbi and his wife always had guests but there was a second table laid on the last Friday of each month. Arthur tied to guess how many faces there were – twenty? – the Rabbi's wife introducing him to everyone, asking if he would sit next to Rachel –

'You must,' she said, her hand on the back of a chair, eyes following him as his glass of wine was poured.

He didn't know if it was the syrupy wine or Rachel bending to take his plate, smiling at him as he looked up, but when the Rabbi's wife insisted he was part of the family and laid her hand on his, he felt all the faces in the room trying to close in on him. The Rabbi had looked over at him then, given the faintest of smiles and drawn everyone's attention to a letter he had been sent from a violinist and former student who would be coming from America.

'Clever boy,' the Rabbi said. 'I have little doubt he is closer to God than I am!'

Arthur would have to come again, the Rabbi's wife said as she was clearing away. He heard himself say yes and number of thank yous – but he had that sense of being pulled underwater again and came back up onto the shore with weak, liquid legs. He wanted to go back – but a sickness rose as he saw himself there again: the noise, the food, the faces – too much, it was all too much.

He slipped behind one of the guests looking through a photograph album on a table by the window.

'Unbelievable to think it's all gone,' the guest said.

'All too believable,' the Rabbi said, putting his hand on the guest's arm before following Arthur to the door.

'Leo, I don't like him walking back by himself so late,' the Rabbi's wife said, getting Arthur's coat, asking if he'd be warm enough.

'I'm just at Llanvanor,' Arthur said.

'Simon,' the Rabbi's wife called out, her hand on Arthur's shoulder, 'where is he? Why don't you walk with Simon.'

The Rabbi looked between Arthur and his wife before he held Arthur's eyes and took his hand, 'Shabbat shalom.' And then, seeing him out and slipping the latch off the gate, he said Arthur could knock on his door on Wednesday at four-thirty if he had any more questions.

He let himself imagine that what he'd discovered during those Wednesday afternoons with the Rabbi might be found at the college, as though it rested in the language and the liturgy alone rather than the second chair the Rabbi used to pull up to his desk for Arthur, or the way the Rabbi's eyes would seem to smile, a sudden brightness in them as he took a book off the shelf and turned the page, setting it between him and Arthur. Gestures that might have given so little, yet gave so much – but there was something else too, harder to identify, dislocated from word or action, unwrapped in the prompt made by the long pause the Rabbi left after he read – yes, it was there, in that pause – just – slight but significant as an ellipsis, where the sounds could sink in, sink in and speak again. The Rabbi would ask Arthur to try himself then, to see if he might make them his own, helping him link them to shape the words that built kings and deserts and temples and oceans, the clamour of voices, unlocked, carrying stories that had travelled thousands of miles on a journey that seemed to have no end. And the questions – with the Rabbi it was always the questions – and the Rabbi would put his hand on Arthur's arm, wondering if Arthur might look a little closer, *go on,* he'd say, *see where you end up*, and the Rabbi right there when Arthur couldn't find his way. Arthur would sometimes try and hurry, rub his knee and take a breath, reel off guesses and the Rabbi would shake his head gently and give Arthur a hint of smile, *Take your time, it is OK to take your time.* But once there at the college, sitting in the seminar, he couldn't touch what the Rabbi had drawn him towards any more than he could find an anchor in the months of tutorials and the cramming that had followed. The voices on the page sounded still but they were incomprehensible – incomprehensible but insistent, no longer offerings but a demand he couldn't answer, a hollering that couldn't be distinguished from the mix of strange tongues he used to hear some nights, nights when he thought he wasn't asleep only to wake to a chorus of cries soaring and fading.

*Close your eyes, just –*

Hadn't heard them again until that first seminar. Somehow thought he might beat them down as though dry, forensic detachment would be enough to silence them. Well, he'd got away from them now – the flames would curl up over the last two years at the college, catch and burn everything that went before.

Standing in the garden at Llanvanor, Arthur set the blaze going a bit further down than where Gerald had that day. The flare was mesmeric this time, spitting black and gold and blue – but there was no victory to be had, only an obliteration. His eyes drank themselves blind until a pair of jointless legs crossed his vision and a sober lens drew Sylvie into focus just as she was reaching her hands into the flames. He tried to call out as he lunged forward but the damp air had caught the smoke, choking his voice, tripping him back a step. *Ma, Ma,* he managed, pulling himself up, unable to see for a moment, only the fire bursting bright before Sylvie became clear again. He locked his arm round her waist, her moan stifled and body thrashing –

*Leave me, leave –*

*Please, Ma, please –*

Her breath began to ease as Arthur repeated the same two words over and over, not daring to offer another or to ask why, just let those two words become familiar, as though anything more than the smallest token of another world entering hers might throw her back –

*Please, Ma, please –*

He tried to draw her inside then but her head dropped forward and she froze at the next step, closing off a sob before it could break.

That evening, hands bandaged, she was laughing about what a butterfingers she'd been with the pot of peas.

'No one likes peas,' Gerald said, getting up. He pushed his chair in and stood behind it for a moment, sighing as he turned to leave.

Arthur waited for the sound of Gerald's last steps to fall away before he covered one of Sylvie's bandaged hands with his.

'What did you do that for, Ma?'

'I just get so cold,' she said, 'so cold.'

*September 1947*

The boy's face had started to open – but it twitched with every movement Sylvie made.

'It's not normal,' Gerald said, looking up from his paper. Sylvie wrung out the milk from the cloth and took a breath. So the boy had knocked his milk over. So what.

'It was an accident,' she said, thankful the constriction in her throat kept her voice from transgressing the careful volume she had tried to preserve since the boy had arrived.

'Funny how we keep having the same *accident* every morning,' Gerald went on, flicking another page without reading it. 'We'll have to do something about it – and the way his eyes keep following you –'

'No they don't –'

'Because that certainly isn't normal.'

'Oh for goodness' sake,' Sylvie said, dropping the cloth as her voice breached the limit she'd set. She turned round and felt the glassy black tremor catch her. 'Go and sit with Harry,' she said – but only his eyes moved, their sudden light tracking Sylvie's face, hands, steps.

'Arthur,' Gerald began, maintaining an even tone. 'Arthur, look at me when I'm talking to you.' The boy had been with them for almost three months but he still wouldn't answer to the name he'd been given – according to Gerald he never answered to anything at all. He smacked his hands over his ears and ducked behind the sofa. Sylvie's eyes flicked at Gerald, clamping his mouth over a livid *What!* Gerald pushed the paper aside and wrenched Arthur upright. This was not the way for a proper little Englishman to behave. The rigid body looked tiny in Gerald's grip and it was a moment before it jerked like a caught fish.

'Please, Gerald,' Sylvie sent her whisper through hesitant lips, saving what quiet she could. The boy seemed to hear gunshots going off in his head at the slightest sound, shrivelling him just as Sylvie felt sure he was at last becoming life-size. Gerald had been saying he had to wonder if the boy they'd taken in wasn't the runt of an abandoned litter – couldn't tell if it would yelp or flee. Runt or not, he was Arthur – or would be; Sylvie couldn't look at the eyes flashing out of the crushed bundle she took out of Gerald's hands into her own. They weren't the boy's eyes, they were the eyes of his dead mother: she looked out of them, asking how Sylvie could have stolen her child – she hadn't – the boy's mother had to understand – it was Sylvie's child who had been stolen – but for a twig-baby and a scattering of buds, she hadn't even been able to touch his death.

*Arthur*, Sylvie mouthed.

So small, so dark, so quiet. But there was the defiant pulse of survival in that quietness, a vigilance that had held its breath. *Twice hidden* – was that what she had been told? Told or imagined? The voice that would have spoken to her had faded, perhaps no one had spoken at all – at least no more than to explain that the child would be sent on what amounted to a 'sale or return' basis. Always fresh horror on the wireless and in the paper, muddled too soon with her Thursday nightmare: a twig baby, the token gesture of buds; buds white bled red by the nameless faces and uncounted bodies, the headlines and the newsreels, caught and heard in flashes that shook the senses but failed to pierce the mind – the mind chased daily to hunt new tricks to shield itself, refusing what it could not bear to believe – refuse or be shattered. No one could confirm what little information she'd been given about the child she was learning to hold in her arms: *mother presumed shot... nationality: doubtful...* or was it *uncertain*, she'd slowly erased the those few details along with the name printed on the document, inserting *Arthur* in its place. The one voice that had stayed clear was one on the home service, so clear still – she was holding Harry and she'd turned it on just to hear something beyond them and their tiny airless world – it was a soldier's, his accent northern, yes, and his voice was barely holding, saying how he'd uncovered the blackened face of a baby and a woman had begged him for milk and he'd given her milk and she'd run, staggered, fallen.

Sylvie folded the boy in towards her, taking in the warmth she meant to give. *Mother presumed shot…* Even this frail speculation had been recorded in parentheses. Russian soldiers had found the baby in a hut, his body wrapped in paper amongst the splayed limbs of the dead. Always at night, just as she was at last falling asleep, Sylvie would catch sight of the woman who would never hold her child – but there was no face – only two blind voids puncturing a mask of skin fitted to a skull. Her own Arthur's eyes were the only ones to flash – seeing Sylvie holding this strange small darkness, seeing himself replaced. Mrs Cohen would never do that. She would go on waiting for the post that would never come.

'Well now, who's this smart young man?' Mrs Cohen had asked, coming to the end of her lawn as Sylvie came back with the boys from their first Thursday at the park.

They hadn't really spoken these past couple of years, not since London lit up and Sylvie's world went dark. Mrs Cohen wouldn't let her world go dark, though. Sylvie had asked Arthur to tell the nice lady his name but he dropped to the ground and tied his arms round her legs. Harry shouted his name across. Mrs Cohen laughed, 'Well how do you do, Mr Harry?'

'Sorry,' Sylvie had said, 'Arthur's a bit of a shy one.' It took a moment for Mrs Cohen to connect the name with the boy.

Mrs Cohen came towards them but stopped at the curb, 'I think that's a marvellous name!' she said. Her voice was too loud, her intonation too buoyant. 'I think that's just… as it should be. Do come in for a little something.'

'Thank you but we can't stop,' Sylvie had said, prizing Arthur from her leg so she could get Harry before he trundled to Mrs Cohen's gate. Harry shouted his name again.

'Goodbye for now, Mr Harry.' Mrs Cohen stepped back and went on waiting.

*March 1949*

'Absolutely mad,' Gerald was saying as Sylvie buttoned up the boys' coats, stark raving she was, it was pouring. Well then she'd take the brolly and the boys had their wellies, besides they'd been stuck in all day and it was a Thursday – she always took the boys to the park on a Thursday. Sylvie opened the door and the wind snatched it away from her, swinging it wide. 'I'll say no more,' Gerald said, except to say that not only was she stark raving mad she was a lunatic – 'do you hear me Sylvie? You're a lunatic – that's what I'll have to tell the doctor when the three of you get pneumonia.' They wouldn't get pneumonia, she said, stepping outside, the umbrella turned inside out as Harold ran to jump in the puddles along the front path, Arthur keeping a step behind, face turned up and tongue stuck out, catching drops of rain.

'Water,' Arthur explained to Sylvie when she tried to pull him along.

'Rain,' Gerald barked. 'Get back inside all three of you or I swear to God I'll—'

'You'll what?' Sylvie dropped Arthur's hand, her eyes and smile shimmering. 'Or you'll what, Gerald?' His open mouth let her go on. 'Tell me Gerald, what will you do?' Sylvie watched the threat puff and deflate in his cheeks. 'You're not in the army now, General Gerald, we're not your little soldiers.'

The words had been corroding unsaid since the first night Sylvie had had to feel the heat and weight of another body beside her again, flesh voluble as breath, smothering her numb with the General's homecoming. *General Gerald*. Sylvie would never have let herself call him that back then, however deliciously crisp. The mockery would have been another lash to his great bulk. He'd spent his life giving orders and his time in the army taking them, it wasn't until he got demobbed that he could set about restoring the balance. He was answerable to no one now – not after those last months, held up in a depot camp, the end drawn out in case he might be sent East, the last four years creeping up to catch him. And coming back to what? Snide comments from civvies asking if he'd had a fine time of it at the country's expense. He'd quipped he should have signed his letters as the General – *Mother seems to think I was running the show, be good enough not to put her right,* a bit of a joke between them, Sylvie had thought. He'd explode now, surely. But he didn't – not yet. Sylvie would learn Gerald's various strategies for keeping his soldiers in place. That calm with which he could take a long breath and give his slow nod, his light tut, in an instant making all the sharp, terrifying satisfaction she imagined she'd taste a floury mouthful. *Go on, Sylvie,* she'd tell herself, *go back to Maldon, you know where the door is.* But she couldn't. Now that the war was over there had to be something else to make sense of all the sleepless fear and waiting rage.

'I've never heard anything so mad in all my life,' Gerald muttered. Sylvie saluted the door that didn't require the wind to slam it and turned.

Between Harry's refusal to miss out on a single puddle and Arthur's insistence that he 'Stop! Stop!' and that Sylvie 'Stop! Stop!', trying to show them how to taste the rain, Sylvie heard her voice trip into Gerald's, 'I'll leave you both here if you don't hurry up.' So brisk. It wasn't her voice. How did Gerald keep finding his way inside her? Maybe it was the pills. Might have got her up but pushed her off the edge of sharper dreams. She'd give both of the bottles back to Mrs Cohen. She shouldn't have let her start talking to her the other week, she knew how Mrs Cohen would only get her to come in, tell Sylvie not to worry, she'd keep her ear out for the post, Mrs Cohen's unfailing illusion hypnotic as a lullaby. Sylvie had listened again to the same details that made the story of the son Mrs Cohen had never stopped waiting for more real than his death, too sudden and anonymous to be true. He was there in front of them, the air carved out to accommodate him – the way she did that, etching a life with her hands and her words, brought Sylvie's Arthur back to life too. Sylvie had fallen asleep then, only for about ten minutes but she juddered awake, startled by the shawl Mrs Cohen had laid over her –

'The boys!'

'Don't distress yourself, dear,' Mrs Cohen had said, taking Sylvie onto her lawn to see Arthur and Harry had been set to work with their own toy spades, 'We all have our little spells.'

'Look at me digging, Ma!'

Mrs Cohen had handed Sylvie two brown bottles before she left. A little something to pick her up and another to help her drop off.

'Mrs Cohen, I really don't think—' Sylvie's objection fractured as Mrs Cohen's eyes moved towards the boys – they were huddling together in the corner. 'They're playing, isn't it lovely how they play together.'

'Lovely,' Mrs Cohen said, 'But Sylvie—'

'Really, Mrs Cohen, they never squabble,' she said, bright as she could, a quick, sheer smile as she turned to the boys. 'Come along now. Arthur, Harry, come along.'

No, she didn't need Mrs Cohen's pills, she was fine. Well just in case, Mrs Cohen had said, putting them into Sylvie's bag.

She'd stop taking them. Get rid of them before Gerald found them. He didn't believe in pills and he certainly didn't believe in spells – not after what happened to his father. Gerald had asked how he could be expected to have time for a man who couldn't hold on to his nerve – 'Still got my nerve,' Gerald was prone to reminding Sylvie, checking his hands, his guts – 'see that, never lost my nerve.'

'I'm cold,' Harry whined.

'I told you to hurry up,' Sylvie said, the rain smacking her face and hands.

'I'm cold cold cold!' Harry was starting to cry.

'Well that won't get you warm – we'll be home soon enough.' They would be, they'd have to be, she'd be very quick this time and get them back, run them a hot bath – 'come on, quickly now.'

There was a bench by the pond under an arch but she'd never sat the boys there before, it was too far in any case, she'd have to put them where she always did, where there was no going off, where it was Harry's job to hold Arthur's hand and Arthur's job to hold Harry's hand and not to talk to anyone – not that she'd have to worry about that today – the rain had emptied the park. Harry's face was swollen with tearless sobs –

'Who's going to be a good soldier and look after Arthur?'

Harry sang that he was. Sylvie looked at Arthur's face, sewn shut the way it had been in those first weeks.

'And who's going to…' She'd only be a minute, she could tell him later how she'd just gone to visit that other little Arthur she'd told him all about, gone to see how big and strong he was getting – he'd come with her one day and then the sewn shut face would open and she'd promise that next time there'd be lots of time to play because the sun would have his hat on –

Looking back never did anyone any good so she went straight to where she'd planted him – just the other side of the bandstand. Her pocketful of dried buds were wet and stuck to her palms. She wiped them off, said he'd have to hold tight, that there was someone she wanted him to meet, another little Arthur just like him.

'Look at my two brave soldiers!' Harry had his arms wrapped round Arthur whose face was crushed against his shoulder. Sylvie squeezed them both. 'See now,' she said, 'we're all brave soldiers, aren't we?' All brave and blue and shivering. Neither of the boys made a sound on the way back, they were so good Sylvie said as she reached the front door to find it locked, so so good, she said knocking, so very –

At least the rain meant Mrs Cohen was inside. She'd seen them, though, and was coming out with her umbrella.

'Are you shut out?'

A quick cool gust from Sylvie's last reserves: 'We're fine, thank you.'

'Well dear, if you need anything…' Mrs Cohen seemed to dissolve into the rain. Sylvie's eyes closed over the heat welling in them. There was something in Mrs Cohen's kindness that made her ache. He'll be home to you soon, Sylvie thought – *let her keep him, let her keep her lie,* the truth was savage but Mrs Cohen's lie was as kind as she was.

Sylvie gave a weak knock and sat herself and the boys down on the front step. The car was gone. The sun has got his… she tried to sing, rocking the boys a little. Must think this is all very clever, very funny, make Sylvie learn, teach silly Sylvie a lesson. Silly silly Sylvie, clever clever Gerald. The sun has – come on sing! Sing! The boys seemed to have shrunk under her arms, she dropped to a vague hum, stop shivering, stop it – Sylvie heard the car door and Gerald's steps crunching up to them.

'Looks like you've been having fun and games,' he said.

'That was a nasty trick.'

'Good God! I was frightened out of my life and you—'

'They'd be dry by now—'

'Mad, absolutely mad,' Gerald was muttering as he turned the key. 'Well for God's sake get in!' Sylvie felt limp. She squeezed the boys tighter to try and feel her strength against something but they went slack and a moment later Gerald was lifting her ragdoll soldiers up, saying he was going to get them into a hot bath –

'I was going to do that,' Sylvie said, closing the door behind her, 'I was—'

'Now don't you worry about that,' Gerald's voice was clean and sleek as a licked cat. Pitched against the boys' silence, his words measured out a lecture for her. At least Harry was beginning to whimper a little, enough to say that he was alright, that she was alright. She shut her eyes, holding on to the sound of Harry's short, sharp breaths, as though they might shield her from the silence of her two little Arthurs, the wound opening as she heard now what she had then – she had failed them both.

*June 1967*

Arthur could feel the silence begin to press itself against the edges of the trudge and bustle up the hill behind the park. He had to pop the gold locks of his briefcase just to pinch the quiet. The inevitable emptiness of the case made it no less disappointing – familiarity does not always bring comfort, but it was preferable to the humiliation of carting about whatever it was he might have carted about – whatever it was that might have told the world (or, rather told his father and his brother Harry), that this young man is going somewhere, this young man will some day be someone we shall wonder how we ever did without.

Less than a week after Arthur had set light to every last scrap of evidence of his *unmet potential*, Gerald and Harry had him kitted out – *not bad for a college man, eh Harry* – telling him that, if he played his cards right, he could work his way up from playing secretary to front of house in no time – he must have been a worse player than he'd thought since he ended up spending as long rearranging the filing cabinet as he had under Epstein's surveillance. He'd had it with both of them.

*First you quit the college, now here – I won't have a boy who's a quitter. That's what you are, Arthur – you're a quitter. Can't stick at anything.*

Gerald gave him a day before he was back:

*What else are you going to do with yourself, chum?*

Never. He was on his way up – or would be; the labour exchange would come good, wouldn't it? It had to. *It's just a matter of persistence*, he was told again last week. *I've been persisting for six months*, the man behind him in the queue snorted when Arthur quoted this wisdom, another snort as the man noted Arthur's case. The last interview was at Alderson & Co. – Mr Alderson, sucking his breath through his teeth, had put both his hands on his desk and asked Arthur what price he would put on time. Arthur's eyes fixed on Mr Alderson's hands.

'Price? I – er – I'm not too sure I can answer that, sir.'

Arthur was already turning off Lisson Grove by the time he realised Mr Alderson was referring to the fact Arthur had turned up ten minutes late.

'Chin up, dear.'

Arthur presented his card to the woman at the cash desk and strained a smile, teeth clenching as he took the dole he'd be handing over to Gerald. Gerald had held it out in front of him the first time, not looking up at Arthur as he said there were barrow boys making a tidier sum – Arthur had tried to mumble that line about persistence, claiming he was starting somewhere the following Monday, the conviction in his tone straining to counter his own incredulity as much as Gerald's – somewhere, he went on, with *prospects*.

'Prospects! Well I never! Do you hear that, Harry?'

Someone would take him on. *I'm a quick learner*, he'd say. But he wasn't – he gathered slowly, making sure of each step before considering the next. Still, he had the case – that had to count for something, gave the right impression, didn't it? Less convincing was the third-hand tie and, perhaps less convincing still, the park bench – it had seemed a refuge at first, an interval of anonymity, even invisibility, until passing eyes, curious or irritable, forced him to take shelter under the arch more quickly than a turning sky – and yet, by now, each return filled him with a sense of dread and duty worthy of the working man. Except Thursdays – there was, if his luck was in and the sun was kind, a Thursday to look forward to: as soon as the bells had chimed the half hour the twin girls would cartwheel past, disappear behind the bandstand and then, just before the park folded back in on him, came the voice that called out that it was time to go. He'd watch the woman hold her hands out and the twins take one each, swinging their arms up before they raced to the gates, the woman patting her bun as she ran after. But it would be a whole summer of Thursdays before Arthur would know that woman to be Lydia.

In the absence of a lone pair of black wings to cross the sky, Arthur made do with the pigeon investigating the crusts he'd dropped at noon. It was always during these last minutes, his homecoming all too imminent, sitting out the remainder of his post, that all the sluggish hours since nine at once bounced up to chase each other round the clock and Arthur out the gates, down the hill and back to Llanvanor Road, during which time he would take the opportunity to prepare himself, rehearsing various alternatives of a day he hadn't had – because today was always at last the day that they would start quizzing him all over again – yes they would want to know – today was the day they would catch him out!

*Tell us Arthur, we're intrigued, what exactly is the nature of your employment?*

The vein on Arthur's forehead sprouted a whole new tree life, branching out towards his temple and up to his hairline –

*Prospects!*

Of course his father hadn't bought it. Of course not. And to think how he'd gone, day after day, preparing and rehearsing exactly what he'd say to make his father sit up and swallow his words – with such diligence, in such detail – only to get a weekly snipe about *earning his keep.* That and Gerald's spluttering laugh. One of them might have at least wondered how his day was. Hardly. Unless he counted Gerald's performance – just last week it was – playing the dogged inspector –

*Perhaps young Arthur's been wandering incognito? Hiding from the knock at the door like an enemy alien –*

Harry had looked up at Gerald, his chuckle a little too loud in an effort to compensate for the delay. 'Enemy alien! That's a good one, Dad.'

'It's alright, Arthur, they've been and gone.'

Arthur had looked over at Sylvie, she wasn't laughing. 'Laugh!' His father had commanded, leaning forward – but then his hardened eyes closed and he sat back, 'For God's sake, love,' he muttered into his lap, 'can't you just—'

Arthur watched her face contort. His father used to like to remind him what had happened to Mrs Cohen's husband. People said he'd been interned, that a car had come in the early hours right at the start of the war – *before you boys were even twinkling in anyone's eyes* – and no one had ever seen him again. *That's right, Arthur, the crack of dawn: collar the lot!* They said it was one of the reasons Mrs Cohen wasn't right in the head.

'People shouldn't say things like that about Mrs Cohen,' Sylvie had said.

Gerald said he could say what he damn well liked. It seemed to Arthur as though Gerald had kept the story about Mrs Cohen's husband close to hand for the best part of twenty years, ready to expound ever since a certain small dark quietness arrived, a warning of sorts. A car drove up for Mrs Cohen too one day – but that was years later and his father always kept his eyes on Sylvie whenever he told that one.

Arthur offered several hellos to the empty kitchen and front room – his father's hat had reserved his armchair should Goldilocks be tempted. *No, he would never let them dress him up in that!* Arthur lifted the hat, turned it over and back, put it on. He would need to pick his briefcase back up to be sure. The two, he could only admit, were not incompatible. He sat down in the armchair the hat had reserved – just to consider –

'Hello there, Arthur!'

'Harry!' The name (though blurted) and the hat (though tossed) seemed to Arthur to have flown across the room with unquestionable autonomy, landing together at Harry's feet while their supposed agent attempted to extricate himself from the armchair that had swallowed him – he would be more appreciative of his park bench tomorrow. Harry shared a look with the hat, let a chuckle roll around his mouth and, taking the two necessary strides up towards Arthur, thrust the bowl of nuts under Arthur's chin: 'Nut?'

'No thank you,' Arthur said, a little off balance as he came upright. To return the hat to its rightful place would admit responsibility for the indignity it had suffered; to leave it as it was would allow it to accuse him from the floor – a verdict Harry would have no choice but to agree with. Arthur might have been able to commend himself on the speed with which he was able to improvise an escape route into the hallway had another overlooked variable not at that moment come through the front door – or rather was being urged through the front door but was, in fact, immobilised on the front step:

'Come on Sylvie, that's my girl.'

It was now that Arthur would gladly have been eaten whole by the voracious armchair where he would gladly have returned to his park bench where –

'Mind your back, Arthur.' His father, standing behind his mother, palm hardened against her back, had fixed his eyes on their destination – the end of the hall – and until this was reached neither his hand nor his eyes would release their pressure.

'Not much further now, Sylvie,' a taut band of encouragement accompanying their every step. They stopped, his father came round in front of her, stroked her cheek and took her chin between his fingers, 'Has my Sylvie lost her smile? Has she? Where's my Sylvie's smile?'

It had been months since this routine which now averaged three or four times a year: his father would bring his mother back from wherever it was he'd taken her off to a week or so before –

'Where are you going, Dad? You alright, Ma?'

'We're off to find your mother's smile,' his father would say, summoning a hollow chuckle, sinking a little as he stared dumb at some unidentifiable point, a moustache of crevices gathering and darkening over his upper lip, hands rubbing together, refuelling an empty tank. While she was away his words dwindled to the *Oh, I don't know* on his way up to bed, just audible through a sigh, not directed towards anyone, jolting if Harry responded.

Unmoored without his father's cues, Harry drifted round the house until he found a guide in Arthur's careful steps and voice. Their fractional nods, perceptible only to one another, became identical, one starting their supper as the other finished, tacitly acknowledging this interval until Sylvie came back, still without her smile. Sometimes she was given another, but even Gerald said they might have given her one that fit properly, no wonder they slid right off.

Arthur occupied his eyes with the carpet and his hands with each other behind his back, guarding himself by making a guard of himself until the scene had safely passed through and the danger of catching his mother's half-closed eyes averted.

'My Sylvie had a nice smile, didn't she? I wonder what happened to my Sylvie's smile.' There was a pause. His father was clicking his tongue; his brother was coming though, humming:

'Everything alright?' Harry asked, nonchalance unsteadied, stalling as he tried and failed to resume his hum.

'Everything's just fine, we're just trying to find your mother's smile – you haven't seen it anywhere, have you?'

'I'm afraid not.'

'Arthur?'

No, he would not answer, he would not look up.

'Arthur!'

'Yes, Dad,' he said, voice and eyes tricked away from their office.

'We're missing something and I'm wondering if you can help us.' He was squeezing their mother's chin again, turning it a little each way before he looked at Arthur.

'I don't think so.'

'Well of course you can't.' His father dropped the chin. 'Get yourself upstairs, Sylvie, and wash your hands and face, I need a sit-down,' he said, dusting off her shoulders. Arthur looked up as she turned. Too soon: the half-closed eyes caught his. He tried a smile. The half-closed eyes tried to shut, the lids twitching.

'Right,' his father concluded, going into the front room. 'I'm having my sit-down – Harold!'

'Dad.'

'My hat seems to be on the floor.'

'Yes, Dad.'

'What is my hat doing on the floor?'

'I don't know, Dad.'

'Does my hat go on the floor?'

'No Dad, it goes on your chair.'

'And who's been sitting in my—' His father's chuckle had returned to form.

'Ask Arthur!' Harry said, chuckling along.

'I'm asking you.'

Arthur was contemplating the door, the stairs, the end of the hall. None would rescue him.

'Arthur!'

'Yes?'

'Take a cup of tea up to your mother.'

Arthur stood outside her door, blowing over the cup in his hand. He usually only knocked once, left the tea on the landing and waited halfway down the stairs for a few minutes, listening for her to take it. She never did, though, so he'd gulp it down before Gerald found it had gone cold. But Arthur wanted to give it to her himself this time, sit with her while she drank it. He made a succession of knocks. 'Ma,' he whispered, 'Ma, it's me.' He knocked again and opened the door. She was sitting on the edge of the bed, pulling at her lank ponytail.

'It's all knotted,' she said.

'Do you want tea, I've got you some tea,' Arthur said, putting the cup down.

'All tangled.' She looked up at him, eyes open now.

'It's alright, Ma, it's me, Arthur.'

'No,' she said, smiling her broken-toothed smile. 'You're not Arthur. Not my Arthur.'

*March 1950*

Sylvie drew her arm over her eyes before she put the lamp back on. Gerald was on his second round of gargling, rinsing, spitting. He'd be on to the cupboards in a moment – yes, and now rattling each of the bottles. He hadn't said a word about the pills this week, instead he allowed the rattle to serve as oracle: *You wait,* the rattled bottles said, *you'll be just like my old man.* The extended throat-clearing confirmed the prediction.

Light off, thuds, sighs.

Sylvie slid a little further under the tight sheets, one side of her body pulled down by Gerald's weight sinking the mattress. She opened her eyes into the darkness, waiting for him to give the shudder that told her he'd be closed up in sleep any minute. It was only ever when she heard the drop in his breath, deepening but still clear, not yet heavy, viscous, harsh, that she sensed again how fragile his great, bursting mass was – it would have crushed her a moment ago, but sleep emptied him, bound him. She'd heard his snore thicken, catch and break one night. Little more than a nick in the rhythm but it felt like a rupture and she knew he'd been flung by a nightmare into a world she'd never seen and he'd never share. Not General Gerald. But he wasn't Gerald then – woke as the man he must have been or become in the years he was away. His hands had shot in front of him as he sat up and he seemed to be trying to pull something towards him, saying he couldn't move. He hadn't heard her saying his name, but then his hand flew back to push her away. He put his shaking hands under the covers, an impulse to protect them or hide them she didn't know – but he let her hold them, hadn't pushed her away again, just let hands make sense of what they could, speaking more than they had since before the war. 'Not like my father,' he insisted, but his hands wouldn't listen. *Of course not,* Sylvie thought, believing it for him, for herself, instinct making her keep the words silent; unspoken they couldn't give away the lie that would crack his fear wide open and her heart with it. But that heart wasn't hers and the hands she was holding weren't Gerald's. She'd looked at his hands for too long the next morning. 'What?' He'd asked. 'What are you looking at?' 'Nothing,' she'd said and finished her tea.

That was only a few weeks ago but she knew they would never mention it. His sleep was deep enough for her to get up now but she tested slight movements even so, standing at the door before she slipped through it and down the hall to check on the boys again. Just as she'd left them. Always the nights she didn't check she'd hear the footsteps along the hall and have to rush down, bundle Arthur up and coax him back to bed. Both as they were then: one, splayed on his back, open-mouthed, one curled up foetal, face sewn shut – one little Harry and one little Arthur – but not her little Arthur. Sylvie tried to clench her hands to release them from the numb grip that locked them but her fingers were thick with senselessness, separate from her as she touched the child's shoulder. His eyes were on her, flashing their questions. 'Ssh,' she said, turning to see if Harry had been woken, 'ssh.' Fingers still numb as they passed over his head. She went rigid as she walked backwards and stood outside their room, knowing her legs would not take her to see again what she already knew: this Arthur was not her Arthur – her Arthur had gone. Whether he'd died again in the womb of the ground or left to find a grave that would keep him; where he could share in the mourning his corpse was due, steal a prayer's echo, a blown petal, where it wasn't just the gesture of dried buds and a quick word on a Thursday, the corset froze round Sylvie's heart and lungs clamped the impervious truth. The scream she'd held but never heard coursed through her for what would be the third and last time. It did not so much cease as freeze. But the scream that would not be melted until she made her way back to him was the same scream that iced her lungs, her heart, iced her legs rigid – they couldn't take her – not to the gates she'd have to climb over, not past the bench she sat the boys on, not behind the bandstand and up to where she'd planted him. Knowing was not and would never be enough. She would have to dig and dig – she'd dig up the entire park if she had to, tunnelling through damp soil to know what she already knew but the sun was just about to put his hat on when her legs entombed her with their protest: they would not take her any further than the gas heater.

It was past four the next afternoon when Sylvie heard Harry singing 'the sun has got his hat on, Harry's got his hat on! Harry's got his hat on!' Arthur patted his head and looked at Sylvie, 'Hat, hat, hat,' he said.

The sun may well have had his hat on but no, they were not going to the park.

Her skin was burning but her calves and feet, still iced, would not let her move. Arthur was dragging her coat along behind him, landing it on Sylvie like a puppy with a lead, 'hat,' he said, 'hat for little Arthur.'

Sylvie drew her knees up to her chest and turned her face away. 'Not today, Arthur.' Gerald would be back soon and Harry would be jumping up and down, and Arthur still *hat, hat, hat*... Well she was sorry and Gerald could say what he liked but she was not going to the park, if he felt so strongly about it, she would say, why didn't *he* take the boys to the park? Any moment now he would be walking through the door, solid and steady and no, *nothing like my father*. If anyone was going to turn into a vegetable it would be Sylvie, Sylvie who was still exactly where he'd told her to get the hell up from that morning –

Hadn't she even moved? he'd ask. Well of course she had, how else would the boys have been fed and if he started on about the dishes and the milk being left out to spoil at least there was evidence that she hadn't let the boys starve.

She had to get up. If she tried, though, it seemed some part of her might snap off, a limb, a hand, her head – perhaps she should, then, to see what would come off first, perhaps she could snap herself to pieces and one of her snapped off hands would pick her all up and put her in a pot to boil and feed her piece by piece to Gerald, let him taste that scream frozen inside boiled flesh, the iced flame of emptiness.

'The sun has got his hat on!'

'Not today, Harry. Not today.'

Arthur crawled under Sylvie's coat and put his head on her lap. It was a moment before her hand let her stroke his hair. 'Not today, Arthur. Not—'

Then tell him about that other little Arthur, the one just like him.

## *July 1967*

'Can I get you something, Ma?' Arthur asked as Sylvie got up. She shook her head, jointless legs insistent towards the door. She stopped. 'There was a pot here – what did you do with it?'

'It's right here, Ma,' Arthur said, reaching for the pot on the ledge.

She shook her head and came up to the ledge, running her hands over it – 'not that – another, another,' she said, tutting at the ledge, 'there was a pot – a pot with my last handful.'

'Are you alright? What is it, Ma?'

'Someone must have taken it – someone must have stolen it,' she said, flitting back from Arthur's arm as it reached for her shoulder.

'Stolen what?'

'Who's locked this?' the embers of Sylvie's voice sputtered. She pulled at the door handle, 'Who's locked me in?'

'No one's locked it; here, see,' Arthur said, opening the door. 'Where is it you want to go? I'll come with you.' Sylvie snatched her hand back before Arthur could reach again for her shoulder, leaving both to drop their hands, Arthur pocketing his, Sylvie examining her fingers as they strained to curl and uncurl, stretching the tight shiny heel of her palm, her eyes closing while her finger tips read the scarred maps of her hands, a puckered geography of ivory dips and bridges.

'Did you take my last handful of buds?'

Arthur blinked away the conviction that had crystallised over Sylvie's face, the question mark hammered off like a chip from an ice sculpture.

'I had a last handful and now they're gone.'

'It's alright Ma, it's me, it's—' Sylvie's brittle pivot round stopped him: her hand was veering back again, striking up, fingers uncurling. It hovered, the crooked splay of fingers softening, curving towards Arthur, stroking her scarred palm down his cheek, disclosing the reading her fingertips had taken,

'All creases and caverns,' Sylvie said. 'I never thought you'd take my last handful.'

Arthur opened his mouth to speak, closed it, let her palm repeat: Someone else's someone where her Arthur should have been.

Someone stood then, just inside the last door of Llanvanor Road, watching a woman totter by on toy stilts, her head always a pace further along, her legs unable to catch up, a paper doll by the time she reached the end, blown round the corner in a whirling cloak of crisped leaves snipped from a picture book and onto the Finchley Road.

'Afternoon.'

Next door was pruning back the rose tree. Arthur nodded, missing what next door had gone on to ask as he looked up towards the corner the paper doll had blown round.

'Don't see much of your mother these days.'

'No.'

'Alright is she?'

'Who?'

Next door wanted to assure Arthur that he wasn't one to pry but the only time he'd seen Sylvie of late was when Gerald was putting her in the car and when next door had called cheerio there was no cheery-bye back – and what's more, next door just so happened to be on his way for his constitutional when the car came back, but there was no Sylvie so, naturally, next door felt a little concern, especially after what happened with Mrs Cohen all those years ago – did Arthur remember Mrs Cohen?

'Yes, no, not really.'

'Such a shame.'

Now that she was out of view, Arthur could see Sylvie as she had been, as she still saw herself – agile, urgent. He could see her and himself beside her, as though they had taken her last handful together: up the hill and through the gates and back behind the bandstand –

'But your mother,' next door was saying,

'Fine, she's…'

Arthur turned inside. The pot. Buds. He would get her some buds. Dried. A handful that would be the last. Always the last, she'd said, as though this final scattering would let that other little Arthur lie, let him rest, let her rest. Arthur opened the pot, took the spare key out –

'What's this door doing wide open?' Gerald wiped his shoes off and strode past Arthur. 'Sylvie?'

Arthur flinched as he heard his father call out for his mother again. The key was dropped straight back into the pot, Arthur's coat put on and he was out the door, next door's 'Be seeing you,' jabbing him from behind, legs taking him up and on and through –

THESE GATES CLOSE AT SUNSET

Arthur hadn't noticed the darkening sky. He looked through and made out Sylvie's shape on the bench she'd always sat him and Harry on.

'Park's closed, pal.'

'Yes, I know, but that's my mother there.'

'No one in after dark.'

Arthur pointed towards the bench but, as he did, saw that Sylvie's shape had disappeared.

'Funny sort of mother you've got,' the keeper said, 'off you trot.'

No, he would not *trot off*. He would wait. That keeper would be gone soon and he'd climb over, find Sylvie –

*Ma – Ma, it's me –*

Arthur felt again the stroke of her palm down his cheek, saw her brittle pivot, her legs rigid – legs that seemed to totter on toy stilts, legs that couldn't take her –

Yet, still, she must have come, surely she must – where else she could have gone? Up and through and back behind the bandstand, stopping only to collect –

If someone hadn't taken the last handful –

Arthur pictured the paper cut-out being blown up and down Llanvanor Road before it was tossed through the last door to be charred by Gerald's interrogation. Ashes for Cinders to sweep. No, he couldn't go back – Harry poking his head in – he couldn't *trot off*. Couldn't he just sit in the Old Bull and have a pint? Sammy might be in there – or Pete – one of them might put him up for the night, perhaps longer, perhaps he'd never have to go back at all, never have to hear what was said by the stroke of a palm scarred and puckered, by the glove of silver-pink skin, by the sound of her fractured step and Gerald's striding thuds coming after, never have to see what he'd never stopped hearing even after there'd been no more telling – but even if Sammy or Pete were there he hadn't spoken to them since he'd left the college – another passport confiscated, they'd never let him over that border now, not that he imagined anyone had ever taken him for anything but an imposter –

*Enemy Alien!*

It was only a matter of time before he was defrauded – better to take matters into his own hands, leave before he was exiled. Sammy and Pete had been different of course – hadn't they? Still, he couldn't go into the Old Bull, he couldn't sit there while his mother was being blown and tossed and charred, funny sort or not.

Not so very funny, Sylvie had never made it further than the corner Arthur had kept his eyes on but hadn't seen as his legs sped him intent on going where Sylvie's had been intent on going, intent but –

*Funny sort of* –

'Oh Ma.'

'Why don't they work?' she asked. 'My legs, they won't work.'

'Let me help you,' Arthur said, putting his arm through hers. Sylvie lurched, pulling her arm back. There seemed to be no reflex to put her hands out, nothing to break her fall. Arthur hauled up the crumpled body, grappling with the strange heaviness of frailty. Eyes passed, peered over, passed on.

'It's OK Ma, you're OK, you're not hurt – you're not, are you?' She was slipping from his grasp, her head flopped down – 'you're alright' – oh Christ, he'd killed her – he was standing at the corner of Llanvanor and Finchley Road with a corpse in his arms! 'You're alright aren't you, Ma?'

Her eyes flicked half open and she smiled the first of her broken-toothed smiles.

*June 1950*

Harry was running through the kitchen into the hall, Arthur just behind. He stopped and looked back at Sylvie. She shook her head. 'Harry,' she called out, urging her feet as far as the cupboard to get a puzzle out.

'No going to the park?' Harry asked, puffing his cheeks and folding his arms, solemnity upheld until he spied what Sylvie had in her hands.

'For me!' he announced, rushing towards her, taking the lid off the box as she set it down.

Sylvie felt the tug in her chest release, Harry's eager hands drawing out a smile, 'Yes darling, for you *and* Arthur. To share.' Arthur looked up at her and her smile fell, *not today*. 'Go on,' she said to Arthur, pointing to a corner piece. He picked it up, studying it for a moment before a knock at the door sent his eyes back to Sylvie. Her hand came up to her forehead, the heel of her palm sliding down her temple. She couldn't answer it – *not today, not* –

'Hello dear,' Mrs Cohen said, holding out a bunch of flowers, 'oh, I don't want to trouble you, only I saw these and –'

Sylvie looked at the flowers, unable to take them for a moment, swallowing as she lifted her eyes to Mrs Cohen, 'Goodness, thank you, you're too…' she murmured.

'Nonsense, dear! Nothing like a fresh bunch to brighten one's day!' She paused, 'it's been a little while – and I thought –'

'Thank you,' Sylvie said, taking the flowers, her step inside sudden as her corrected tone, instructing herself to find a vase –

*Just flowers, that's all, simply Mrs Cohen being kind –*

But, cutting the stems, they seemed to Sylvie a reminder that no, she still hadn't been back, she had broken her Thursday promise –

*Just flowers, that's all, simply –*

'I won't stay,' Mrs Cohen said. Sylvie looked at her, attention caught between the flowers and the boys – Arthur crouching, studying Harry's determination to jam two pieces of the puzzle together.

'Harry, let Arthur do some,' Sylvie said, nodding as Arthur looked up at her before her eyes were drawn back to the flowers. Her hand came up to her throat – 'thank you, Mrs Cohen, so – so thoughtful.'

Mrs Cohen shook her head, trying to hold Sylvie's gaze, 'Well, I suppose – unless there is anything that wants doing?'

'Nothing at all,' Sylvie said, disconnected from the calm in her own voice. She gave a taut smile, her head dipping as she went towards the door. Mrs Cohen paused, a caught gasp and a glance at the boys before she followed, turning back as she stepped out, her hand opening towards Sylvie.

*Just flowers – just Mrs Cohen being kind –*

Sylvie shut the door, her eyes closing as she leaned against it, resisting the little hand pulling at her skirt and the small voice she could just make out.

'What is it, darling?' she asked, the foetal ghost receding as she took Arthur's hand. 'I'll be in in a minute. Go and help Harry with the puzzle – go on now.' But he just kept his eyes on her hand, holding it tighter.

No. There'd be no more going to the park now – not on a Thursday or any other day – at least not with her. But week after week, this someone else's little someone dragged her coat over to her and, in answer to her tightened breath, huddled under it, nestling his head in her lap as she sat down. Sylvie pushed the unbearable warmth of his head away, her head folding towards her chest as he got up, listening to him dragging the coat across the floor, trailing the knock, brush and scrape of buttons and cloth behind him.

The sunlight plunged into the kitchen and, leaching the oblivion from closed eyes, made Sylvie trace through shut lids the outline of the little head she'd just pushed away, the shape of that small dark quietness pasted over the bloodless body that only hope engendered by grief could weave and plant and tend. Sylvie saw the countless pairs of feet that must have walked over his makeshift grave, the weeds that must have grown and been cut back, the tall grass and dropped wrappers, the kicked balls and picnics spread – just any patch of earth, oblivious steps trampling, blown petals falling, her Thursday promise decaying beneath.

Though Gerald wasn't back yet she felt as if he was standing over her, his face a parody of concern. She flinched from the imagined hand miming a kindness that, now touching her cheek, now touching her shoulder –

*Allow me –*

Adjusted the sunlight with polished sympathy, helping her see a little better the face, the body, she saw only too well –

*Please – please don't –*

*There now, Sylvie, open your eyes, there's a good girl –*

Throwing a shadow to double a small dark quiet. Gerald's breath seemed to be closing round her, mammalian blood heat radiating from him, sucking up the air and saturating her every pore, insulating the untouchable cold, the inaudible scream. More than five years since they'd taken her Arthur before she'd held him, but the moment still came right up to meet her, showing her what might have been the flicker of his unlived life, sending her to assemble the carcass she'd line with moss and soil and load with stones that outweighed the weight of grief, swaddling it in the wreaths that were her Arthur's due, strapped her work of her earth and death across her –

Gerald, just demobbed, had appeared to return as untouched as the house. He'd counted windows, heads, noting they were a soldier short – but he and his four walls were still intact so it was surely safe to presume that Sylvie must be too. When silenced mouths first threatened to whisper through an unseen crack General Gerald arrived to gag them and that joke about the General didn't sound much like a joke anymore.

'We'll soon have another,' he'd told Sylvie, handing Harry back to her.

Not if Sylvie could help it. She didn't have to. Gerald said there must be something wrong with her – she was doing it on purpose. Caught something while he was away, had she? Sylvie said he could think what he pleased and thanked her womb for refusing to let anything grow inside it again. If she'd never come to London, never met Gerald, those first walks with him by the river –

*Sweet Thames run softly for I speak not –*

Words were better kept in your head unless you wanted them turned inside out. What words? She didn't know the prayer for this one.

'Chop chop!'

Sylvie looked up: an immaculate Gerald was standing in an immaculate kitchen with two immaculate boys – one hatted, one not – close behind him.

'Cheerio, Sylvie.'

The immaculate man, kitchen and children said the rest. No trace of his hidden terrors, seeming to escape only on the occasional night, while hers, refusing confinement, followed her into the day. Well good. Go then. Let him take them to the park –

*It is a Thursday. Don't you always take the boys to park on a Thursday?*

Gerald, brushing off his shoes, checking the time as he waited for Harry and Arthur, may not have asked the question –

*Yes I always –*

But Sylvie always heard it.

'Say goodbye to your mother, boys.'

So he took them, every Thursday, leaving Sylvie in that immaculate kitchen, arms wrapped around her knees, feeling nothing but a changeless season.

Gerald directed their entrance as he had their exit: a single file led by the General, that someone else's little someone at the tail, a hatted Harry between – but why was it, Gerald asked as he brushed out the matted rear, that their orderly line was never quite so orderly on the way back in as it had been on the way out? Perhaps Sylvie could explain –

Why that someone else's little someone, now mud-caked, earth-caked –

Perhaps Sylvie might be able to tell him why Arthur did not want to play or race or –

'Harry won! Harry's the winner! Ma! Ma! Harry's—'

'Wonderful darling, wonderful—'

'Perhaps Sylvie might know why the boy ran off behind the bandstand?'

'No, I don't,' Sylvie said, pressing her hands into the floor to lever herself up, one protesting leg then the other.

'Do you have any idea what a fool I looked?' Gerald hissed.

'Well you should have been keeping an—'

'How dare you! You tell me why—'

'I can't, Gerald, I can't—'

'Like hell you don't – tearing up grass and—'

Sylvie looked at Arthur, at Gerald, her hand coming up to her head, heel of her palm crossing her brow. Gerald lunged for Arthur's arm, but Sylvie's hand shot between them, a glittering ferocity that had lain dormant woken as she pulled the boy in towards her. Gerald drew back, his glare locking her for a moment before he turned away.

*

Sylvie's hands admitted some of the heat from the flannel she wiped across the dirtied cheeks. The whites of black eyes gleamed out of a blackened face.

'Digging and digging,' Arthur said.

'You mustn't, Arthur, you mustn't – how could—' Her caught breath cutting off the question she didn't dare ask.

'What a little mess you are,' she said, trying to glide over the tremor in her voice, putting his hands in the water.

'Digging,' Arthur persisted. Sylvie could hear the tears waiting, in him, in her.

'Shhh, now, shhh…'

'But Ma, Ma—'

She shook her head, eyes prickling. No. No digging. She dried off his hands, 'No more.' It was no good, she told him, he wasn't there. No more other little Arthur.

'No other little—'

But she'd told him, told him. Sylvie took in the open eyes, the open face, unsewn, asking: tell him, tell him. Well then she would, just while she scrubbed his nails, just while Gerald was still asking Harry who the winner was –

'Harry's the winner!'

And, leaving the warmth of his little head on her lap, she'd begun again all about that other little Arthur, the one –

'Just like me!'

'Sssh now—'

'Just like me?' he whispered, mouthing along every few lines. Sylvie stopped, watching him shape the words in her silence. Enough now. That was enough. The warmth of a dead stranger's child where her Arthur should have been. Again she saw the boy's mother run, turn and drop. She checked his nails. They were done. But the little head would not be pushed away, instead it nestled again into the comfort it found in the folds of her skirt.

And, while the General commended his victorious soldier, Arthur, word perfect, played a vanquished Sylvie back to herself, proceeding automatically, silent repetitions softening creases and caverns – if she would not tell him, tell him, he would tell her, tell her: tell her all about that other little Arthur, now big enough and strong enough for them to pull up and out of the ground for the whole wide world to see.

'Harry's the—'

'Shut up! Shut up! Shut up!'

The soundless mouth stopped, the little head sprang up, the face flickered out, sewed itself shut.

'Dear God, Sylvie! What on earth's the matter now?' Gerald jerked round.

'Nothing, nothing.'

The General erected himself and leaned over towards Harry who was blinking back the tears that neither winners nor soldiers cried. Gerald snapped the eyes up: 'Who's the winner?' he demanded.

*Say Harry*, Sylvie willed him, *say Harry is.*

But Harry didn't want to be a winner anymore.

'Everyone wants to be a winner,' Gerald said. 'Isn't that right, Sylvie?'

'Everyone.'

Not Harry.

Well that was rather a shame because anyone who didn't want to be a winner obviously didn't want to go to the park ever again.

*August 1967*

A pair of squeaks behind him, below him, flipped Arthur's eyelids up, threw his head down, and out scrabbled the twins from under the bench, squeaks escalating to shrieks, leaving Arthur with his head suspended between his legs. His head found its way back up as they ran off – there was the woman chasing after them – and now marching them towards him – what had they told her? He hadn't done anything! He was innocent! But already Arthur was back in the playground swearing on his life, his mother's life, on the Queen, that he never pulled anyone's hair!

'Apologise to the gentleman!' the woman said. The twins looked down before they peered up at Arthur. 'Apologise!'

Arthur gripped his knees, smiled – could the woman see his nose was twitching? The twins could, he was sure; their mouths had formed tiny o's.

'I'm sorry,' the woman said, shaking her hands out of the two tugging hers.

'No, please – there's nothing to be—'

'They can be dreadful! Girls – apologise to the gentleman!'

*Gentleman* – that was twice! What would Harry and his father have to say about that? He had met a… lady – yes, he would tell them that he had met a lady who just happened, as it so happens, to think that he, Arthur, was a gentleman –

'Girls, say—'

'Sorry! Sorry, sorry, sorry!' They were running off again, a token cartwheel each and there it came as the woman turned, her voice calling out that it was time to go –

Going! Arthur got up, dashed towards them –

'Excuse me! Excuse me!'

'Yes?'

'Excuse me!' Three mouths tightened. Arthur slipped his hands into his pockets and glanced back towards the bench – oh why hadn't he just stayed put with his briefcase? Stayed and waited till next Thursday by which time, neither breathless nor flustered he would have Worked It All Out – he might even have improved the contents of his briefcase should she enquire –

'If you're going down towards the station,' he managed – there now, that wasn't so bad was it?

'No, up towards the pond.'

'Oh...' Arthur launched himself in the direction of the bench, snatched his briefcase and, before he'd quite caught up with the woman, sent a hopeful flurry towards her, 'If you're going up towards the pond.'

'Down towards the station,' the woman laughed over her shoulder. Arthur's eyes followed them to the gates before they returned the sky's blankness: 'Next Thursday,' he told it and soon he would be telling his father and Harry with the same solemnity that he, Arthur, a gentleman, having met a lady of some... responsibility, would need to consider moving on –

*Moving on! Where to? What lady?* –

And having been offered a... promotion – or perhaps having been promoted would be better –

*Promoted? To what?* –

Would naturally need to find alternative accommodation –

*What sort of alternative accommodation?* –

One that could accommodate his newly promoted, soon-to-be-wed-with-twins-inclusive self –

It did seem there was quite a bit to get All Worked Out – next Thursday had seemed agonisingly far away and now it had snuck up, waiting to meet him any moment – the course of events would have to be deprived of their brilliant simultaneity, in dull succession he would become employable, promotable – then, the flat, well really they needed a house, the four of them – and how to propose? He'd need to get a name off her first –

'Bit funny isn't it, man like you pissing the afternoon away like this—'

'It's only on a Thursday – I finish early on Thursdays – don't you want to sit down?'

'Not really,' she said as she sat, propping her elbows on her lap, her chin dipping to perch on interlaced fingers. 'Lydia. Well there it is then, I don't suppose there can be much harm in you having that.'

The twins skipped up to them, four ribboned plaits flying backwards, whispered into cupped ears, investigated Arthur with potion-green eyes and skipped off. Lydia was leaning forward, she seemed to be drinking them in.

'They're beautiful aren't they?' she said.

Arthur realised that he was behind, he was still consumed by the miracle that this woman, whose voice he had waited for every Thursday, had just given him her name – Lydia! – and this Lydia had remained seated in unimaginably close proximity for several thousands of seconds.

'I was beautiful too,' she said.

'Beautiful!' His assent sprang out of him with a little too much exuberance, edging the woman – Lydia! – along – only a fraction, but it wasn't a fraction Arthur felt he could sacrifice. Carefully, as though the word were new to him, he measured out a repetition. It had its own faults, coming out in a strained whisper. She hadn't seemed to hear him though, her ear was following the twins – they could be heard but not seen. Arthur watched her scanning for them. He should get up, show his concern –

'Don't worry,' he said, placing an unsure hand on her shoulder. The lightless glass of her eyes considered the hand until he removed it. She leaned back, smiling, hands coming together for a soundless clap – she didn't want reassuring. She was either marvellously reckless or marvellously composed. Either way it was marvellous – still, Arthur felt he ought to pocket his rejected hand.

'Oh dear,' Lydia said with a slight shrug, thumb and index finger flicking the back of her hand as though an insect had landed there. 'I suppose you had better kiss me now, hadn't you. It's usually best to get the first one out the way.'

*January 1951*

Sylvie had always said not to be frightened –

*It's only a dream –*

But it couldn't have been, he hadn't been asleep, he'd been trapped under all these bodies and his mouth was all filled up with them, he could taste it –

*Just close your eyes darling –*

He couldn't, he would have to stay up all night. Sometimes, if he went downstairs, Sylvie would be there and she'd let him sit next to her by the gas heater. She never seemed to see him at first but then she'd gasp – that always made him gasp too. Oh Arthur, she'd say, come here then, and she'd make it just like when they'd first stopped going to the park, with him curled up on the floor and his head on her lap and her coat over him. She didn't tell that story about the other little Arthur very much anymore and never told it right the way to the end. He would try and finish it for her but she'd make him get up and wouldn't let him put his head in her lap. He wasn't sure if that other little Arthur would ever come up out of the ground like she said – but if she said then he must – Sylvie wouldn't lie. But then where would Arthur go? Sylvie never said anything about that – she never said what happened next – the story just stopped… maybe that other little Arthur would have to sleep in Arthur's bed and Gerald would send Arthur back –

*Where you belong.*

Only some stories were true stories – Harry knew which were which but he couldn't ask him because the story about that other little Arthur was a secret – *No one else in the whole wide world*, Sylvie had said. Maybe that other little Arthur had bad dreams and couldn't wake up.

'Harry?' Arthur whispered.

Harry never had bad dreams. That, Gerald had said, was because he was a proper little soldier. Proper little soldiers didn't get out of bed until the curtains were opened, either – Sylvie wouldn't tell though, she had bad dreams too.

'Buck up, old boy.'

Gerald's voice. It didn't sound like him though – except for when he was talking to himself, like the words were being heaved out of his throat. Arthur had better not move – if Gerald caught him now he'd say it was time Arthur was sent back to where he belonged. Arthur didn't know where that was – only that it wasn't somewhere he wanted to go, where he'd be trapped under all those bodies, where he couldn't call out for Sylvie.

'Never lost my nerve.'

*Straight and still as a soldier –*

'Not once.'

Arthur leaned forward – just a bit – he had to see if Sylvie was there, if he could just see her face –

'Dad, where's –'

'What the hell are you doing?'

'Nothing Dad, I promise –' Arthur looked at the gas heater – maybe Gerald had done something to her. Maybe she'd gone – maybe she was dead –

'Ma. Where's Ma?'

'Asleep, like you should be.'

The General's hands seemed to grow as Gerald took a step towards Arthur, fists unlocking to cuff Arthur's wrists. Arthur ran up to Sylvie and Gerald's room, 'Ma! Ma!' He pulled the covers off the bed, opened all the cupboards, 'Ma!', freezing at the sound of Gerald's step.

'Do you want a hiding?'

Arthur squeezed his eyes – he wouldn't cry. Proper little soldiers didn't –

'Well do you?'

Arthur's head dropped but Gerald had pulled him round and had him by the arms so he couldn't put his hands over his face. He looked up at Gerald, determined eyes wide. Gerald's grip tightened until he drew a yelp out of Arthur. The release burned no less than his arrest, but Arthur wouldn't let Gerald have another yelp – he watched Gerald's face lower and, before it could meet his, ducked, rushed for the stairs, aiming for the front door.

'Arthur!'

Sylvie was standing in the hall, the blue china pot in one hand – there was something else in the other.

'Ma?'

She didn't look at him, not until Gerald's steps brought her eyes up to Arthur being dragged backwards. Sylvie opened her mouth but she didn't speak. She just put the pot back on the ledge and emptied the other hand into it. Huge snowflakes seemed to fall from her palm.

'That's it,' Gerald said. He dropped Arthur and threw the pot against the wall. 'Enough of all this. That,' he said to Sylvie, 'is going back where it belongs. I'm telling you, I…' Arthur looked up at him as his voice faded, the General seeming to fade with it.

Dried white flower buds flecked the hall. Slowly, silently, Sylvie gathered them, picking round the broken pot. Arthur crouched with his arms round his legs, head pressed against his knees, juddering with each of Gerald's steps away. The steps had little more power than his failed voice, but Arthur waited for the sign of the General. He always came back – and Arthur had to be ready.

'Every Thursday,' Sylvie was saying, 'and when he's big enough and strong enough…' She raised herself back up, eyes drifting over the broken pot. She bent to pick up a piece and laid it on the ledge, her other hand folded softly round the buds. 'My last handful,' she said, opening her palm towards Arthur, 'you take them.'

*September 1967*

The landlord assured Arthur he couldn't miss the place –

*And just remember, once you get to the little yellow chap with the accordion, walk another fifty paces. If you pass the Crown, you've gone too far.*

The voice on the end of the line broke off into a wheeze. Forehead creasing as he heard the landlord drop the receiver, Arthur took another coin from his pocket, straining to decode the muffled fumbling –

'Hello?'

A cough, tinkling, several gulps, a crack –

Arthur tightened his grip round the phone. Gerald had been right, of course, he'd never find anywhere – *No Blacks, No Dogs, No Irish – and No –*

'Arnold?'

'Arthur –'

'Arthur – righto. Four o'clock, then – and give the door a good bang.'

A day later and Arthur was hauling himself along from the labour exchange for the *Grand Tour* the landlord had promised. Arthur checked the card with the address against the numbers precariously nailed to the door. Almost half past. He stepped back onto the Holloway Road – no sign of the accordion player – was that the Crown? A man in a patched corduroy jacket and slippers standing two doors along raised his head and trundled up to Arthur, tapping his stick.

'You after Keith?' he asked, pointing his stick at the boarded-up second storey window.

Arthur squinted at the card and held it out towards the man, 'Mr James?' he asked. Leaning on his stick, the man checked his watch, laughed and cupped a hand round his mouth, 'Oi Keith!' He turned back to Arthur, 'We haven't seen him for weeks,' he said with a grin and then, eyeing Arthur's briefcase, 'you're not causing any bother, I hope.'

'No, I've – I've come to see the room,' Arthur said, drawing his briefcase behind him.

The man nodded, 'Here's y'man,' he said as a red whiskery face appeared through the opening door, 'wotcha', Keith, looks like you've got a customer.'

'Alright, Solly, just a sec,' Keith ducked back inside and came out, wallet in hand, slipping a note into Solly's breast pocket. Arthur tried to feign interest in the pavement as Keith gave Solly a wink, 'put a lady on that mare your boy was on about, eh?'

'Oh, she's a fine one,' Solly said, patting his pocket, eyes pausing on Arthur before he went.

'We spoke yesterday,' Arthur said, trying to catch Keith before he closed the door, 'about the room.'

Keith rubbed his face and sucked in his lips, 'Aha, yes – Arnold!'

'Arthur.'

'Come on in,' he said, giving Arthur's hand a vigorous shake and bending to gather the scattered post from the mat, adding it to the pile next to a tumble of shoes in the hallway. He stopped by the mirror, cleaned a circle with his sleeve, pulled back his top lip with a finger and rubbed his teeth with another. 'Follow me,' a firm hand on the banister before he took a step up, breathing laboured as he reached the half landing. He smacked his chest, 'old lung plays up from time to time – now here's the bathroom,' he said, pushing the door open, 'all fully functional.' He stepped over the broken toilet seat on the floor to turn the tap and slapped a hand on Arthur's shoulder – 'what more could you ask for, eh?' – reaching for the chain to demonstrate the flush was in working order. 'Now remind me,' he said, leading Arthur up the next half flight, 'what line of work did you say you were in? I can see you're not a medical man, which is a pity, I have to say, I wouldn't mind having someone about in an emergency.' He paused and turned back to Arthur, lowering his voice, 'How are you in an emergency?'

Arthur blinked, 'Emergency? Well I don't know.'

Keith smacked his chest and cleared his throat, 'You're an office man, correct?'

Arthur's eyes fell to his briefcase, 'Theoretically – I'm sort of… *between positions*,' he looked up at Keith, lips tight.

Keith's smile broadened, '*Between positions* – a word of advice, Arnold – Arthur – take it from me, that dole queue *eats* a man's soul.'

Arthur nodded, gaze set on Keith's folded arms, 'I'm – I'm looking into it.'

'Of course you are,' he said, 'Right, now, kitchen in there,' he put his head round a door, 'second thought, let's show you the room first,' he tapped a finger against his lips, 'your lucky break will come. Just look at Solly's boy – years idle and now a *commissioning agent*. Me, I've been in all lines – furs, antiques, skins and that was before I even got started on the Monopoly Board. Nothing much I haven't dabbled in. But there comes a time,' he said, putting his weight behind the jammed door, 'when a man has to think about his *contribution*.' His head disappeared behind the door before he turned back round to Arthur. Arthur's face tightened – *contribution*? – but hearing Gerald's chuckle warned him away from trying the line about perseverance.

'I might get an interview this week – or next –' Arthur ventured but Keith was scrutinising the crumpled piece of paper he'd taken out from his pocket, '*The Ballad of the Hollow Way* – it's almost there, I can feel it – no,' he said, smoothing the paper out and holding it under his nose, 'I can *smell* it.' He folded it into four and waved it in front of Arthur, 'Did I tell you that I am, in fact – no, *in truth* – a poet?'

Arthur shook his head, squinting, no less baffled than relieved, eyes on the door behind Keith. Keith sniffed, scratching his ginger whiskers as he scanned Arthur – 'I have an inkling there might well be a poet in you, have you ever thought…' he waved a hand over his shoulder, 'now,' he said, showing Arthur into the room, 'this was home to my one-time muse.' He picked a cigarette off the floor and put it behind his ear. Arthur looked up, eyes moving over the cracked ceiling, down the torn poster of fluorescent swirls and lozenges to the mattress, home to three bags of rubbish and a small wicker cage –

'What was that?' Arthur asked, eyes darting round to Keith.

'What was what?' Keith was attempting to pour a glass of congealed milk down the sink.

Arthur took a half turn – 'That – the scratching.'

'Inevitable in these parts.' Keith jabbed a thumb over his shoulder at the wall – 'Next door might be more up your street. Never seen a rat in there – honest to God. We used to put my mother-in-law up there – once upon another lifetime.'

*

Arthur waited while Lydia's eyes took a tour of the room. And another. She was getting her bearings, familiarising herself. The third circuit halted at the lamp. The lamp! Of course, the lamp! Arthur snapped it on. Well now, that was better. The bulb flickered but it worked, that was the main thing. No, the main thing had been to find somewhere, anywhere at all, the main thing had been to get out and he had and now here he was, not being clocked or watched, questioned – or unquestioned – yes here he was, and here was Lydia – even if she wouldn't let him take her coat and still hadn't taken off her gloves, even if she still had that little bag of hers clutched in one of those obstinately gloved hands, even if – the room was getting smaller and smaller now that her eyes were on it, eyes that simply *had* to point out the damp – he would have to do something about it, the cracks too – perhaps he had been a little too rash pulling the posters down – no, he could never have slept with a stoned Buddha over him, worse than the psychedelic swirls next door. He would talk to Keith about it – he would risk having to endure another recital of *The Ballad of the Hollow Way* –

*Or Ode to the Hollow Way – what do you reckon?*

Followed by Keith's unnerving insistence that he was sure there was a poet in Arthur too somewhere – yet Arthur would endure – he'd have a word about the damp and get Keith to do something about the cigarette burns while he was at it.

'You might at least get a shade,' Lydia said, the relief of her voice sufficient to both pause the rapid shrinkage of the room before it disappeared entirely and blunt her words so that it was a moment before their significance engraved itself on Arthur's optimistically subdued consciousness but, once sharpened and registered, they made their brisk snips at the missed square inches with each tug Lydia made at the fingers of her gloves – still, she was taking off her gloves, her little bag under her arm now – why couldn't she just put it down? Why couldn't she just put her bag down and let him take her coat?

'The lamp by my bed at Mrs Simons's has a very nice shade,' she said.

Yes, well the lamp by his bed at Llanvanor Road had a very nice shade too. A shade – why hadn't he thought? Arthur loosened his tie – he should never have put the lamp on. Lydia circled the toe of her shoe round a stain. He hadn't noticed that one but now he would never fail to notice it, yes he would go on noticing that stain long after it had become invisible to Lydia, long after she was even there to notice it at all. She'd be gone but the stain would still be there and he would still be meaning to be doing something about it. It was a formative moment: Arthur had never known it was possible to feel such animosity towards a lamp.

The mighty thud overhead was premature – Keith never usually got up before three.

'What was that!' Lydia's eyes had been pulled up to the ceiling, her arm clamped to her bag.

'Keith, I think – he falls out of bed sometimes—'

'It's two o'clock in the afternoon!'

'I know! He doesn't usually…' Arthur trailed, caught himself, noted the gloves – he must deliver them both before those gloves went back on and all hope was aborted. He should never have invited her round – he knew he wasn't quite ready. It had been her, cornering him into it, saying she was sure a *gentleman* like him, a suit like that – a *case* like that – must surely be very well set up, very well set up indeed. Arthur had put the case on his lap and looked up at Lydia, her words and eyes, lingering, delaying his efforts to object. It was a seductive premise: Arthur, the well-set-up gentleman. Yes, he'd heard himself saying, a set-up she would have to see to believe. Oh Lydia would like that, she'd like that very much.

Cornered him when all he needed was another day or two and his humble but homely habitat wouldn't be vanishing under her gaze. Preparation for his defence lunged him a step back, landing him just inside the doorless threshold – of course! Salvation! He had meant to show her this first!

'For the twins!' Arthur burst.

'The twins?' Lydia dropped into the chair, her bag on the floor –

'Yes! Look at this! You have to have a look at this!'

Lydia crossed and re-crossed her legs. 'Look at what?' she asked while Arthur, one foot either side of the threshold, flapped an arm towards the windowless cavity whose usage, Keith had explained, was limited only by the imagination. Keith had gone on to explain that not only was he a poet but a *born* Poet –

*I think this sort of thing is congenital.*

Arthur considered it best not to doubt Keith on this point, especially while Keith was quite so wondrously indifferent to the question of Arthur's rent – an indifference that would be sustained by Shelley and whiskey until the mighty thud overhead cracked its last, one Sabbath three years later. A cliché shaped in flesh and blood is no less vulnerable to being ravaged by all that cliché entails and it would seem odd to think almost half a century later, passing by the old place when it would be nothing like the old place, that really none of it would have ended up as it had if it hadn't been for Keith.

Lydia moved a little closer, peering in, 'What am I looking at?'

'We'll have to get them beds and everything, but they'll fit, don't you think?'

'The twins or the beds?'

'Both, obviously – and shades, I'll get lampshades. And lamps! One each! Two lamps, two shades and—'

'Arthur, it's a cupboard.'

It was not a cupboard: it was, as Keith said, only the imagination – and he had imagined, him and Lydia, the twins – it was not a cupboard! It was –

'Storage space!'

'The twins aren't storage—'

'I never said – did I say?'

Lydia sat back down, a laugh, delicate as a bubble, floating up. It popped.

'The twins in there? Oh Arthur… besides, they already have two perfectly nice lamps with perfectly nice shades—'

'And perfectly nice beds too, I suppose?'

'Yes. Perfectly nice.'

'Well good.' Arthur rolled up his sleeves, went over to the sink and plunged a hand in, fishing out a mug, a cup and – there must be one in here – a spoon – well good, so they had beds and lamps and shades – he had a sink! They probably had a sink too. Well of course they had a sink. Even next door had a sink. Arthur heard the filmy laugh bubble up and pop again –

'I'm not sure what Mrs Simons would make of all this,' Lydia said. Arthur was staring at the bottom of the tin of coffee – how could there not be a single granule in there? 'She'd have a fit!'

Not that Arthur had anything against Mrs Simons – at least not personally – but at that moment Mrs Simons could have had a seizure for all he cared – Arthur could, at that moment, have quite happily wrung Mrs Simons's neck –

'What the hell does it matter what Mrs Simons thinks! Anyone would think she was your mother!'

'Oh if only she were! She's marvellous! How she puts herself together. If I could put myself together like that I'd – well you would hardly recognise me—' Lydia yanked her bun free and patted wispy curls over her face.

'I'm not sure I'd like to.'

'You would if you were Mr Simons.'

'Well I'm not!'

'No, I can see that…'

Arthur tipped the empty tin upside down and bashed it with the heel of his hand – not one granule –

'It's alright,' Lydia said, unbuttoning the top button of her coat. 'I didn't really want any.'

'But I do! I want coffee, a cup of coffee, a tin full of coffee and I don't want to hear another word about your mother!'

'She's not my mother!'

'Anyone would think—'

'Well she's not, the twins have her all to themselves and that's that.' Lydia's voice had caught, split.

Arthur dropped the mug back into the sink. What was this all about? Her mother, the twins' mother, she was probably Mr Simons's mother too. Well now that made him feel a little less despairing, things could have been worse – he could have been Mr Simons. A surge of pity flooded Arthur's uncontainable heart. It was all going to be alright now, he was rescuing Lydia and her precious girls from this madcap couple, he was – or would be – just as well set up as she had imagined, she would love it – love it! She would love it and the twins would love it and they'd have lamps with shades and –

'Please let me take your coat, Lydia.'

'Of course,' Lydia's face and voice were marble smooth again.

Yes, he knew she loved it: the room was resuming its former size. He hung her coat up.

'I will get a shade, you know.'

'What? Oh alright, if you like.'

Surely that confirmed it all then – yes, clearly now it was unconditional: with or without the shade Lydia loved it – loved it!

'You must promise me you won't miss Mrs Simons too much, will you?'

'I don't see how I should miss her at all.'

No, indeed, how could she? Once they were all set up and settled. She and the twins would forget all about this Mrs Simons – they could all forget about Mrs Simons – except Mr Simons of course, poor poor Mr Simons. Arthur really must buy him a drink.

'But I'm sure she'll miss you – and the twins – but you could take them round I suppose – or she could pop in, say –'

Lydia's hand flew up with her popped bubbles of laughter, 'Arthur, you really are the strangest creature!'

He wasn't in the least bit strange! He was quite ordinary, he just happened to have an extraordinary sensitivity to the fact that, regardless of how intolerable Mr and Mrs Simons were, Lydia and the twins had become used to them and they, naturally, might have grown attached –

'We'll have them over once a fortnight—' Arthur stopped, Lydia was getting up, picking up her gloves, her bag, her unparted lips drawing a dimple into her cheek.

'I'd never leave Mrs. Simons,' she said. 'And I couldn't very well leave the twins.'

Arthur took his lunge back to the doorless threshold, flapped an arm – 'Well of course you wouldn't leave the twins!' He wouldn't dream of it! Well, he'd better not, Lydia said, she'd been with them since… well since they were born!

Arthur could see what Harry's chuckle would be doing now, threatening to explode, restraining it only so he could take Arthur through the finer points of reproduction, *Shagging has been my preferred subject for some time now, chum.*

'I know quite enough about shagging, thank you –'

'Arthur!'

'Lydia – sorry, what I meant was—'

'I'll pretend you didn't say that, fancy going on about your sordid escapades while I'm telling you about the tiny treasures who'll be lost without me. Seven years I've been with them, Arthur! Seven years! Do you have any idea how long that is?'

'Yes I—'

'You can't imagine it, I never could have – no one could.' Lydia's head whisked round. It felt to Arthur as though she'd been sucked down by those supposedly unimaginable seven years and, by the time she had found her way back, the woman he'd met at the park had been peeled away. 'But then I never thought the Grande Dame would send me to London either. Well I'm only too glad she did – what would I want to be stuck with her and the Old Bear for? Woolacombe Bay? I only wish they'd *removed* me sooner. *Removed*? – I'm not a piece of furniture, Arthur.'

'Of course you're not.'

'Mrs Simons can you tell I'm not a piece of furniture if you don't believe me.'

'I do believe—'

'Mrs Simons loves me—'

'I love—'

'Don't be silly, Arthur!' Lydia flicked his cut declaration away and dragged a neat channel down the grimy windowpane with her fingertip, 'The twins love me—' She swallowed, holding her fingertip up to her eye, 'funny when you think about it,' she murmured, her hand dropping to her side.

'What?' Arthur had lost her again. He took her hand and she let him have it for a moment before she pulled it away and closed her eyes.

'Please don't, Arthur – don't pester me.'

'What did I –?'

'The Dame was always pestering me,' she said, turning back towards the window. 'The Bear was always pestering me too – the wolf and the witch more like – hardly my fault if the grizzly beast couldn't keep his hands to himself.'

The wolf? That was it! Arthur would go to Woolacombe Bay and slay the beast! He would rip the claws and –

'Lydia?' He was trying to take her hand again. 'Don't be upset, please—'

'I'm not upset! Who's upset? I'm not—' The next word was clipped away and Arthur's eyes made an automatic copy of Lydia's, shut tight after a blink. His hand came to his forehead, checking for tree life. Maybe this was all a little beyond what he had All Worked Out.

'I'm not upset,' she said, quiet, steady, 'because there's nothing to be upset about: I never have to see the Old Bear again.'

*The Old?*

But Lydia caught Arthur's questions before he could ask them, placing a finger on her lips and turning to walk the tour her eyes had taken on arrival. 'So you see,' she said, 'I would *never* leave Mrs Simons. And I would *never* leave the twins. I've done practically everything for those girls but give birth to them.'

*But?* Arthur looked for clues in her face but its marble surface, restored, told him nothing. 'They're not yours?'

'Mine? Oh Arthur!'

'But I – and you said yourself, you've been with them since…' It was unravelling – him, Lydia, the twins, taking her in, taking them in, Noble Honourable Arthur… but Arthur's Honour and Nobility were not Lydia's concern – nothing, it appeared, was her concern, she had been sheathed in that wondrous indifference all over again. She put her gloves and her bag back down and tiptoed back up to Arthur, 'You are very clever,' she whispered.

'I am?'

'Very clever.'

Perhaps nothing was unravelling in the slightest – and perhaps, if Lydia's slowing tip-toe were to be believed, nothing needed to be Worked Out: it was all as tidily composed as the bells and the cartwheels and the voice calling out that it was time to go.

'The way you've arranged everything,' Lydia said.

Arthur checked her face again… still marble smooth… Yes, of course, everything.

'The way you… see things,' Lydia paused, her touring eyes making an elegant hop over the stains, past the damp, enlarging Arthur's more than humble, more than homely habitat. The way *she* saw things! 'Not everyone would see things the way you do – but you're right – absolutely right. After all, who plaits their hair and takes them to the park and tells them stories so they can go to sleep? Not Mrs Simons! Yes, Arthur you really are absolutely—'

Of course he was – absolutely!

'Absolutely what?'

'But then I suppose the twins do rather look like me, don't they? Yes, they do look like me, just like me. They have big round brown eyes, just like me – not black little buttons like Mrs Simons – and big brown curls just like me – and the sweetest whitest little teeth just like you—'

Arthur's jaw clenched. She was laughing at him. There he was with the wrong end of the stick again – of course his father would find this very amusing –

*It seems our old chum Goldilocks has got the wrong end of the stick, wouldn't you say, Harry?*

Always somehow managed to end up with the wrong end – yes well one day he'd take that stick and he'd show them just what – they might not all think he was quite so funny then – his father, Harry – and Lydia too, he'd show her – no, not with her, Arthur the Gentleman would let her have her little laugh at him with the wrong end of the stick in his hands and his awful teeth. He was resolved: from tomorrow not a day would go by with unbrushed teeth.

'Were you very sweet?' she asked. 'I bet you were adorable, I'm sure you never cried. I know I never did – not once!'

Arthur returned to his sink, dropping back all he'd fished out – he would probably never find that spoon again – put the empty tin of coffee back for future regret and studied the damp's consumption of the room: neither humble nor homely, this was a hole! But it was his hole and in less than half an hour had endured several deaths and resurrections – it was exhausted. Inside the safety of his closed mouth, Arthur examined his teeth. Four orange-gold plaits and four green eyes crossed the wall. The twins were no more like Lydia than they were like him. It was just that was how he held it all in his mind. He couldn't imagine her without them, it was how he saw and heard her – how he saw and heard himself: noble, honourable Arthur, taking them in as his own. He had been looking forward to saying that – taking them in, taking her in, and not giving a damn what anyone had to say about any of it… perhaps he wouldn't have minded being Mr Simons after all – not poor poor Mr Simons but poor poor Arthur! It should be Mr Simons buying him a drink! No – no one was buying anyone anything!

'I'll find somewhere else,' Arthur told the sink.

'No Arthur! This is perfect – for someone like you.'

*

Perfect for someone like Lydia too, particularly when, just three days later, that someone was kindly informed her services were no longer required, kindly advised to pack up her things and instructed in no uncertain terms to be out by the time – and here Mrs Simons had stopped to relieve Lydia's neck of the pearls that had found their way round it, her dressing table of the dolls that, having been bought, boxed and ribboned for the twins that morning, were now propped up against the mirror which held Lydia's placid face and into which Mrs Simons spoke –

Lydia understood, but she had to suggest, for Mrs Simons's own sake, for the twins' sake, that she didn't make such a hasty decision until she had calmed down –

'I am quite calm, thank you Lydia.'

'But Mrs Simons, I was going to take the twins to get fitted for their uniforms today and there's all the tidying to be done and—'

'Goodbye, Lydia.'

Lydia's coat was already unbuttoned before she rapped an ungloved hand on Arthur's door. He didn't have to worry, she told him, prompting his eyes up from her suitcase, she wouldn't be missing that Mrs Simons any more than she missed The Dame and The Bear – though she was quite sure, just like Arthur had said – oh you are always right about everything! – that that Mrs Simons would miss her. Maybe not yet, but she would.

'Well, aren't you going to ask me in or are we going to stand in the doorway all night?'

Stepping inside, Lydia answered for Arthur, leaving him to picture the room shrinking as she entered – the room which, in her absence, had held firmly to its original dimensions. Arthur put a hand on her suitcase and waited before her 'you might at least look a little more pleased to see me' ushered him in.

Didn't he look pleased? He had meant to look pleased. He was – of course he was! More than pleased – delighted! Or would have been had that rapturously ungloved hand not knocked quite so soon. Though the first hours of Lydia's absence had left Arthur with the inevitable conclusion that she was as irretrievably lost to him as the spoon languishing in his bottomless sink, a conclusion that would have made any hand – gloved or ungloved – more than welcome. Yet he, aided by Keith's unwarranted arrival, (no gloved or ungloved rapping, rather more an instance of breaking and entering), had survived to that endless day's end – and the next. Neither Arthur or Keith had indulged in the performance about the rent, instead Keith assumed a ready audience for his compilation of quotes and anecdotes designed, in this instance, to tend and mend the wanting wounded heart. Wisdom laced with whiskey served both well and induced in Arthur a bout of optimism which enabled him to displace all former certainties: no, Lydia's absence did not presage all the torments of eternal damnation, but the provision that would secure their reunion. Now Arthur had precisely what was needed – the opportunity to rearrange all he had previously arranged – not least the whole idea of Lydia and the twins and himself. He had the right end of the stick now and he wasn't about to let it be snatched away: if she couldn't be Lydia with the twins then he could hardly be Noble Honourable Arthur taking them in and not giving a damn what anyone – no, he would have to be another Arthur altogether – but that Arthur would suit him just as well, it would suit him better – he would be Lydia's Arthur! There was of course the question of who she'd be… that wasn't so difficult to clear up – she would be Arthur's Lydia. All that required was paring away everything other than what stood before him. He thought again of that moment she'd let him have her name – how he'd heard it then and how he heard it now – in possession of his own: *Lydia's* Arthur. Yes, now that he was Lydia's Arthur all that was left to be done was to find Lydia and *her* Arthur somewhere just right for just the two of them. Somewhere with not only their own sink but where the tin of coffee would always be full, where bulbs did not flicker and lamps had shades, where – but that ungloved hand had rapped without giving him a chance, dragging him up from the mattress, rapping again before he'd managed to pull on his grubby towelling robe and the room still reeking and convalescing from Keith's visit –

'You had a party without me!' Lydia said, attending to the incontinent ashtrays. Arthur pounced to take them from her hands, 'Please Lydia, let me –'

'I love parties!'

'We didn't – there wasn't. Oh, please don't worry about all that. I was only this minute about to have a clean-up—' Arthur gave the ceiling his glare. Immediately Keith went from being a convenient inconvenience to the sole cause of Arthur's grief-stricken future – for the next thirty seconds there was no man Arthur could imagine so worthy of his wrath: it was all a complete disaster and now Lydia was rolling up her sleeves and – please dear Lord no! – plunging bare arms into the bottomless sink, striking back up with –

'Spoons!'

Defeated, Arthur slid his feet along towards the mattress, sank down and listened to the splash, clink, clatter –

'Not one bit!' Lydia sang. 'How right, how right you were! Are we sorry, Mrs Simons? Oh dearest Lydia, ever so. Good – and Grande Dame? Ever so. So you should be. What about Mr Wolf?' Lydia growled, laughed. Arthur sat himself up, his senses blurred by the cast of voices Lydia was breezing through.

'Lydia,' he began, trying to steady the scene.

But she was attending to the set, wiping off her hands on the tea towel that had wrapped the pair of china cups she'd just taken out of her case, 'Pretty, no?'

'We've got mugs!' Arthur protested. He went to the cupboard. Well then they were in the sink – somewhere – but Lydia was busy not missing Mrs Simons one little bit, she was busy unveiling a lampshade from a tablecloth – but he was going to get –

'Lydia, what on earth?'

'Which one do you think will have which?' Lydia asked, holding up the dolls.

'Which one what?'

'Oh it's perfect!' Lydia said, bouncing up towards the doorless threshold – she stopped, glancing back at Arthur before she ventured over and showed the dolls in. 'Oh Arthur, they are going to love it!'

'They're dolls!' Arthur cried, tightening his robe a little too fiercely. He coughed, swallowed, breathed. 'Dolls.'

'Don't be silly Arthur, of course they're dolls. Presents for the twins – a little surprise for when they get here.' The dolls were dangling from her hands now.

The stain on the floor was thwarting Arthur's attempts to vocalise. He slid a foot over it –

'Now, Lydia—' but she was kneeling down, cartwheeling the dolls around him, dancing them up his legs –

'Perfect!' she said, making each of the dolls kiss Arthur's cheeks. 'And they are going to love you! They'll be over the moon!' Lydia was leaping the dolls over Arthur's head before pressing them into his arms. 'And you are going to love them!'

But they were dolls – dolls! The hands on Lydia's hips suggested to Arthur he was again guilty of not looking quite as pleased as he ought. She snatched the dolls out of his arms and dropped them on the floor.

'That's no way to treat them,' she snapped.

A reflex sprang Arthur to the dolls' rescue, uprooting his careful footing so that in the next moment he not only found himself cradling the dolls, but betrayed by the stain. The stain failed to have any effect on Lydia, however, not now the dolls were in Arthur's arms – oh how they'd love him! – it was all going to be just right, just like he'd said, oh he really was such a clever Arthur – and no one was going to be missing anyone one little bit! How could they when they'd be just like Mr and Mrs Simons – except she wouldn't have those little black button eyes and he wouldn't –

'Wait! There's something else.'

Oh please no, nothing else, please dear Lord –

Lydia was kneeling at the case again, throwing out socks and skirts and bottles until she came to a plastic-covered dress. She held it up against herself and twirled. 'How I put myself together,' she said, letting those cautious lips open into a smile. Arthur nodded. Lydia flung the dress down to pull her final trophy out of the case: a plastic-covered suit. She pinned it against Arthur. 'But oh, how I put Mr Simons together.'

Arthur stepped back but she stepped with him. 'Very smart,' she said, brushing the back of her hand against a plastic-covered lapel. Arthur's cradling arms forgot their care of the twins – the dolls! He had meant the dolls! – as he pushed Lydia away – he was not going to let her, not let anyone dress him like –

'Mr Simons!' It was Lydia's turn to rescue the dolls. 'There, there,' she cooed, 'Daddy's just a little bit angry. Oh don't be angry, Arthur!' She sat on the floor, the dolls in her lap, and began plaiting their hair. 'I just thought you might like a nice suit.'

'I have a nice suit!'

'I just thought you might like to be all smart, all suave.'

'Well I don't.'

'Oh go on Arthur, try it on, just to see.'

'No.' There, he had said it, once and for all: No.

'For me? Please.' No, he had said no, he had said –

'I will have nothing to do with… stolen property.'

Lydia laughed, 'Stolen property? My, aren't we…'

Another ferocious tightening of the belt. Arthur almost winded himself – he would have to sit down. Yes, he would sit down, collect himself – himself! – and then all this was going back to where it came from and that would be the end of that and he would find his mugs which were somewhere in his sink and get his own shade and his own –

'You know what, Arthur? You really must be the most adorable—'

'I am not adorable!'

'I think you are,' she persisted and held up the suit in one hand, the dress in the other. 'Well hello Mr Simons. Well hello Mrs Simons. Did Mr Simons have a very nice day? He had a very nice day indeed, Mrs Simons, did Mrs Simons have a very nice day? The nicest. Mr Simons is pleased. Mrs Simons is pleased Mr Simons is pleased. Mr Simons loves Mrs Simons very much. Mrs Simons loves Mr Simons very much. Mr Simons would do anything for Mrs Simons. Mrs Simons would do anything for—'

'No! I am not—'

'But what is Mr Simons doing home so early? Why Mrs Simons, it *is* a Thursday – don't I always finish early on a Thursday?'

*May 1952*

Gerald followed the trail of Arthur's footprints through the hall and up the stairs – it was VE day and this was not quite what he had had in mind: mud-covered, earth-caked, this proper little soldier didn't look much more like anything to Gerald than a proper little mess.

'And what have you got to say for yourself?'

The caked face didn't crack.

'I thought you'd stopped all this nonsense.'

The silence, dried dense over Arthur's mouth, told Gerald, nonsense or not, nothing had ever stopped at all.

'You like digging, do you?'

Arthur shook his head.

'Oh, I think you do – and I've got just the thing for little boys who like to dig,' Gerald said, pulling Arthur by the arm down the stairs and through the backroom into the garden. There was a shed at the end of the lawn hidden behind the trellis that was warped by a jungle of weeds. Arthur had spent an hour that might as well have been forever in there after Harry had dared him to go inside it. Harry would count to one hundred and then he'd knock and if Arthur came out before he was a big –

*OK, OK* –

Arthur couldn't hear if Harry was still counting but he hadn't knocked and Arthur didn't want to be a big anything – except for big; that would be quite good – big enough and strong enough, just like that Other Little Arthur was getting and one day the two of them would come out for the whole wide world to see. They'd show that whole wide world…

Arthur had tried to jump high enough to see through the window but he only caught a blur of murk and green. Harry? Couldn't he come out? No, else Harry would tell everyone at Cubs what a tell-tale he was if he said when Gerald asked what sort of cheek they had, playing up like a pair of children.

'But Gerald,' Sylvie had said, 'they are children.'

'Don't you undermine me.'

Not another word then and not one now. Gerald selected a shovel and neither Arthur's caked silence nor his shaking head would make Gerald withdraw its imperative: he wanted to see this digging Arthur liked so very much.

*No digging no digging no digging* – dislocated from their origin, the words reverberated in Arthur's ears as insistently as the compulsion, asking him *why, why –*

*Don't know, don't – didn't mean – oh sorry, Ma, sorry –*

*No digging –*

*I didn't, I promise –*

*He's not there, Arthur – he's not –*

The raised shovel sent Arthur a step back.

Gerald wasn't in the mood for one of Arthur's little games. Not on today of all days. Today was no ordinary anniversary. The boys were now in their seventh year and it was time they made good use of the army caps they had been given. Today their training would begin. Considering the most efficient method of transforming a proper little mess into anything that might be even the slightest bit less improper, Gerald stamped the shovel against the grass. He looked at Arthur – was he going to have to repeat himself?

Arthur crouched down and wrapped his arms round his legs, pressing his head against his knees, eyes squeezed tight as Gerald bashed the shovel against the ground.

'Right then,' Gerald muttered, dropping the shovel. He came behind Arthur, pulled him up by the scruff of his neck and dropped him, drawing back as he saw Arthur's body curl up. He looked down at his hands and clenched them before his eyes came back to Arthur, the tightened body now perfectly still.

'Alright, now, up you get,' Gerald said, his voice quiet, measured. He straightened his hands out, assuring himself the tremor was only slight – just lost his grip sometimes, that was all –

*Occasionally, only occasionally –*

Arthur pressed his head into the grassless patch again.

'For goodness' sake, boy – what are you playing at? Testing my nerves? – well, I will not have you testing my nerves. Understood?' Gerald flattened his hands against his sides –

*A slight tremor – nothing like the old man – never lost my nerve – never –*

He took a breath and straightened, stiffening against the sight of himself coming down the stairs the previous night. He'd been jolted awake by the face of one of the lads who didn't make it back –

*Damn bright, that lad, strong as a horse. Stop it old boy, getting sentimental. Can't get sentimental. Not over one lad. One lad – one in how many million? Can't be a gibbering wreck over every blasted body you lugged along. A large Scotch'll set you right.*

He'd taken a tumbler out of the cabinet, hand against the counter to steady himself, staggering back the moment he heard Sylvie's voice.

*Gerald, are you –?*

*Heaven above, woman!*

She was hunched by the gas heater, spectral eyes setting his hands going, her body a tangle of limbs untwisting, pulling herself up, step by step towards him, her hand reaching, almost touching his, their trembling matched.

'Go to bed, Sylvie.'

Yes, he told himself, still had his nerve alright – nothing like his father. They'd tried everything on his old man and he was still the same bedwetting mute – had a soft spot for Sylvie, though – made you wonder if it wasn't all a bit of a performance – perked up as soon as she arrived, Gerald's mother had said. Not that she was about to trust one of these girls that came to London after a good time. She'd been through a least a dozen of these types and they were all the same, but since Sylvie was the only one to last longer than a week, came on time, fresh and smart enough, managing to get Gerald's father washed and changed without too much fuss and a bit of soup down him it seemed, in the end, against her better judgement to let the girl go. She had to, though. Sylvie may not have been after the sort of good time Gerald's mother suspected but Gerald, mortified by the sight of this bright young thing cleaning up his incontinent father, was rather keen to show her one. He would show her London. His London. *The* London.

'I'm sure I knew London better when I was still in Maldon,' Sylvie had said.

'Give me just one evening,' Gerald had said, 'and I'll change all that.'

Gerald's mother said he wouldn't dare. She wasn't Jewish for a start – a shiksa. Common. Like your father. Being common's what they have in common.

She wasn't common. That house hadn't felt a living breath before she walked inside it. He wasn't being rash. He wasn't being naive. Later he would tell himself that nothing but studious observation had led to the conclusion that Sylvie was not an unreasonable choice – had she not demonstrated precisely the qualities required? Patience, efficiency, sacrifice. Yes, and it was this, not the walks along the river or the way she went mad for the flicks and could do all the voices and certainly not the start of the bloody war. Nothing but the oracle could have foreseen the woman he would come back to, arms still empty even filled with Harry, would be so many women away from the one who had waved him off. She had waved him off, hadn't she? That was what they all did, wasn't it? Tried to see it but here she was, so many women away, standing in front of him, reaching towards him, stepping back, curled and hunched again, against that damn gas heater of hers.

Gerald checked the backs of his hands. His palms –

*Yes, still got my nerve alright.*

He watched the boy rubbing his head against the ground, folded his arms and took a step towards him, feet at the boy's head.

'Alright now, old chap,' Gerald offered. 'What's say we get you and Harry your caps on and go out for a knickerbocker glory.' Arthur's head was still, hands crossed under him.

'Did you hear me, old chap? I said you, me and Harry – Arthur!' Gerald circled him, hands beginning to shake. He clenched and flexed them, eyes straight ahead, staring past the point of seeing. 'Arthur if you don't get up – I'm warning you—' He looked back down at Arthur's frozen body, nudging a toecap into his side. Gentle, quite gentle.

'Arthur—'

Gerald bent down. Arthur was lucky Gerald was such a soft touch.

'You're a lucky bastard, you are. Do you know that? Did you hear me?' Gerald straightened and nudged Arthur with the other toecap – gently gently. 'You know what you are, don't you Arthur? No? Well I'll tell you. You, Arthur, are A. Dirty. Little. Semite. And do you know what dirty little Semites do? They dig us a bad name. Dirty, little… I should never have let them bring you back.'

They didn't have knickerbocker glories that day. Or wear their army caps. Army caps and knickerbocker glories were only for proper little soldiers.

'But I am a proper soldier,' Harry said when the lights had been put out.

'Harry.'

'What?'

'What's a Semite?'

'Don't be stupid Arthur, everyone knows what a sea mite is – it's a thing that lives in the sea.'

*October 1967*

Arthur opened the suitcase he had just closed. It was all going back. Oh was it now? It most certainly was, Arthur told Lydia, the attention given to knotting the tie that was *his* tie securing a note of authority –

'Here, let me—' Lydia offered, sliding off the chair and round behind him, slipping her arms through his –

Oh no she wouldn't! He was perfectly capable.

'Goodness! I was only trying to be helpful,' she told him, slinking back to the chair.

'What's wrong with how I do my tie?'

'Nothing, it's just a bit… wonky.'

'Wonky?'

It was not – no, he wouldn't be drawn – it was all going back – all of it –

'Except the dress,' Lydia said.

Arthur turned to Lydia – he was sorry but it had to go – yes, the dress was going back too.

'No.'

'Yes.'

Lydia twirled a brown curl, making a roller out of her index finger. She couldn't possibly take it off, she only had a little slip underneath, she'd freeze –

'That didn't stop you from stripping down to put it on in the first place.'

'That was different… please let me redo your tie.'

'No!'

'Well go about with a wonky tie then.'

'I'm not going about. I'm going straight to Mrs Simons's, I'm taking it all back this minute – including the dress.'

Lydia wasn't quite so certain. She was curious, however, how he imagined he'd be taking anything anywhere when, surely, she said, twirling another curl, he couldn't possibly know the house or the street because really, as far as *she* understood, he couldn't possibly have had the faintest idea where he was going – Lydia's lips were keeping their smile to themselves –

'I most certainly do,' Arthur said, trying to ease the knot of his tie, 'I know exactly—'

Perhaps – only she'd never told him where she lived, she'd never actually given him an address now, had she, so unless he'd been following her –

'What? Of course not!'

The stain, the damp, the mugs, the empty tin – all turned at once on Arthur.

A twitching nose and a loosened tie won Lydia his confession and she let her red heart of a mouth split with a reward. He had her smile now and she wouldn't take it back.

So then, she knew, well fine, he had only been trying to do the right thing – besides he had not been *following* her; he had, on one single occasion, ensured her safe return. Noble Honourable Arthur was still in the making then and what else could be uppermost in such a consciousness but a young lady's very best interests? If he'd had her name it would have been different altogether, he'd simply have called after her, but he couldn't start crying out with that 'Excuse me!' all over again, galloping up the hill – so it was up towards the pond! – like an unbroken horse.

It had been after that hideous night he should never have agreed to – Oh come on Arthur, it'll be a laugh, Harry insisted, slapping him on the back, elbowing him in the ribs and at the time it seemed that only agreeing what a laugh they'd have would prevent any further bruising. He wouldn't regret it, Harry promised, his girl was bringing a friend of hers – a friend? No: Noble, Honourable Arthur still-in-the-making would have to say – but he was still smarting a little from that down-to-the-station-up-to-the-pond business – he was still Working It All Out and Lydia was still that woman with the twins; she had only just developed a physicality beyond the voice calling out that it was time to go. Well alright then, but only so this friend didn't end up having to spend the evening poking at the glacé cherry halves in the bottom of an empty cocktail glass while Harry and whoever this girl of his he had on the go consumed each other's necks and faces. Arthur was nudged to reconsider: perhaps so far from threatening to diminish Noble Honourable Arthur still-in-the-making it might well be the evening in which Noble Honourable Arthur would be made. Yes, he would distract this friend out of courtesy, common feeling, amuse her, perhaps even have a little dance, he wasn't such a terrible dancer was he? Arthur, Harry said gravely, you are a terrific dancer! And then, after a slap on the back that was surely undeserved, had him kitted out in some of his Carnaby Street get-up – no arguing, if he wanted to come –

He did not want to come!

Oh, Harry thought he rather did and yes, he was going to have to let himself be dressed up like that.

'Just don't go spilling anything down it.'

Another slap. At least he'd spared him his crack about getting him a bib.

'We really should get you a bib.'

Bastard.

Never again.

*

The chased chasers (chased to fortify him while he attempted to distract and amuse over the band's thrashing drums) were now conspiring in his guts with the strobe lights. Internal revolutions suggested Charlotte or Scarlett was likely to be deprived of his gallant efforts when he vomited all over Harry's Carnaby costume. Arthur wasn't sure a bib would have been sufficient protection. The dance floor was an indivisible writhing monster that would, without any warning whatsoever, erupt at spasmodic intervals with a flying body or shower of beer – he had to get out – he had to leave.

'Hey! Where are you going? Let's have a dance!' Harry yelled out into the wash of unbacked vocals allowed to surface between songs. He threw his arm round Arthur's shoulder and treated his back – which, having gone unmolested for almost two hours had become more complacent than was wise – to a good thump. Charlotte or Scarlett was shouting something into Harry's girl's ear who shouted into Harry's who, explosive with chuckles, threw it down Arthur's: his girl's friend wanted to know if there was something wrong with him. Something wrong? Something wrong! There was nothing wrong with him. Why did everyone always think there was *something wrong* with him? Arthur glanced at Scarlett/Charlotte and received two formerly giggling now glowering faces in return. No, there was nothing *wrong* with him – perhaps though, there was something wrong with them. Another shouted enquiry was passed along – Harry's girl this time –

'Is he a mute?'

As Arthur's failure to pass an answer back did not provide sufficient evidence to confirm, Charlotte/Scarlett suggested an alternative – was he, she asked Harry's girl who asked Harry who asked Arthur, deaf?

'Funny you should say that,' Harry chuckled, 'Dad always thought the same.'

Arthur's privately churning insides threatened to publicise themselves. That was it. He dodged Harry's arm, squeezed through the tangle of limbs, ducking and swerving where apparently detached hands swung bottles and glasses, until he found himself outside, sweat cooling, guts settling.

Tube, home, bed and one hell of a head in the morning – not that he could very well be worrying about the morning when he still had this Carnaby costume to get out of and the relish his father would take in hearing Cinderella come in well before Pumpkin Time to endure. Cinders. The endearment was quite new and they couldn't get enough of it – either that or Goldilocks. Harry was shuffled through a few of the seven dwarfs depending on Gerald's mood but none of them stuck, while Arthur had been Goldilocks for as long as he could remember – that was on account of his being so dark (or so they said, next to Harry with his dirty blond mop) and, of course, for sleeping in baby bear's bed and gobbling baby bear's porridge –

Never! He'd only ever taken what was given, he was a good boy, a good honest boy that became a good honest man who was now – or would very soon be – Noble, Honourable Arthur who had naturally taken it upon his Noble, Honourable self to ensure a young woman, walking home alone late on a Saturday night, returned safely. And now, wearing *his* tie that he alone had tied, and being the good, honest man that he was, the Noble Honourable Arthur he had become – a law-abiding citizen, bringing justice and order, taking everything – yes, *everything*, Lydia – back where it belonged. His resolve both dissipated any lurking shame about Lydia knowing he'd gone after her and inoculated him against being reeled in while Lydia sat, twirling brown curls – Once! It was only once! And he'd been so discreet! (practically invisible) – In any case, it almost seemed it was she who had something to hide – all wrapped up in a feather boa and without the twins, she could have been anyone. That was it:

everything but the fact it was all going back was hoisted out of his mind.

*

It never did go back. Number sixty-three was two doors away when he was stopped short by the image of the Mrs Simons Lydia had repeatedly drawn for him: little black button eyes and a little buttoned-up mouth. Those black little buttons would surely pop and hang from black threads, and certainly the mouth would unbutton – how else would it gape? Yes, unbuttoned and gaping that Mrs Simons would be if she opened the door to God-only-knew-who – either a mad man or thief driven up the hill by what could only be fear or remorse (he hadn't even given a sideways glance towards the park as he passed it) standing there with a wonky tie and a rather too familiar case. That his image of Mrs Simons had now come to present her wearing a replica of the dress that was currently in that very suitcase did not help to encourage him. She might call the police – yes, she would have him arrested! Lock him up! Convicted or admitted, either way the key would be dropped down the well and he would never see the light of day again. Well, then, he would have to go back, full suitcase in hand, to Lydia, show himself, a stalker and a thief, incapable of doing his own tie and let her slip off the chair, into the dress, unwrap the cups, the shade, take out the ribboned dolls, the suit – yes, he would have to let her dress him up like –

*'Mr Simons, don't you look—'*

Uncanny, yes. He would, in the end, have to let this Mr and Mrs Simons move in. Halfway up the stairs Keith informed Arthur that Mrs Simons already had.

'What?'

'I hadn't expected you to be the type to be knocking about with a married woman – not that I'm one to judge—' Keith had said, conserving a smile.

'Mrs who? No, that's just—'

Oh why bother? Keith was another one with an alarming propensity for getting the wrong end of the stick – more alarming, however, was his preference for it (the right end having considerably less potential). Well let him have it then, he was welcome to it. Keith gave Arthur a double-time double raise of his eyebrows and tapped his nose.

'Hang about,' Keith said, bringing a handful of change out of his pocket, 'pick up a bottle for us later, would you? Go on – and a couple of tins while you're at it. I've got a few lines I want to run by you tonight.' Arthur rolled his eyes. 'Tomorrow then,' Keith said, urging his fistful towards Arthur. Arthur sighed and held out his hand. 'That's my boy,' Keith said, winking as he put his hand on Arthur's shoulder.

The stairs had undoubtedly become steeper since Arthur had left but laboured steps assisted him in his resignation to what less than two hours had made of him: a stalking, thieving home-breaker who couldn't even do his own tie. Forgetting it was not for the first time that being Mr Simons was a strikingly appealing alternative, Arthur decided the sooner he let himself be dressed up the better.

'You know,' Lydia said, doing his tie, 'It really was so good of you to see me home that night.'

'But I—'

'Anyone else following me like that and I would have thought – but not you. No, as a matter of fact it was what convinced me.'

'Of what?'

'That really and truly you were and are a gentleman.'

A gentleman! Yes he was. Arthur's face, having been chalked out by a day that was meant for no more that padding about in his grubby robe round his respectably proportioned room, Working It All Out, but had, in the end, sent him up the hill without his Jill and sentenced him on three counts at least, breaking a good deal more than his crown on the way, flushed at this renewed proclamation of himself as he was indeed: A Gentleman – a gentleman whose chalked out face, now flushed, confirmed Lydia's victory with a reiteration of his confession. Well if he must be a stalking, thieving home-breaker whose tie had been superlatively tied for him, he was also a gentleman, a gentleman whose likeness to Mr Simons was nothing less than –

'Uncanny,' Lydia affirmed, placing a doll in each of their laps.

*

If it meant Lydia would not miss Mrs Simons too much –

Not one little bit! –

Then Arthur would, on a Thursday, having finished early, return to find the lamp lit under its shade, the cups and spoons laid over the table that had suffered the improvements of a tablecloth (lace), a vase of flowers (lilac, dried), a fruit bowl (plastic, apples glued down, grapes and bananas unglued – an inconsistency Arthur found not mildly unsettling), mats and coasters (both cork, featuring members of the royal family), and say that yes, Mr Simons had had a good day and yes he had made lots of money –

Lots and lots? –

Yes, lots and lots and that yes, he was very clever –

Three weeks of scaling up and skidding down a greased ladder to the moon had made Arthur an expert if weary performer. From the giddy height of the top rung Noble Honourable Arthur oversaw the company climbing beneath – just below was Lydia's Arthur (so close! So close!) – a little further down, persevering against the constrictions of both his fancy dress and his reluctance, came a likeness to Mr Simons (Lydia's imperturbable enthusiasm for this likeness as 'Uncanny!' testing Arthur's most beleaguered representative, clinging now to a middling rung) – while a thieving, stalking, home-breaker slipped, his fall broken by Goldilocks and Cinders who, between receiving their endless supply of thumps and slaps on the back, always avoiding ever catching a pair of half-closed eyes, a broken-toothed smile, always seeking never catching hands that reached for the gold black and blue, admitted him at the foot of the ladder with neither welcome nor complaint. Of course Noble Honourable Arthur was not without sympathy for the plight of the various Arthurs under his watch, but neither nobility nor honour could provide an extra hand and, frankly, his own were full as it was with the twins and the mass of brown curls he helped to untwirl.

His portion as Mr Simons (Uncanny! – Oh would she stop! Just stop! Lydia, dearest) almost complete, Arthur would sit and stay sitting without a word while Lydia sat the dolls up and set their tea before them, telling them not to speak with their mouths full. Nor would he say a word when she said they must be very sleepy –

'We had such fun at the park today, Mr Simons.'

'Did Mrs Simons take the twins to the park herself?'

'Mr Simons!'

'What?' (careful, Mr Simons – Arthur was repeatedly floored by this variation) 'But I thought you' – he stopped, took a breath, jaw unlocking – 'Lydia – I thought it was *Lydia* who took the twins to the park.'

'Well who else since my Lydia was so cruelly taken from me!' A tear streaked the anaemic sheen that had made up Lydia's face as Mrs Simons's: 'Oh Arthur,' Lydia said, Mrs Simons's buttoned-up mouth unbuttoning a red heart, 'you don't think she's got someone else, do you? You don't think she's forgotten me – or the twins… They couldn't – not after—'

'Well I suppose—'

'Well you're wrong! She would never replace me just like that. The Grande Dame might, but not Mrs Simons. She couldn't! Say she couldn't, Arthur. Arthur, say—'

'She couldn't.'

'You're right, she couldn't. Mrs Simons loves me. She always said she didn't know what she'd do without me—' Lydia reached her hand behind her neck, a faint nod before she went on – 'funny how the twins' eyes would stay open just a little while they slept, this tiny pulse in the lids – I remember their eyes changing colour – yes, and flecked with yellow they were, these tiny shards of light, yellow and green and brown…' She looked up at Arthur, 'I never meant any harm – really I didn't – never. You do believe –?'

'Yes?'

'You love me, don't you?'

'I said I – yes, of course.'

'Yes,' Lydia said, turning round, 'and one day we'll have twins of our own and we'll take them to the park and tell them stories and—' She stopped, blinking, waiting.

'If you like,' Arthur said, a little disconcerted by how easily the words could be said, formed and loosed aloud by Lydia's blinking eyes: she'd made them come free and hardened them into a promise. She reached her arms over his shoulders, dissolving the edges of her frame against his – what was it he had said? His own arms reciprocated before his mind could interfere, drafted into the mix of smoke and moss as he breathed her hair in – Lydia, but someone and somewhere else too. She pulled away and the mix of smoke and moss evaporated, leaving Arthur to steady himself: he hadn't been holding Lydia – no, she had been holding him. She was looking down now, chin squashed into her throat as she checked her dress for creases. A finely cut smile then, brief as it was sudden, and at once her paling lips tightened, Lydia's face disappearing again behind Mrs Simons's. Arthur watched as she recomposed herself stage by stage – an arrangement of eyes and mouth and hands that left the air around her dry and cool. It seemed impossible, this effortless yet scrupulous method, a set of scales immediately recalibrated. He tried to bring his head up, resisting the urge to slide into the chair – *Lydia?* – He wanted to hear her answer to her name but caught himself. At least so long as Lydia was Mrs Simons, Mrs Simons could hardly be missed –

'Not one little bit!'

Nor would he say anything about the sleeves –

'So what if they're a bit short?' Lydia had said when Arthur's shoulders ejected two elbowless planks, the inches of exposed forearms making his protest for him – there was the evidence, right before her and Arthur hadn't had to say a word. Lydia sat herself in his lap and the dolls in her own. 'Never mind,' she said, one hand on his bare wrist, another freeing brown curls from their bun, 'Mr Simons always was a bit stubby.'

'Stubby?'

'Yes,' Lydia said, her once more unbuttoned mouth spilling generous smiles over Arthur and the dolls. Bubbles of Lydia's laughter, floating and popping, made a wonderland out of the room. Poor poor stubby Mr Simons. Arthur reconsidered the sleeves: he, at least, was not stubby; he, by some miracle of fortune, was not Mr Simons but Arthur – Arthur with Lydia on his lap, Lydia who was not missing Mrs Simons even when she wasn't Mrs Simons, Lydia who, plaiting and replaiting the dolls' hair now, was returning Arthur back to himself as the Noble Honourable Arthur he'd originally conceived, an Arthur aloft a greased ladder to the moon, taking in Lydia and the twins and not giving a damn what anyone else had to say about any of it at all because he, Noble Honourable Arthur, was a gentleman.

'Your turn now,' Lydia said, thrusting a doll in his hands as she got up.

It was time, Lydia explained, that Arthur learned how to do their hair himself. Lydia would teach by example and Arthur would practise.

'What? No! Whatever for?' Arthur halted, sighed – alright, alright, if it meant Lydia wouldn't miss Mrs Simons too—

Lydia smiled and settled into the chair, the dolls in her lap, *practice makes perfect,* she said, nodding, a curious serenity softening her voice. Arthur studied her, drawn forward, almost lulled – no, he couldn't, he'd never get the hang of this, he was simply no good –

Pair after pair of knotted ropes followed. Arthur suspected Mr Simons would never have had to do any of this. If the suit had allowed, Arthur would have slumped but instead his back was kept rigidly aligned. His eyes found themselves wandering over a pool of disappointment ribbed in widening circles of damp on the wall opposite; a disenchanted Narcissus failed to glimmer back at him. Arthur undid his jacket, tugged at the sleeves, wriggled out and, at last, slumped.

'Just have one more try,' Lydia pleaded.

Arthur picked the doll up, its painted lips for a moment displaced by one of the twins' tiny o's – and his nose hadn't even twitched! 'Well I suppose I could have another go.'

'Why of course.' Lydia spilled a smile of congratulation – and practice, even if it didn't make perfect, made for an unexpectedly satisfied Arthur – he was, he had to say, getting rather good indeed – he never knew he had it in him –

'That's right,' Lydia said, standing behind him. She slid a hand round to retouch the ribbon at the end of a plait. The pair of tiny o's appeared and disappeared. They really were very life-like.

'Aren't they?' Lydia bent to rest her chin on Arthur's shoulder. 'But you do realise Arthur, they're just—'

Dolls! Yes of course, he – Arthur jerked round but Lydia's back was turned, unzipping the dress and letting it fall to the floor.

'You wouldn't mind putting it away for me, would you?' she said, stepping out of the layers of silk round her feet. 'And take that suit off, you look ridiculous, the sleeves are too short.'

Ridiculous? Too short? Just because he wasn't –

The hands of a less than uncanny likeness slid, and bumping down the rungs came nothing-like-Mr-Simons. Noble, Honourable Arthur strained his eyes past Lydia's Arthur to see the party gathered at the foot of the ladder. They did not look altogether happy.

Lydia, having put on Arthur's robe, was lying on the mattress, her hand on her stomach, toes poking at the tumble of sheets and blankets at her feet.

'Put the covers over me, Arthur.'

'I thought you wanted me to put the dress away, I thought you wanted—'

'Don't worry about that – just put the covers over me, I'm cold. Arthur?' Lydia's eyes were closed, her whole face unbuttoned, waiting. 'I'm not trouble, you do believe me, don't you?'

Arthur's mouth opened with the assurance that was becoming automatic but Lydia had already heard another answer, turning onto her side, telling the crumbling patch of wall that if he didn't believe her he obviously didn't love her.

'But of course I do,' Arthur said, trying to hold his hand back before it grabbed the back of his neck. He went over to her, interposing himself between her closed eyes and the crumbling patch of wall.

'Yes, well the Old Bear said he did too. Put the covers over me and tell me a story.'

What story? He didn't know any stories and besides, it was time to put Mr and Mrs Simons away, it was time they were put back under their plastic and into the cupboard.

'I used to tell the twins a story every night,' Lydia said, sitting up. 'Couldn't sleep if I didn't. Oh go on Arthur, tell me a story and I'll go to sleep.' But they hadn't even had any supper yet – why didn't he go out and get them some supper? But Lydia didn't want any supper, she wanted Arthur to put the blankets over her the way he did, smoothing out all the creases, she wanted to be under the blankets hearing a story – if he told her a story she'd go to sleep. Tell her, yes tell her – tell her that story about that other little Arthur –

'What other little Arthur?'

That other little Arthur – the one just like him.

# Part Two

*September 1953*

Gerald was at the window, keeping an eye on Arthur standing sentry at the end of the lawn. Mrs Cohen's tabby was sunning itself in the middle of the road. Gerald craned his head closer to the glass, 'Bloody asking for it, that cat,' he muttered, folding his arms. He rocked onto the balls of his feet, settling back onto his heels as he saw Mrs Cohen coming outside –

'Arthur, get in here!' Gerald was about to go after him but the sound of running water turned him round to see Sylvie. He hadn't heard her come in. It seemed to Gerald as though she always appeared just as he'd reconfigured his sense of order – ten days at a time in her room, not a word, hardly a mouthful, her body still in the house but Sylvie vanished.

'What are you doing down here?'

She sent a laugh into the sink.

'Sylvie?'

She dropped the plates back into the sink but left the tap running, 'What, Gerald? Would you rather I went back upstairs?'

'No, don't put words into my mouth. You won't get up, you won't dress for God knows how long, the boys ask… and now here you are, bouncing round like—'

'I can assure you, Gerald, I am not *bouncing* round like anything—'

'Wait—' He had taken his eye off Arthur. 'I don't like that way Mrs Cohen has of smiling at him.'

'She's probably just being friendly.'

'Does Mrs Cohen smile at you like that?'

'Well yes, as matter of fact she does.' Sylvie ran her nails over her palm. Mrs Cohen smiled differently at her now – her kind smile, mouth ever so gently parted, head ever so gently tilted. Sylvie knew those smiles too well, she'd given them to Aunt Cynthia, to her mother, and now it was her turn.

'That might explain a thing or two,' Gerald muttered and returned to observing his charge. 'I don't want that woman talking to Arthur.'

'Keep your voice down, Gerald.'

'Don't tell me what to—'

'Dad, am I finished?' Arthur was coming in, taking his cap off.

'What did she say to you?' Gerald wanted to know.

'That she liked my cap.'

'Anything else?'

'No.'

'Good. Keep it that way.'

Arthur didn't mind talking to her. She was nice. She liked his cap. She said her boy used to have a cap like that. Her boy had always wanted to be a soldier. Arthur said he didn't want to be a soldier.

'Doesn't every little boy want to be a soldier?'

'Not me.'

'Oh, well then, what do you want to be?' Arthur crouched down to stroke the tabby that had been lured away from its post and up the path where a full saucer sat waiting. 'Maybe,' Arthur said, 'maybe I could be a sea mite.'

Mrs Cohen had laughed then. 'A Semite?'

'Yes,' Arthur was soldier-serious about this. 'What's a sea mite?'

Mrs Cohen poured a little more milk into the saucer.

'Well it's a Jew, isn't it?'

'What's a Jew?'

*

Arthur never saw Mrs Cohen again after that. But then neither did anyone else – only the car that had pulled up and pulled off –

'Neglecting to run the tabby over,' Gerald remarked.

'But it's not there,' Arthur said. 'What did they do with it?'

'I'm sure Mrs Cohen wouldn't have gone without taking the cat,' Sylvie said.

Harry was sure Mrs Cohen had eaten it. Gerald was sure they should all get on with their tea and never talk about Mrs Cohen again.

'What have you got there?' Sylvie asked Arthur, always the last to get up from the table.

'Nothing.'

'It doesn't look like nothing.'

Arthur looked down and handed over the napkin stuffed with the forkfuls of chicken he'd slid off his plate into it. 'In case it's hungry.'

'Oh Arthur, you can't go doing that,' Sylvie said.

'Maybe it's scared,' Arthur stopped to verify this with Sylvie. She shook her head, glanced over at Gerald easing himself into the armchair and bent down to Arthur. 'Go and get a saucer and then no more about it.'

'I've got eyes in the back of my head,' Gerald reminded them.

'It's only a bit of chicken,' Sylvie said.

'I won't have you encouraging strays.' Gerald didn't need to raise his voice. 'One's enough, don't you think?'

*November 1967*

*Well if he would not tell her, tell her then she would tell him, tell him –*

'Don't sigh,' Lydia said, rolling over, 'you're always sighing.'

'I'm not.'

'You are, always, like an old man.' Lydia sat up and rummaged for a doll lost under the covers, pressing it first over her stomach before offering the tiny o of a mouth her schoolgirl breast. 'My goodness, aren't we hungry.'

'Famished,' Arthur said, picking up his keys.

Lydia let the doll fall into her lap and looked up. 'You're not going out, are you? You said you wouldn't. You said you'd stay.' There was an aching translucence in Lydia's voice, sudden, fragile, a match just struck behind stained glass.

'I was only going to get us some supper,' Arthur said, not hearing his old-man sigh until he caught the curve of Lydia's mouth. He waited for another giddy shower of bubbles to giggle over the room but the rainbow-filmed wand just swelled, trembled, popped and the curve withdrew.

'Funny how it flows,' she said, the cool sweet cream of her neck blotching as she shaped her drained mouth into a smile. It wasn't a face Arthur had let himself see her wear before, it twitched round the pinned lips. Arthur shifted back, this unknown face of Lydia's lost to his glazing eyes. He waited for her to look up with another before it took hold.

'All this milk I had,' she said, her neat smile oblivious to the face it was set in, 'like being all dressed up with nowhere to go.'

Except to Mrs Simons whose advertisement for assistance with her newborn twin girls the Grande Dame had helpfully circled. The

Grande Dame had been very helpful with all of it, doing a good clean thorough job on Lydia – the fact that it was the Old Bear, the Grande Dame's husband, who'd made such a job necessary was not a point the Grande Dame felt it was particularly ladylike for Lydia to make – while recommending Lydia cover herself up a bit more in the future.

'The Grande Dame was very professional,' Lydia said through a brittle laugh, 'you'd think she'd done that sort of thing before, so efficient – and I didn't cry, you know – I didn't – but then it was hardly the first time my legs had been prized apart and a foreign body rammed into… I suppose the Old Bear was rather efficient too…' She pulled in her lips, swerving round as Arthur's eyes met hers. 'Don't look at me like that—'

He blinked, taking a step towards her, his hand reaching out –

'Don't – it was all a long – anyway –' she shook her head, managing a frail smile to bridge her words – 'Poor old Uncle Teddy.'

'Poor nothing!' Arthur burst. Hadn't he said he was going to slay the beast –

*If you go down to the woods today –*

'Oh he was harmless, really, everyone said he was just a few sandwiches short—'

No. It was quite simple: Arthur would have to kill him. Woolacombe Bay, was it? It wouldn't take more than a few hours to get to Woolacombe Bay.

The Grande Dame booked Lydia on the ten-fifteen to Kings Cross and Mr Simons would pick her up. Mrs Simons had everything prepared. Seemed the milk started up on arrival – there hadn't been any sign of it before that.

'You'd think a crone like the Dame might have warned me,' Lydia said. 'Get rid of the bloody thing and there you are.'

If Mrs Simons had only been after someone to do the nappies and get the tea she found herself a wet nurse into the bargain.

'Waste not, want not,' Mrs Simons said, her own breasts having dried up the moment she gave birth, 'not a drop.' She'd taken Lydia straight into the nursery and combed her curls as the twins suckled.

He would stay then, yes, he would stay until she fell asleep –

'And you'll tell?'

'Alright.'

'All about that other little—'

'Yes' – and then he would go to Woolacombe Bay and slay the beast! But yes, Lydia, yes, first he would tell.

He couldn't find the words until he found Sylvie's voice, followed it, rewound it, hearing himself in unison with her: planting that other little Arthur out in the earth that would keep him safe, planting him out in a second womb – but then Lydia began to echo the story until she made the words her own. The sound of Sylvie faded under Lydia and Arthur stopped.

'You can't stop now – you have to tell what happened next.'

Lydia wanted more – more, yes, so what then? Every Thursday, until he's big enough, strong enough –

'And then?'

But there was no then, only the blue china pot smashed into pieces and the buds flecking the carpet, the little brown pot he'd found, thinking it might replace what it never could replace –

*For the buds, Ma, for the buds –*

Found it in a pram filled with junk and rubbish – chipped and covered in dust and dirt – a little chipped brown pot engraved with flowers –

All those days when he didn't see her, all those nights he saw her, hunched and curled and cold, so cold –

*No buds, no stories, no telling, no other little* –

Only this Arthur who had gone back through her dream and taken Lydia with him, Lydia who was now playing back to Arthur what Arthur had played back to Sylvie –

As Lydia laid one of her hands palm up in Arthur's, he revised the geography of unscarred palms, finding relief in a terrain lightly veined as a new leaf. Lydia stroked it down his cheek, then her own.

'Am I not a little bit like her?'

'Who?'

'Your mother.'

'No!' Arthur got up, the back of his hand brushing out the sense of Lydia's palm – how had she made him tell like that? He'd never told before – not when Gerald threatened – never. He picked up the keys again.

'Well I suppose I must be if you're going to lock me in too –'

'We never – and I wasn't –' He wasn't locking anybody and had never locked anybody and as for taking his keys – well he was averting the catastrophe of standing at the door knocking and knocking, his arms full with the supper he couldn't afford going cold – and that was assuming he could get in downstairs – no: he was going out, he was taking his keys, he was getting their supper – he could kill the wolf later.

'Tell me what she was like.'

'She's not dead.'

'Well then,' Lydia said, that terrible transparency now washed out of her voice as a face Arthur had stopped waiting for was slipped on, 'I should like to meet her. If my mother wasn't dead I'd let you meet her. I wouldn't keep her all to myself.'

Arthur's old-man sigh accompanied squeezed eyes. He pinched the bridge of his nose as a hideous scene unveiled itself: Harry pulling out a chair for Lydia and pushing her in, jamming her right up against the table, plunging the ramekin of nuts down over her shoulder and onto her dinner plate as he poured her wine over the brim, giving him cause to supply Arthur's back with a good succession of thumps and then Gerald, engorged with pride, would enter, leading Sylvie in like a circus act, presenting the spectacle of the jointless-legged lady on toy stilts, silver-pink skin-gloved hands turned up for all to see: 'Come on now, my lovely,' Gerald would say, 'let's show our new friend what you can do. Harry, pass your father the nuts.'

Arthur returned his eyes to Lydia. That was it: he would never close them again.

'Don't you think she'd like me?'

'Well of course she would—'

'Yes she would, and I would like her – very much. She would like to help me, I'm sure. Do you think she would?'

'With what?'

'Planting out, yes she would show me where and how – how to weave the twigs and scatter the buds – and we'd go to the park every Thursday – a handful for her and one for me.'

*And then when he's big enough and strong enough –*

*When she's big enough and –*

Tell her, tell her, she'd said.

No.

But she wanted to hear –

Not now.

Hear all about – yes, she had to hear it again – hear all about that other little –

No, there should never have been any telling at all: keys, out, supper – oh don't, please don't, she wasn't, was she? Neck and face blotching –

'Don't cry, please don't—'

'I'm not.'

'Look, I'll just be a few minutes.'

'Arthur.'

'Yes.'

'If you go I might not be here when you get back.'

Arthur stood at the door without opening it.

'Oh it's alright,' Lydia said. 'Go on, go and get your damn supper. Lock me in if you like. I'll still be here – of course I'll still be here – it's not as if I have anywhere to go.'

*

Stepping into the hallway was stepping into another country and onto the street another world: the flash of cars and lights and faces multiplying under the clash of horns and voices merged into a single unintelligible stream. The momentum was inexorable, keeping Arthur as invisible to this alien territory and its inhabitants as they were unrecognisable to him.

'Just the man!' Keith's waving arms transported Arthur with all the brutal suddenness of an emergency landing to the pavement of the

Holloway Road. The waving arms abandoned him almost immediately, now engaged in a routine of circling, swinging and flapping in the effort to sustain if not quicken the progress of a plastic-bag-laden silhouette of a man towards him. Once the silhouette appeared to be navigating its fractured course independently, Keith bent over. With his elbows out, palms on thighs, shirt sleeves billowing between, he seemed to have been equipped with a pair of giant triangular wings. He panted a moment and found a breath to slap his hand on the trunk at his feet.

'Help us up with this, would you, Arthur.'

The trunk looked as incongruous as Arthur had felt – cracked and scuffed, unidentifiable by its tangle of brown tags, it might have been taken from the prop cupboard.

'Go on, Arthur,' Keith said, taking his palm from the trunk to pummel his back, encouraging the deepest recesses of his lungs to supply him with the convincing dose he now shot with an archer's accuracy between Arthur and the trunk. 'Come on, I've had Solly and his boy to deal with all bloody afternoon, I'm dying here.' Keith raised an arm and the silhouette disappeared behind a bus, reappeared and began to gather dimensions and detail as he made his way across the road to them, dropping a bag to clutch his hat to his head as though there were a fierce wind.

'Arthur, allow me to introduce Professor—'

The clutched hat was snatched off and shaken in objection –

'Not Professor! Professional!' The man shrank, taken aback by his own volume. 'Professional,' he mouthed, replacing his hat.

'Blimey, yes alright, no need to shout,' Keith said.

'I no mean to shout!' The man shrank again and, for the first time Arthur could remember, Keith made no effort to either laugh off or conceal bafflement, left to scratch exposed skin until the line of rescue was thrown. Well it was no use widening his eyes at Arthur. Keith's eyes were pleading. No.

'Well our *Professional* here,' Keith said, 'will be your neighbour – I'm putting him next door to you.'

Next door? He couldn't! Next door was not fit for human life to endure – his room might have been a hole – his hole, with his Lydia – his Lydia who he should never have left, his Lydia who might not be there when he got back – no, no one could possibly be put next door – worse than a hole – his hole! – next door was a pit!

'Our Prof works in a *university*,' Keith said, drawing in his lips as he gave Arthur a nod.

The man raised his hand to protest but let it fall with a mild shrug, concentrating his watery vision on Arthur, his hooded half-moon eyes sunk deep in the soft pouches beneath like rings embedded in the silk folds of a jewellery box.

'Ah, Arthur,' he said, holding out his hand, 'so now I know,' his articulation as distinct and certain as his nod.

Know? Know what? Arthur observed the waiting hand: silent, stationary, its inaudible message extended in the unending moments after it was made. It seemed, like the man himself waiting, silent, stationary, to have been chiselled from stone – another looted prop.

'Arthur!' Keith nudged him and one of Arthur's pockets gave up a hand just as the stone figure was displaced by the man its maker had sought to duplicate and the waiting hand dropped.

'Know what?' Keith asked as the two hands at last managed to synchronise.

'Arthur, yes, yes – it is nice to know again, so pleased,' the man went on, his accent and face familiar, but both too soft to locate, his eyes taking up Arthur's own with a quiet intensity. He wanted them back – he wanted his hand back too, for that matter – but it was only when he yanked it away that he could feel how gently it had been held. It was going back in his pocket nevertheless.

'Know again what?' Not knowing not only what was known but known again was driving Keith's nails up his arm, his neck, his scalp. Arthur's eyes freed themselves and escaped on to Keith.

'Don't look at me like that,' Keith said.

Like what? He wasn't looking at him like anything. If anyone was looking at anyone like anything at all it was this man looking at him like – like what? – Well, like… *that.*

'I am sorry not to see you again,' the man said. Both Keith and Arthur looked at the man a moment, lids slipping down over his eyes. 'Ah, perhaps I confuse,' he said.

'Confuse!' The word brought a clarity so delightful to Keith that he lunged to grip the man's shoulder. A trio of uneven laughs followed – or, rather, a pair: Keith's rotund, multiple, Arthur's strained, singular, the man's just visible if not audible.

'Well not to worry Prof, we'll have you parleying like a native in no time. Our Arthur here is a total layabout but he's an excellent teacher and I'm sure there's a poet in him somewhere – though I'm yet to find it – did I tell you that I, as a matter of fact, in truth, am a poet myself?'

'Yes, yes…'

'Hey Arthur, hold up – where are you – ?'

Arthur felt the stream, alien only minutes ago, readily absorb him, a hand on the keys in his pocket a raft, drifting back even as he heard Keith say something about Solly –

'Think you know a man and then – Prof, tell me – can you ever really know a man? I mean, me and Solly – we cut our teeth together –'

'Cut teeth?'

'Yes, Prof – so to speak. Ah, poor bugger, wonder how long he'll get…'

Something about giving him a hand –

'Do us a favour, Arthur – you wouldn't want me pegging it halfway up the stairs—'

Something about the trunk, saw him whacking his chest, saw the stone carving animate, moving down to pick up the trunk –

Arthur jolted.

'Arthur's my right-hand man. Anything you want, you ask Arthur. Has a very receptive ear.'

'I was just going to get—' What was he just going to get? He turned back to Keith and looked at the trunk, 'supper!' Yes, that was why he had left his Lydia who he should never have left – oh dear Lord let her still be there when he got back. She would, she must – and he must now keep solidly to his purpose – he would hold this in his mind and nothing else: supper, Lydia, purpose; supper, Lydia, purpose – this and this alone.

'Thank you,' the man said.

Thank him? For what? The man was rummaging in a plastic bag and shook a parcel at Arthur. 'Please, please,' he said. Arthur's pockets were less obliging now.

'Take, take,' the grooves in the man's face deepened with the imperative. There was a kindness, a concern, that was almost ferocious. 'Please,' he said, grooves and voice softening, 'always I make too much,' and then retrieved another parcel, immediately unwrapped and devoured by Keith.

'Excellent pickle!'

The man smiled a slight smile, grey lips not quite able to part, and nodded at Keith, the hoods over his eyes just lifting then dropping again as he tucked the still wrapped unaccepted offering back into the bag.

*

Supper, Lydia, purpose; supper, Lydia, purpose – the faithful triple mantra that set Arthur before the counter and his eyes up at the board behind it had repeated itself beyond sense into a collection of sounds that couldn't explain what he was doing, standing there, staring at rows and rows of chalk letters rearranging themselves in and out of meaning. The mantra continued, as useless as it was persistent. Perspective. Yes, that was what was needed: perspective. Supper, Lydia, purpose – purpose, yes – yes it was all falling into place now. Arthur stepped back and into a table behind. He felt for the keys in his pockets – this needn't unsettle things.

'We're not a bus stop.'

The owner turned, leaving Arthur to confront the broad white back wedged behind the counter, while a pink chest, squeezed into and squeezing out of a pink plastic top, squeezed past.

'What can I get you, darling?' Batting lashes suggested to Arthur he would need to risk stepping back again. Perspective! Greater perspective! The step back was a triumph but still the board meant nothing to him.

*Then perhaps I confuse you –*

Keith and the man would be making a whole racket with the trunk by now and Lydia wondering what the hell was going on, all that little and large to me to you banging about up the stairs, the frustrations of an ear and tongue foreign to one another trying to establish a workable mode of communication, comprehensibility plummeting, decibel levels soaring – how could Lydia possibly still be there when he got back? A mechanical chop-chopping replaced the mantra –

chop chop chop; chop chop chop – thoroughly satisfying until it, too, slipped out of sense.

'Did you want something or not?' A knife dropped down beside the broad white back.

Arthur searched –

*Then perhaps I confuse* –

And found –

'Pickle?'

A chuckle came from the direction of the broad white back and the chop-chopping, invigorated, began again. 'Shel, I think you've got a customer.'

Shel, Arthur presumed, smiled, rolled a lollipop down her blue tongue and tucked it into a hamster cheek. 'Don't mind him, darling,' she said, cramming a cup with pickle. 'This do for you?'

Arthur nodded, marvelling at the blue lips, the bulging cheek sucked hollow again. He reached into his pocket –

'You're alright, darling, it's on me.'

On her? The blue lips grinned – he would have to come here again.

Chop chop chop –

Chop chop indeed! Back to Lydia – pickle, Lydia, purpose; pickle, Lydia – Arthur looked at his pink-plastic-clad, blue-lipped benefactor – what was he supposed to do with pickle? Shel – Arthur could only presume again – gave him a blue-frothed smile before she tilted forward, eyes burrowing round past Arthur, lips first pursing, then smacking –

'Are you getting under those tables or just round them?' she called over Arthur's head.

'Mind! Mind! Wet, still wet!' A mop was swirling in Arthur's direction.

Of course, yes! That was it!

*Then perhaps I confuse –*

Or rather, that was him –

'Wet, still wet!'

The urgent burble and the swirling mop carried the plastic-bag-laden silhouette coming towards him and Keith along with the man waving his hat before them, his waiting hand, his paper-wrapped parcels and, dragging Arthur back well over a year, and then another, and placed them with the same silence of his likeness carved in stone into the corridor outside Epstein's study at the college.

It must have been the only time Arthur had ever spoken to the caretaker – he hardly remembered having even seen him. Well he'd be seeing enough of him now, he supposed –

*Then perhaps I –*

The caretaker, the pocket dictionary, the photograph – Arthur ducked, seeing that urgent hand coming towards him again –

*So long I search –*

And holding the photograph up to Arthur's face like that –

*Check every list –*

So insistent, so… what was it? Obviously something not right about the man. In any case, the caretaker had *confused* –

*Indeed you do –*

And Arthur would let him confuse away, he would keep hold of the right end of the stick and it was no business of his if the caretaker had come into possession of the other. Good. Well now, chop chop and back to Lydia – only what to do with this damn cup of pickle? He couldn't go into Lydia with a cup of pickle – but how to dispose of it? It had been a gift, on Shel – it seemed he would have to hang onto it – but he must get back to Lydia –

She would still be there, wouldn't she? Lydia who had nowhere to go – but of course there were no doubt countless places she might have gone – he could see her now, outside number sixty-three, the twins cartwheeling round her – or worse, the Old Bear opening the door to her – never mind the Grande Dame – a witch was a witch but the Bear was beast! He'd be dragging her up some sandy creek within the hour. He should never have gone out, or else he should have gone straight to Woolacombe Bay and done what was only right – he could have been on his way to being Noble, Honourable Arthur after all. Arthur tried to picture the Old Bear – he needed to get a sense of his foe, his proportions, he needed to be sure of the tone of him in order to find the most appropriate way to dispose of him – how odd that disposing of Old Uncle Teddy should seem significantly less awkward than disposing of this cup of pickle. Arthur was on to old Ted though – if one was on the lookout for a beast, one must be alert to anything that *appeared* as a lamb. Yet Arthur could envisage neither beast nor lamb – all he could see was Gerald: Gerald dragging his Lydia up a sandy creek on Woolacombe Bay. And all he would have to explain himself with was a cup of pickle.

*

The trunk had made it inside but not up the stairs. Arthur looked up towards the landing, the door next to his was open, feet were padding about, plastic bags rustling. He might have taken the trunk up – not that he was going to let it, unattended, reprimand him from the bottom step, recall for him Keith's ghastly cough. Arthur put the cup down, picked the trunk up – alright then, alright, he would take it – but this was neither an act of submission nor admission – it did not mean he was responsible – not for Keith, not for the caretaker, not for the trunk. Keith was a grown man, he could get the quack to have a listen to his chest if it was so awful – it was pretty awful and that funny colour he went sometimes – Arthur rubbed his face – he felt like he might be going a funny colour himself – was that what happened if you lived on the Holloway Road long enough? No, he was alright and, as for Keith, he'd looked rosy-cheeked enough this evening, that hacking and wheezing was all just a bit of a performance – still, maybe Arthur could pop into the chemist tomorrow, he had to show his face at the labour exchange in any case, could go on his way back, leave something outside Keith's door. Arthur lugged the trunk up over the last step – so much for hunting down the Old Bear and slaying the beast – this was battle enough.

The rustling stopped with Arthur's steps, resumed, 'Please, please, a minute, a minute.'

Arthur's own door was closed – Lydia would still be there –

Two half-moons lit first on the trunk, then the arms that carried it and at last on Arthur.

'Look how you have,' the caretaker began, the stone face at once flushed alive, etched lines deepening and smoothing in the relay of smiles that kept trying to form but fell. He unloaded the stack of books from under his arm, leaving them in a row of knocked dominoes between him and Arthur. 'Please, please,' he said, taking the trunk. Arthur stepped over the books while the caretaker deliberated with the trunk at various points of the room, standing over it once he'd set it down. 'Later I find it place,' he concluded, scrunching a tuft of hair at his temple.

*Its*, Arthur might have said, *its* – could he not? A small thing. Just one more small thing –

'Its.'

The caretaker's eyes came up.

'Its place.'

'Ah.'

'*Its*, not *it*.'

'Not?'

Oh God it was hateful to be corrected. The caretaker's smile formed, held. 'Its?'

'Yes.' Absolutely hateful.

'Its, its,' the caretaker's smile grew with the repetition, 'thank you,' he said, 'it is too lucky to know you again.'

'Lucky?'

'Yes.'

Yes. A small thing. Arthur's eyes skidded past the caretaker, scanning the walls, the floor – a murky oblong hung over the mattress where the florescent poster had been removed, now neatly rolled by the door along with the wicker basket – before they came to the caretaker's hand, watching for a tremor – something to explain the discomfort wriggling through him. But there was nothing. It was just a hand that happened to be attached to the end of a string-tied sleeve, that same pocket dictionary protruding beneath – no one had the wrong end of the stick – least of all the smiling caretaker, utterly sincere, utterly benign, this little nod that said he understood. The hoods over his eyes dropped then lifted, half-moons clouding, unclouding, 'Five years I come and every day my English speaks worse,' he said and his face shared a laugh first with itself, then with Arthur.

The caretaker began unlacing his shoes, stopping after one, eyes searching round the room before he got up, dragged a box to the table and unfolded a hand towards the chair. 'Please,' he said as he sat on the box, a foot up on his knee to unlace the other shoe, aligning the pair beside the box.

The chair eyed Arthur, noted his delay: it was expecting him. His hands sneaked into his pockets, he felt for his keys – Lydia? – she must still be there.

The caretaker commiserated with the empty chair, 'You do not very much like to sit.'

'Oh no, I like very much to sit,' Arthur enthused, key-holding hand skittering up from his pocket, 'only I have to—'

The slight smile was forming again, forming, settling, holding, horribly sincere, horribly benign. Could he not sit? A small thing? Just this one more small thing. No. He had to get back to Lydia –

The caretaker was untying the string round his sleeve, releasing the pocket dictionary it secured.

'Hold on a tic—' Arthur said and went to reclaim the cup of pickle from the bottom step. Without the trunk he felt deliriously light back up the stairs and through the door, but within a moment, the chuckle that had come from behind the broad white back caught him. Arthur was sure he could hear the General chuckling along. A dizzy hand (certainly not Arthur's own) set, knocked over and steadied the cup on the table.

'Please,' Arthur said.

With the immediacy of the touch of a magic wand the caretaker's furrowed concentration cleared, 'For me?'

'Yes, yes, for you. A gift. Just a small thing.'

As soon as the caretaker picked up the cup, the magic wand reversed its trick. He hooked a finger over his chin and began going through the plastic bags until he fished out the paper-wrapped parcel, his slight smile forming, settling, holding – utterly sincere, utterly benign. Arthur swallowed, his eyes dipping to the parcel held towards him, a moment before he took it and looked up, catching and returning the little nod that said he understood.

'Pickle?' the caretaker asked, peeling off the lid, 'We must to taste.' He opened the cupboard and drawers, 'Ah, why no spoons! Ah here, here,' and, having handed one to Arthur, took a sample with his own. 'Excellent pickle!' he pronounced, holding his spoon up, dipping it back towards the cup he now held out towards Arthur. Arthur was not sure he could stomach pickle.

'You must to try!' the caretaker encouraged, taking Arthur's spoon from him, extracting a neat portion and urging it towards Arthur's reluctant hand. Arthur chewed, winced, swallowed.

'Excellent, no?'

'Excellent.'

*

Arthur sat down to the empty room, laid the paper-wrapped parcel on the table. Well of course she had somewhere to go. He pushed the parcel aside and made a pillow out of his arms until closed eyes booked him on a train to Woolacombe Bay while walking him up to number sixty-three; one Lydia drawn up a sandy creek, another Lydia just returned from the park, the twins cartwheeling round. Arthur lurched up: the contents of the case that never did go back had been piled up on the chair opposite, elevating one of the dolls just enough so that it seemed to be peering over the table. Arthur was sure it had shrivelled a little in Lydia's absence. His eyes caught on the tiny o of a mouth. Oh Lydia-not-his-Lydia –

Arthur's head fell back onto his makeshift pillow – not his Lydia, no – but then he wasn't her Arthur either: the application of the possessive was his own and, clipped from it, he felt himself dangle mid-air and tumble. Arthur looked back up to see the tiny o had closed into varnished lips. He picked it up and searched about for the other but there was no tiny o to tell him where it might be and it wasn't for varnished lips to say what had already been said: one for telling stories to and one for planting out –

*Up the hill and over the gates –*

Would she? Those gates would have been closed hours ago – gates Arthur would have stared through, the dark helping him to make out the shapes that weren't there: Lydia, Sylvie – Sylvie who'd fallen and looked up at him with the first of her broken-toothed smiles, Sylvie who he'd found where he found Lydia now – standing on the corner of Llanvanor and Finchley Road –

'Oh Lydia – please –' Arthur pulled her towards him, anticipating a re-enactment of Sylvie's fall.

'I just wanted to see,' she said.

'How did you even get here?' The distance between Llanvanor and the Holloway Road seemed hundreds, thousands of miles away.

'What does that matter?' She drifted a step towards Llanvanor and then looked back at Arthur. 'Am I not a little bit like her?' she asked.

'Let's get you home, I've got us supper and everything,' Arthur said, taking one of her hands to be sure of an unpuckered palm, wondering how long it might be before she, too, looked up at him with a broken-toothed smile.

*

Arthur didn't get up, it might wake her – she was such a light sleeper, he'd sit there all night if he had to. The muffled rustle through the wall that pretended to divide his room from the caretaker's drew Arthur's eyes towards it and back to Lydia. It was alright, the caretaker's movement hadn't touched her – *What's that? Who's that?* – she'd asked every time the wall betrayed the rustle – *Nothing, it's no one*, Arthur would manage, head coming up just as it dropped, trying to sit up in the chair he'd brought up to the mattress, brushing off the sleep that kept thickening round him – but no, curled tight now in Arthur's robe, the doll that was for telling tucked into the curve of her body, a blanket swaddling them both, her breath at last even – it caught then shallowed, tugging Arthur forward to see the curled body twitch and settle on the edge of a dream.

Again she had wanted him to tell her tell her and so he had told her told her – three days of telling it had taken for her to close her eyes (though she would remember it as nine) and, now that she had, Arthur's were locked open, set on the wall as if this might warn off the rustle, the shuffle, the opening of a drawer, the tap, a match struck, the water boiling. All that took his eyes away from the wall was the jerk in his neck, reminding him to check Lydia's shape through the sheets, check the breath still even, every shift beyond the wall intruding with its strain not to intrude; each of the caretaker's movements, hovering on the cusp of being identified, somehow far more voluble than Keith thudding about upstairs, muted by regularity.

'Why did you take me here?' Lydia had asked when he'd brought her back, 'You said we were going home,' and she'd dropped the doll that was for planting out, the doll she'd taken with her, and picked up the doll that was for telling, that had been sat on the case peering at Arthur and the paper-wrapped parcel through the dried lilacs. 'What are you doing here?' she'd asked it. 'Little girls shouldn't be left all by themselves.' She set it down and lifted the doll that was for planting out, rocking it as she walked it round the room –

*Until she's big enough and strong enough…*

Her voice thinned as she set the case on the floor and laid the doll inside. She seemed to Arthur to be encircled by a fine yet impenetrable membrane – but within an instant she was brushing off her hands, closing the case. She stood up and surveyed the table, 'What's that?' her eyes were fastened on the paper-wrapped parcel, 'I don't want that there, or these,' she said, pointing out the treasures the case had supplied and she had so meticulously arranged, dressing it up just as she should for a Mr and Mrs Simons: the dried lilacs, the plastic fruit – 'not this, not this' – all of it tumbling to the floor as she swept up and shook out the tablecloth to make a pall for the doll.

She smiled over the case, 'That's better now, isn't it?'

Arthur looked at the fallen fruit, the lilacs, the parcel. Lydia tucked her chin in, pressed her knuckles against it, she wasn't finished: everything that never did go back was going in the case that never would go back. The stripped room gaped at Arthur. Lydia zipped up the case and dragged it over to the cupboard. A patch of crushed lilacs caught her – she stopped, her vision circumscribed by the buds before her eyes came up in intervals to Arthur, flitting on and off him. He tried to hold them but they slid onto his shoulder and back to the floor, towards the stems.

'Such a mess,' she was saying, 'such a mess in here.'

Arthur opened his mouth before he could find the words. His eyes traced a line between his feet and Lydia's, seeing the edge of his robe on the floor. She tucked herself in under the covers then, the doll that was for telling at her breast, her head lowering, her lips touching the doll's hair.

'Come on now,' she urged it. It was better not to look – he had no business looking – his only business was with the mess of dried lilacs. Arthur drenched a stray sock and began scrubbing, the patch darkening and magnifying under his hands until a mauve oval stretched from the cupboard to the table.

'Something's the matter,' Lydia said, standing Arthur up, the wet sock in his hand. 'Something's wrong.'

'Nothing's wrong.'

'The milk, it must be bad – do you think it's bad, Arthur?'

Arthur's eyes fell over the darkened oval and drank and drank – no, it wasn't bad, it was good – it was good and she was good – a good Lydia and a good Arthur, her Arthur – hers so long as he told her told her –

'Tell us and she'll drink, tell us then she'll sleep – I'll sleep – sleep and sleep and sleep—'

*

Arthur kept his eyes on the curve of Lydia's body as he picked up his coat, paused by her murmurs of dream speech – her sleep seemed impenetrable now but still he wanted to shield it, waiting a few moments by the door before he opened it, his eyes following the barely perceptible rise of her hip and shoulder with each breath. A snatch of her unintelligible babble folded into the shuffle and rustle through the wall. Sluggish but ceaseless, the caretaker's movements had become almost inaudible to him again, as inaccessible and immediate as Lydia's dream world. He wouldn't be more than ten minutes, fifteen at the most – just get them some bread and milk, cheese if there was enough over.

Arthur stopped on the half-landing to check what change he had left, stiffening as he heard the toilet flush and the tap run –

'Morning, morning,' Keith said, coming out of the bathroom, his hand on Arthur's shoulder.

Arthur rubbed his eyes, his forehead – the effort to reply felt beyond him. He nodded and went down the stairs but Keith was right behind him, his hand back on Arthur's shoulder as soon as he got outside.

'You alright, Arthur?' Keith asked, eyes narrowing as his head came forward, 'You're looking a bit… peaky.'

'I thought you were the dying man,' Arthur mumbled, shaking off Keith's hand.

'Now, now—' Keith said, standing back, holding up his hands.

'Sorry, Keith,' Arthur said, letting a sigh go, 'just not much sleep, that's all.'

'Ah, the muse is keeping you awake,' Keith said, a grin undermining the sympathetic hand on Arthur's arm.

Another sigh – what did it matter? Arthur took a breath, put his clenched hands in his pockets.

Keith shook his head, checked Arthur again, 'The dole queue, then – that's it, isn't it? It's eating your soul – I can tell. Didn't I say it eats a man's soul? I've seen it – many a time – you can see it shrivelling a man from the inside, sometimes it's terminal. Can lead a man to desperate measures. Take Solly,' Keith's hand was on Arthur's arm again, this time without the grin, 'hobbling up to the dock – just as his boy came good.' Arthur swallowed – his mouth was dry, a metallic bitterness in the back of his throat, his head seeming to swell and turn, Keith's arm all he had to moor him while he waited for the flood of sensations to pass.

Keith was grinning again, face flushed. He slapped Arthur's cheek – 'I think we need to consider an advance for my right hand man.'

'Advance?'

'Something to keep you afloat.'

'You mean like a loan?'

'An *advance*,' Keith nodded.

'What for?'

'For my right hand man in case anything should go wrong – something might need fixing… mending. And besides, I need you at the ready when this chest packs up on me.'

'It is not going to pack up on you and nothing is going to go wrong!' The turn and swirl round his head again, temple pulsing, the ground under him slipping, sinking, Lydia's murmuring babble and the sound of Sylvie's voice, the story he'd told, lost, caught and told again. All that seemed solid was Keith, the change in his pocket, the bread and the milk he was going to get. Arthur tried to rub the pulse in his temple, brushing off Keith's hand ruffling his hair, pulling himself away. Keith called after him as he crossed the street, assuring Arthur that he, too, was once a poor struggling poet.

*

Arthur slipped back into the chair by the mattress, his coat still on, his eyes on Lydia a moment before they closed and he let his head sink forward. He could only just make out the caretaker's movements but their edges blurred until he found himself straining to hear them and the silence announced itself, waking Lydia. She sat herself up, looking around the room, up at Arthur, at the doll, blinking her way back to familiarity. She reached her hand up towards Arthur, her eyes watching his hand hesitate as it came towards hers.

'Did you go out? Where did you go?' she asked, her questions almost weightless, drained of urgency.

'Just to the shop,' he said, his voice quiet as though trying to save the stillness in hers.

She got up and moved towards the window – 'Why are the curtains closed? Look, Arthur, the curtains are closed,' she said, pulling them back, 'they shouldn't be closed on such a beautiful day.' The vibration in her voice was quickening now, her hands checking her face and neck before she opened the window, casting a gauzy light over the room,

'You are alright, aren't you, Arthur?'

'What? Yes, yes, of course.'

She went over to the cupboard, pulling out a dress, a scarf, shaking her head, putting them back, 'but we're late, we've got to get ourselves ready – and the twins…'

'Late? What for? I don't understand.'

She dropped the clothes in her hands and sank down to the floor

– wasn't it time, she asked, that they knocked at the last door of Llanvanor Road and introduced themselves properly?

'Properly?'

The lid of the jack-in-the-box flipped open and up sprang Arthur: No they couldn't – he couldn't – properly or otherwise! They couldn't just turn up, not like that –

'But you said—'

'Nothing of the sort!'

'Please, Arthur,' she said, getting up, 'shall we get some flowers for your mother? I'm sure she'd like that.'

The mess of dried lilacs and Arthur's subsequent efforts to clean them up sat him back down and closed his eyes. The shuffle and rustle had begun again.

'Funny little man, isn't he?' Lydia said, pulling the case out of the cupboard and lifting the pall off the buried doll. 'What do you think he's *doing* in there?'

The shuffle and rustle paused. Arthur looked at the wall, eyes squeezed over an image of the caretaker frozen mid-step, wincing, his head down – he wouldn't have heard, would he?

'Lydia,' Arthur began, the demands of a stage whisper pulling and bunching his face into a perfect caricature of the uncontainable contained.

'I'm sorry, Arthur, but you'll have to get rid of him,' she said, giving the doll a little shake. 'Wakey wakey sleeping beauty, time to get up.' She looked up at Arthur, 'You'll have to, I can't listen to all that moaning.'

Arthur's mouth tightened – there hadn't been any moaning. Rustling, shuffling, yes, but no moaning.

'What moaning?'

'All night long, worse than you.'

'I don't moan.'

'Terrible – anyone would think you were in some sort of pain.'

'I do not moan and I am not in any pain. Not in the least – not in the slightest – I am not in any—'

'Good. Well you can help me get the twins all pretty for their nanna and when we get back you can see about that funny little—'

'Lydia!'

But she was shaking the disinterred doll – 'Wake up! I said wake up!'

Broken-toothed smiles and silver-pink skin; flowers and dolls and fistfuls of nuts. The impossible miscellany floated behind Arthur's eyes, resurrecting the uncontainable.

'Come on now,' Lydia said, standing over the doll, 'it's time to meet your nanna.'

Arthur grabbed the doll: two brown eyes, roundly unhorrified, drew Arthur to his hand clenched round the doll's neck – Lydia wasn't sure that was a terribly good idea. Arthur dropped the doll and went to consider the teabag he was certain he could wring one last life from. He couldn't. It was dead: dead, dead, dead. Black specks sank to the bottom of the cup. Dead.

'Arthur! At least say goodbye,' Arthur heard Lydia saying as he went down the stairs. 'Say goodbye nicely, Arthur, or I might not—'

He stopped at the end of the Holloway Road, pulling himself along before he turned back. A drinker outside the Crown raised his glass. To be sitting in there now. Nothing like the Old Bull, of course. The split between that last evening with Sammy and Pete and this. He put his hands in his pockets, nodded to the drinker, walked on. That evening and this – polarised. It took him a moment before he could picture their faces, yet the Rabbi's came to him immediately – those soft creases round his eyes, the hint of a smile. There was no thread to join any of these worlds: Llanvanor, the Rabbi, Sammy and Pete, Lydia – only that each had been tacked on to the next. And yet Lydia wound him back somehow – even in her absence – especially in her absence, there to meet him, just as she'd warned, as soon as he got back.

Sleeping beauty, unwoken, left unburied just where he had dropped her, sent him on what was becoming a familiar route: up to number sixty-three where he did not knock, past the park where he did not stop and down to the corner of Llanvanor and Finchley Road, unsure whether it was Lydia or Sylvie he was looking for. With a groggy mix of restlessness and relief he found neither. He wanted to sit there, just sit there, on that corner – for how long he wasn't sure, indefinitely perhaps – not waiting for either Lydia or Sylvie so much as making sure they never arrived. The pavement didn't make the invitation he'd hoped for. Good, well good. He could hardly waste another minute – yes, this minute, he must get back before the last door of Llanvanor Road made its way up to the corner and there he'd be caught by a broken-toothed smile and a *Hello there Goldilocks, we were just wondering where you might have got off to.*

Oh Lydia-not-his-Lydia. Arthur reburied sleeping beauty, Lydia's threat echoing as he put the case back in the cupboard –

*Say goodbye or –*

Attuning him to the moan it might have obscured. Arthur hadn't heard the caretaker's moan before then – but Lydia was right – the funny little man did moan – funny little? – No, the caretaker, he would allow him that at least. Well so what if the caretaker moaned – it was little odd perhaps, but it wasn't so awful. Yes it was. It was awful. Surely he didn't moan like that. Of course he didn't. Oh Lord, it was agony. Arthur, still dressed, put the covers over him and a pillow over his face – but it wasn't volume he needed to remedy –

the moan was so faint – it might have been agony to hear it but there was no pain in the sound itself – it just sounded like… What *did* it sound like? That was the problem – it didn't sound like anything else. It would accommodate neither reference nor comparison, and the standard Saturday night squall coming through from outside couldn't compete. Arthur flattened a hand over the thoroughly useless pillow while the various inevitabilities of Lydia's fate presented themselves in rotation until each was blasted by the prophetic vision of himself blasting a fist through that unforgivable excuse for a wall.

*December 1967*

Sunday hadn't been quite ready to get up but the covers were yanked back nevertheless – a course of explosive bangs as a car, crammed with the previous night's epilogue, lurched off saw to that, a fuggy wake of smog and song dissolving to humiliate the Holloway Road. Rain was starting to spot the windows. A figure slouched over the railings stuck a finger up at it – Arthur couldn't have agreed more: he might have sworn blind on his blind-with-sleeplessness-self that he would never, no matter what, take his eyes off his Lydia again but, since mistakes insist on being repeated more than they object to being forgotten, Arthur had, within a week, attempted to squeeze a third life out of the last teabag and left without saying goodbye. The sight of Lydia on the corner of Llanvanor and Finchley Road flashed up, fading just enough for Arthur to trace Sylvie beneath – Sylvie smiling her broken-toothed smile – doubling the warning Lydia said better without saying: she still wasn't back.

The slouched figure at the railings and the apt finger it had supplied crawled off. No matter, Arthur had taken its message to heart: if Sunday had to get up, the only sensible thing to do was go back to bed.

*

Arthur could honestly say – in fact he could swear on everything under and over the sun – that he did not dream, so whoever the hell it was that woke him from digging and digging, mud-caked, earth-caked, finding then losing, catching then dropping first Sylvie then Lydia, to the sound of little laughing bubbles popping he couldn't say. He went over to the sink, splashed his face – that couldn't be Lydia in there – *Funny little* – she'd said so herself. Must be last night catching up with him – making him hear things – still caught in a muddle of dreams that belonged somewhere else – to someone else – hearing things, yes – but there it was, another laughing bubble – and now her voice, tripping over the caretaker's interjections in a clumsy dance.

Arthur turned back to the wall, shook his head. Hearing things, yes. He would give the caretaker a knock then, just to verify.

Barefooted, silk-gloved, layered in gowns and dresses, skirts and scarves, Lydia, dressed for as many balls as she could tie and button round her, opened the door: 'Oh, it's you.'

'Hello, hello, come in, come in,' the caretaker's quickened shuffle set him rearranging the box and the chair at the table. 'You must to sit, please to sit.'

'You're… here,' Arthur said.

'Well of course, any fool can see that,' Lydia said – it becoming apparent to Arthur that fools had not been invited to the ball.

The caretaker was smiling his benign smile and Lydia found hers, 'Can't you say I look nice?'

Arthur looked at her, at the caretaker. He was too slow, Lydia's bare feet had disappeared under her as she kneeled down over the trunk, putting on each item as she took it out –

'I'll go to the ball as Old Mother Hubbard – who says Old Mother Hubbard shouldn't go to the ball? Or the Lady of Shalott – yes, I could be the Lady of—' She pulled out braces, a waistcoat and then – 'What's this? A clown's nose! What do you have a clown's nose for? And balls too!'

'For to juggle,' the caretaker explained.

'Are you a *real* clown?'

The caretaker shook his head, 'So sad to say no – not… *professional*.'

'But you must put on a show for us.'

'No no no! No showing!'

The caretaker's objections were unnecessary: 'Oh these are just like

Mrs Simons's,' Lydia said, holding up a string of pearls, 'exquisite exquisite exquisite!'

'Here Arthur, help me,' Lydia said. The caretaker nodded and Arthur took his instruction. Too slow again. Already Lydia had dropped the pearls in favour of a hat. 'Can I have this?'

'But of course,' the caretaker said, 'please.'

'Is this really *all* yours?' Lydia asked, twirling, deaf to the caretaker's reply.

'A man. My friend – for his wife – but she is no there – he is no there and the houses all gone, the school gone, the synagogue gone—' He looked up at Arthur but Arthur couldn't hold his eyes.

'How strange,' the twirling Lydia told the hat as she took it off.

'Strange,' the caretaker repeated, exploring the sound of the word rather than confirming its meaning.

'How…' Lydia brought the hat up to her eye-line, 'very strange.'

'Very strange,' the caretaker imitated.

'Oh, is that it? Only all this—' Lydia noted, disappointed the trunk was unable to sustain its generosity.

'No, please,' the caretaker's benign smile hardened itself against his mouth as he got up to catch Lydia's hand and close the trunk. 'Please to leave all paper.'

A soundless bubble rose and rose –

'But the hat, I do like the hat.'

'Keep, keep…' –

And popped.

Arthur pocketed his hands. What did it matter? She was here.

'Well I don't care what you think anyway,' Lydia said. 'Jack thinks I look nice.'

Jack. He'd never thought to ask the caretaker's name. He didn't look like a Jack. He didn't sound like a Jack. He looked and sounded like… the caretaker. The hooded half-moons emerged to appraise the hatted Lydia.

'Jack's been looking after me all morning –'

'But I was here!'

The caretaker offered Arthur a repeat performance: 'Arthur, Arthur,' he said, miming a knock at the door. 'Dead for this world.'

'Dead. *To. The.* World,' Lydia said, eyes on Arthur even as she attended to her new student.

'Where did you go?' Arthur asked, unpocketing his hands, a thumb kneading a palm, a wrist.

'Looking for you of course, it getting so late and you still not back – and on a Thursday too! If there's one thing you must know about Arthur,' Lydia said, turning to the caretaker, 'it's that he *always* finishes early on a Thursday.'

'But,' the caretaker said, 'this is no Thursday.'

*

'Cinders! Long time no—'

'Just pass Dad over, would you—' Arthur said, putting another coin in.

Harry chuckled, 'Dad, Arthur's on the—'

'Yes?'

'Thing is, Dad – I was thinking –'

'Well you better think a bit faster, I'm expecting a call any minute.'

'Thing—'

'Spit it out, boy.'

'There's someone I'd like you to meet. We could come over. Tomorrow, say.'

'Tomorrow's no good.'

'Friday.'

'No good either.'

'When is good?'

'It isn't. Bad time, chum. Your mother's in a funny way. Not all there. Quack had her signed into this place on the double.'

'Where?'

And then, of course, the phone went dead.

*

'Well?' Lydia asked, adjusting the hat the caretaker had given her. She touched her bare neck, 'Maybe I should have asked for the pearls. Your mother will still want to meet me, won't she – even without pearls?'

'No one's meeting anyone.'

Arthur had felt convinced enough of this at the time, and then, a day later, unseen by Sylvie's staring speckled eyes, he wasn't any less so: no one was meeting anyone.

Sylvie turned her face away and Arthur tried to make out what she was saying to the stems of dried buds he'd put in her hands.

She dropped them onto the sheets that had been pulled over her so tightly she seemed almost strapped down. Arthur picked the stems up, brushing the white lilac-grey.

'Don't you like them? Dried. Must be a good few handfuls out of them. We can just put them here for now,' he said, laying them on the table that went over the bed. 'Shall I open the curtains a bit, Ma? Ma? Don't you want the curtains open?' Arthur asked, pulling one back. 'It's nice out – see, sun's got his—' He turned back to look at her, her staring eyes on the stems. 'The nurse said we could go for a little walk if you like, said they have a nice little garden. I suppose she means that,' Arthur said, nose twitching at the dirty green rug – a little walk? They wouldn't manage a step before they had to turn around. Sylvie's body, rigid under the sheets, didn't seem likely to consent to much more. 'Would you like that, Ma?' Sylvie closed her eyes. 'Maybe I should just stop talking,' Arthur said.

'Maybe.'

Arthur smiled, laughed, but Sylvie's face, masked with transparent skin, pinched and went slack. Towels had been left on the chair at the end of the bed; Arthur lifted them and sat, the towels in his lap. Sylvie's hand was reaching for something – what did she want? – retracting, reaching, fingers curling, uncurling – she tugged at the sheets and pulled herself up.

'What do you want, Ma?' Arthur asked a moment before she knocked the empty cup on the table over. 'Water?'

'Rain,' Sylvie said, almost smiling.

'No, Ma—' Arthur stopped, completing the smile Sylvie had begun. 'Shall we get you up and take you to the park? Take these too – if you like,' he said, picking up the stems.

He went and stood at the window, watching the nurse wheeling a patient backwards and forwards over the dirty rug. Hideous. This was hideous. How could they have put her in here? Left it far too long, Gerald had said.

'Ma?'

No, not all there. Not there at all. Somewhere else – but then so was he. Sylvie's empty hand opened and closed over the last handful. Somebody had taken it. Somebody had stolen it. The opening closing hand wanted that last handful back.

'But Ma look, look,' Arthur was picking up the stems of dried buds, holding them towards her – but the staring speckled eyes didn't see them, they were watching the Sylvie that went up the hill and over the gates, the Sylvie that went to dig and dig and go, mud-caked, earth-caked –

'No more digging, Ma,' Arthur said. 'No more other little—'

*September 1953*

It would be light soon but Arthur put the torch into his satchel just in case. It was important to be prepared. An extra pullover and a banana. Ready. He opened his palm to show Sylvie.

'I'm going now Ma. Ma?'

Arthur went and sat by her, looking at his palm and taking it right under her eyes, 'Look, Ma.' She stared over it, Arthur's collection of petals meaningless.

'Ma! Ma, I'm going now.'

Sylvie gasped, her hand coming to her throat, Arthur's coming up to his own almost in the same instant. Couldn't she hear him? He stroked her hair just like she still stroked his sometimes, 'Going to take the buds now, Ma – I'll take the buds and be right back.'

They weren't buds, but they were all Arthur could find: blue petals on Mrs Cohen's lawn. Only Mrs Cohen didn't live there anymore. No one had ever found out what they did with her. Or her cat. There was a new family now and they didn't have a cat. Arthur had taken a vow not to speak to them. Not until he could be sure they weren't the ones who killed Mrs Cohen.

'No one's killed Mrs Cohen,' Sylvie had said – and she'd squeezed Arthur, she'd smiled, her eyes were wide open again – and then they'd closed and she let Arthur go, telling him to hurry along. Wouldn't she tell him to hurry along now? He tried to put his arms round her, the way she used to put her arms round him. Maybe when he got back, then. Arthur tugged at the strap of his satchel, waiting for Sylvie to look up, but she only gasped again, pressing her forehead into her knees.

'Bye then,' Arthur said.

*March 1968*

Sylvie's eyes twitched as she tried to shift under the sheets that bound her, her legs seizing as soon as Arthur spoke.

'Are you too hot, Ma? Do you want the sheets off?'

She'd be better if he could get her up, get her outside – nice little garden, the nurse had said. Well she could keep her *nice little garden*, he didn't want her nice little garden – Sylvie didn't want her nice little garden. It might not have been a Thursday but he had brought her buds and they were going to the park. Sylvie would have her last handful and that was that. Arthur loosened the sheets and brought her legs round, her body on its side, face pressing into the pillow.

'Come on, Ma, sit up. For me, Ma, please.'

Sylvie's hands closed into fists and came up under her chin.

'Oh Ma, I'm – do you want me to go? Do you want me to leave?' But he couldn't just go – not with her all crushed round like that. Arthur lifted her legs back onto the bed and put the sheets over her.

'Ma?'

She jerked onto her other side, pulling her knees up to her chest. He couldn't see her eyes. Maybe she wanted to sleep. Maybe he'd come back – on Thursday – yes, he'd come back then and get her up, get her outside, take her to the park, take the buds of course, let her have her last handful.

'Flying visit?'

It was the nurse with the nice little garden. Arthur felt his nose twitch – yes she could keep her nice little – and, having found his neck too stiff to nod, was now nodding more vigorously than he'd intended. The nurse tilted her head. 'Yes,' she said. 'Yes.' Yes what? But his nod was agreeing with a mechanised enthusiasm. He gripped the back of his neck – yes she could keep –

*Say goodbye nicely, Arthur, or –*

Arthur glanced back down the corridor. Repeating its threat, Lydia's echo displaced rather than recalled its speaker and, framing Sylvie's tumble from the bed to the floor, showed Arthur her scrambling limbs –

But if there had been any tumbling or scrambling Arthur had missed it: he followed the buds scattered from Sylvie's door to a room that, save the stripped bed and a vase on the bedside table, was empty – empty except for Sylvie – budless stems in one hand, a bunch of blown browned flowers in the other.

'They're the wrong ones,' Sylvie said, the stems of the bunch of flowers dripping on her feet.

'Tell me what the right ones are,' Arthur said, 'Tell me and I'll get them.'

Staring speckled eyes stopped staring and saw: 'Whoever took my last handful ought to know.'

*May 1968*

'Lilies! Let's take lilies!'

'No, Lydia.'

'You just want to keep her all for yourself. You don't want the twins to meet their nanna.'

'She's not well.'

'Then we'll make her better. Anyway I don't see what could be so wrong with her.'

There wasn't anything wrong with her – she just wasn't… all there. Arthur hated the way Gerald had said that. Measured up, had he? He didn't need to and neither did anyone else since that incident –

'What incident?'

The nice little nurse with her nice little garden understood that this must all be very distressing but she really must impress upon Arthur that she couldn't simply let an incident such as this pass.

'But *what* incident?'

'I'm sure you'll appreciate we have to take matters such as this very seriously, but since this was a first offence—'

No he did not appreciate it! Offence? She wasn't a criminal – she wasn't a prisoner – she was –

'Entering another patient's room, handling and taking another patient's belongings. It will be discussed, but under the circumstances I advise you to defer any subsequent visits.'

'Until when?'

This, the nurse was forced to regret, was not for her to say.

Arthur was certain he had never seen such a perfect antithesis of regret. And all over some bloody flowers! The place was mad. The nice little nurse with her nice little garden was mad. Gerald was mad for putting her in here and the quack was a quack – that went without saying – but he'd say it anyway, all the way back to the Holloway Road. Mad, all of them. As for Sylvie, she was as sane as he was –

'You just don't want to share,' Lydia said, putting on the hat the caretaker had given her. 'Oh Arthur, we had such fun while you were out. We…' Thuds up the stairs, a knock at the caretaker's door and a duet of ahs and ohs. Lydia let her voice be flattened out by the dissonance on the other side of the wall. She took off the hat and sat down.

'Can't we go away?' Lydia asked.

'Where? Why? I thought you liked it here.'

'Like it!' she said, just as the duet allowed an interval. 'With that? With him?'

'He gave you that hat.'

'Well I don't want his hat and I don't want to be here. I want –' She stopped, listened. 'I don't know.'

'If you want to go away we can—'

'No.'

No. No of course they couldn't. On what? With what? Wherever away was, it was surely further than the end of the Piccadilly line which was more than Arthur had the means for unless – no, he couldn't ask Keith. He might have to – swallow, yes swallow – not that it would really be asking, more agreeing (still swallowing) consenting to accept a modest sum – a loan. No, he wouldn't swallow. There was nothing to swallow – it was Keith's suggestion, Arthur had never asked for a penny and in any case Keith hadn't called it a loan – he'd offered an advance –

No, there was nothing to swallow – he might not be able to take Sylvie to the park but he would take Lydia – his Lydia! –

'I only wanted to sit by her for a bit, say something nice,' Lydia said, the hat on her lap.

That was it! Yes, he would tell the nurse he just wanted to say something nice. That was all he had to do. She could hardly refuse him that – her and the quack and Gerald couldn't very well say he was forbidden from saying something nice to his own mother –

*Not my Arthur* –

They couldn't – and once he'd said something nice, well she might feel like sitting up, she might feel like getting outside – she might – it was possible – feel like going to the park –

Arthur could hear Keith reaching the climax of Shelley's manifesto through the wall – the final words eclipsed by a fit of guttural coughing that hailed from the same era. From the day Arthur had taken the room until the day Lydia arrived he had endured Keith's recitals – it was only now he realised he missed them. They were wasted on the caretaker, surely – funny little indeed – and giving Lydia that hat. She was smoothing the brim again, putting it on, getting up –

'Where are you—?'

The red heart of a mouth caught Arthur.

'Just to say something nice,' Lydia said.

'You can't. Please Lydia, she's not well.'

'I'm so sorry to hear…' Lydia spilled a lie of a smile and watched it fall before she looked up at Arthur. 'I'm only going next door.'

'But you wanted to get away from that – from… him.'

'Why would I want to get away from him? He gave me the hat.'

Lydia's exit, promptly and predictably, emptied the room. Again it gaped at Arthur. Fine, let it gape. Closing his eyes might put the cloth back on the table, find it dressed with lilacs, sit Lydia beside him, the dolls in her lap, but Arthur could not shut out the duet's clamouring invitation to incorporate Lydia. It took a moment for the counterpoint to arrange itself: bubbles of laughter popped in answer to the caretaker's 'please to sit to sit' and Keith's single but imperturbable note, 'Professor! Professor!' – all supported by an orchestra of boxes dragged across the floor. Well then he would just have to wait, that was all there was to it, and by the time he opened his eyes the room would be contently full, blissfully sated with all that closed eyes had so accurately described. Excellent.

'Professor!'

'Caretaker! He's the bloody caretaker!' Arthur was up, open-eyed in his ravenously empty room, wanting nothing but the pitch of dreamless sleep. He fell back onto the mattress – Keith was clearing his throat now, a *sshhhh* from Lydia, a whisper – who? the caretaker – no, Keith again, then steps, all three, silence – and in this last, which seemed to be drawing out as interminably as the seconds Arthur had managed to wait, a bubble rose and rose –

Oh would it just pop and be done with it –

'Arthur, is everything—'

'Fine!'

Lydia's hatted head was just round the door.

'You can't sit here all by yourself—'

'Yes I can.'

'Come and sit with us. Jack's going to put on a show.'

'No show!' And now here was this Jack – so-called – funny little indeed –

'Oh but Professor, you must,' Keith's voice ringing behind.

'Yes, you must,' Lydia said, 'do be a clown for us, just this once – please.'

'But I am not…' The caretaker's eyes wandered, watered, fell.

'I'm sure Arthur would love to see—' Lydia began while Arthur tried to reclaim ownership of the door. Lydia, Keith and the caretaker were concentrating on Arthur's efforts, leaning forward, inverting him from audience to player – neither of which he had any intention of being. But the caretaker drew back then, his softened gaze resting lightly on Arthur as he nodded, one hand on Keith's arm, one on Lydia's, 'We let Arthur to have some peace now,' he said.

'*Give* Arthur some peace,' Lydia corrected, shaking off the caretaker's hand before her eyes shot back to Arthur, 'I just thought you might like to sit with us, that's all.'

'Out of sorts,' Keith said through a yawn. Arthur's mouth opened on the brink of protest, step suspended –

'Give some peace,' the caretaker said, 'yes, yes,' mouth softening into a smile, eyes rising back up to Arthur. Arthur's eyes fell on his feet and drifted along the landing, hearing Keith cough, clear his throat, the caretaker urging Keith and Lydia away, *give some peace, yes, give Arthur* –

Out – he had to get out –

Quite without warning Arthur was being driven down the stairs by nothing less than a compulsion to be nowhere but back on that bench – his bench – with his empty case. The true value of each had only just revealed themselves: for so long they had merely represented his insurmountable predicament which now, properly surmounted, had left multiple insurmountable predicaments in its place, none of which could be tidily deferred to the singular combination of a park bench and an empty case –

*Say goodbye nicely, Arthur, or –*

Oh she could do what she liked. They could all just bloody well do what they liked. Lydia, Keith, the caretaker –

Arthur stopped, his clenched jaw releasing as he saw again how the caretaker had drawn back, his eyes resting gently on Arthur, so still – had something of the Rabbi's quiet glimmer in them –

'Arthur! Hold up!' Keith was only a few steps behind him, hacking and panting as he clutched Arthur's shoulder. 'Easy there, you know I'm a dying man.'

'You are not a dying man.'

Keith thumped his back and chest to argue the contrary.

'Not like you, Arthur,' Keith said, catching back the breath squandered on performance.

It might be. It might be just like him. What wasn't like him?

'All out of sorts,' Keith said, 'I don't like to see my right hand man all out of—'

'I am not out of sorts,' Arthur said, his hand coming up to his forehead, eyes reaching over Keith's shoulder.

'No. Look here, if this is all about being in a tight spot—'

Arthur's capacity was improving: he would contain the uncontainable.

'I've got something of a proposal for you – take it or leave it. Your… Lydia, is it?'

'You know perfectly well—' His-not-his –

'If you might, on occasion, with her consent, make her… available to me – not anything like that – just for dinner, say, take her out, a concert.'

'You don't go to concerts.'

'I might.'

The uncontainable threatened nothing but still there was refuge to be found in his sigh, in his pockets – Keith could have his Lydia, Lydia could have her hat, the nurse could have her nice little garden but he would have his sigh and his pockets – and his bench –

*Take your time, there's no rush –*

The Rabbi's words had never seemed to carry over into the world outside his door – and yet here they were, floating up on the Holloway Road, frantic feet and faces – and yet –

*No rush –*

Seemed as though he might have glimpsed the Rabbi at the crossing. He glanced towards the lights, saw Keith heading back –

No rush, no. He'd make his way to the park then, sit on his bench – no question of the empty briefcase this time, no voice calling out that it was time to go, no twins cartwheeling past. His bench, yes – his and his alone –

If it wasn't for the young man already there. A young man in an old brown three-piece, briefcase in his lap, crusts at his feet. Arthur's hands tightened in his pockets – there was a whole park full of empty benches, could this young man not sit somewhere else? No, no of course not. The young man popped open the gold locks of his briefcase. Arthur let his head drop, waiting for the bells to chime the half hour – he wouldn't have minded asking what a young man like him might keep in a briefcase like that – but the young man was getting up, making his way towards the gates –

Down towards the station?

*Hey*, Arthur called out to himself, *good luck*.

He pictured the young man getting to the bottom of the hill, stalling there before he turned onto the Finchley Road, rehearsing various alternatives of a day he hadn't had, stopping and starting his way back to Llanvanor.

*Good luck, old boy, good luck.*

*

'Something *nice*?' Gerald folded his arms. 'Do you want to get her kicked out?'

Why not? Arthur hadn't thought of that – a superlative idea. The not-so-nice little nurse came out of Sylvie's room, put her clipboard under her arm and picked up the small stuffed plastic sack at her feet, holding it out in front of her as she came towards Gerald and Arthur.

'All changed fresh,' she said, the sight of Arthur sinking the buoyancy in her voice.

'Arthur was just on his way,' Gerald said. 'All tidied up, is she?'

'Oh yes, even got her up in her chair,' the nurse said, bending her head back round Sylvie's door, 'Look who we've got to see you.' The nurse dropped the plastic sack at Arthur's feet and marched back in towards Sylvie, arranging Sylvie's hands, inspecting her face – that wasn't the way to greet a visitor. Sylvie wouldn't be getting a nod from the nice little nurse with a face like that, no, it was Gerald who would have her special nod – Gerald whose care the nurse trusted she could leave Sylvie in – she was sorry but she was supposed to be on break half an hour ago and if she didn't take it now –

'Why of course, say no more.'

Arthur trod an undefeated step behind Gerald and stood just inside the door. The not-so-nice little nurse had picked up just where Gerald's mother had left off almost a quarter of a century before, primping and preening Sylvie in anticipation of Gerald's arrival. Gerald's mother was adamant her son would have the homecoming her husband never did – and if that meant having to get Sylvie out of that miserable blouse and sort out her unmade face so be it – though what she'd do about that screaming child she could only hope and pray – she was sure they could hear him the other side of London. Gerald certainly never cried like that. It had to make one wonder… Another cause to hope and pray. Hadn't she said to mark her words? – well had he? Foolish boy and now here was what could only be an illegitimate – not that she'd say as much – no, she'd have to save that for later – at least until Gerald was in earshot. Not that there was any point trying to say anything at all with that dreadful –

'Does he ever stop?'

Sylvie had got up then, he'd been so good today, settled right down.

'Yes,' Gerald's mother had said, taking a lipstick out of her bag, 'I thought something like this might happen.'

Gerald considered the nurse's efforts.

'I need a wee,' Sylvie said, pulling out one of the slides that had been scraped into her hair.

'Now none of that,' Gerald said, 'the nurse just had you changed fresh.'

'I want the toilet.'

'See what you've gone and done,' Gerald said, barely lowering his voice as he turned to Arthur. Before Arthur's opening mouth could do any more damage Gerald's raised finger closed it – our chum Goldilocks would do well not to interfere. Gerald tucked his chin into his throat and allowed the raised finger to make its descent with a mountaineer's caution. Gerald sent his eyes over Sylvie, then Arthur –

'I'd better get the nurse back in here, won't be a tick.'

Sylvie was touching her mouth – lightly at first, spitting on her fingertips and rubbing until she'd smeared her painted lips up towards her cheeks.

Arthur watched from the doorway before he took another step inside. There was a napkin on the table that went over the bed. Arthur dipped it into the cup of water and took it over to Sylvie, waiting for her to take it, but her eyes were staring again and went on staring as he dabbed the napkin onto her cheeks and chin.

'Sorry Ma, I'm not very good at this.' Sylvie lifted her face, blinked. That was better. Wasn't that better? Sylvie's face ducked. Arthur could hear Gerald coming back with the nurse. He looked at Sylvie – *something nice* – he'd just wanted to come and say something nice.

*July 1968*

'You want to get rid of me.' Lydia was sitting on the floor, the doll that was for telling laid out in front of her, its cut plaits in her hand.

Get rid of her? That was the last thing – what would make her think? – Lydia's unmasked face answered before Arthur could ask: he'd left without saying goodbye. Again.

Lydia took the doll into her arms and stood up, replacing the words of a lullaby with her own: 'Daddy wants to get rid of us,' she sang, 'Daddy wants…'

Arthur took his coat off, leaning on the chair for a moment, rocking forward, eyes falling onto his hands.

'Of course you can't get rid of me now.'

'But I don't want—' He looked up, took a step towards her.

'No, I don't suppose you do – not now that I've become so profitable.'

'Profitable? Lydia—'

Lydia looked up at the ceiling before she continued her lullaby, a weak bounce in her step backwards and forwards, turning away as she sang to the doll, 'Daddy wants, Daddy wants, Daddy wants to get rid…'

Keith – surely he hadn't –

'Daddy wants Daddy wants…'

He must have. Sly bastard. Biding his time till he thought Arthur had forgotten all about his *proposal*.

'You won't touch me,' Lydia whispered, 'but you don't mind renting me out.'

'Oh Christ, Lydia, it's nothing like that.'

Lydia was holding tightly to an unspilt smile and looked up again at the ceiling, 'He didn't seem to think so.'

Waiting for his moment and pouncing –

*Never take your eye off the ball,* Gerald would have been pleased to remind him.

'Dinner, a concert—' Arthur sputtered, stopped – even it had been just that – even then – oh, the whole thing –

'Dinner? A concert?' Lydia's unspilt smile pierced her lips. 'Arthur, if you aren't the most… *Daddy wants, Daddy wants, dada dada dada da*—' She dropped the lullaby with the doll and went to open the cupboard, pulling out the case, throwing out its contents, the doll that was for planting out landing neatly skewed beside its counterpart –

'Here now,' Lydia said, a storm of smiles falling as she lifted out the dress. 'Do you think this will do?'

'Please don't – it's all just a misunderstanding.'

'I'll wear the hat too, I think.'

The hat? Arthur looked at the wall, waited – nothing.

'By the hour, is it?'

'Stop it, Lydia!'

'Well it's only right that I should know.'

The rustle and the shuffle sounded itself for a moment. Arthur and Lydia both looked at the wall.

'Yes,' Lydia said, getting the suit out of the case and handing it to Arthur, 'I shall certainly wear the hat.'

*

That evening they sat at the table, Lydia in her hat and dress, not quite the Mrs Simons she'd thought she'd be, Arthur in the suit nothing like any sort of Mr Simons he'd never thought he'd be, and, having accepted the caretaker's offering –

'Always I make too much!' –

That arrived after a significant period of rustling and shuffling, opened their paper-wrapped parcels which Lydia declared as truly the most exquisite supper she'd ever had, managing to distinguish no less than four courses in a pickle sandwich – exquisite!

*August 1968*

'Mrs who?'

'My mother, she—'

The nurse's eyes repeated the glassy flutter they had given Arthur after *the incident* of Sylvie's *offence* – a flutter that as good as made him an outlaw, belatedly enforcing the sentence only a glassy flutter could make. Ever since Arthur had made a mess of the nurse's fine work the days had hitched themselves together into weeks that went by until Arthur had lost count – a tally he couldn't keep any sort of command over while he stood, back in his grubby robe, not watching Lydia hat and dress herself into anyone but Mrs Simons –

'Lydia, really, you don't have to—'

'Oh I'm not so sure about that, Arthur.'

And decided he could forfeit at least one evening of bearing witness to this procedure to, at last and at least, just come and say something nice. Yes that was all, really all: no buds, no going to the park, nothing but –

'I'm afraid she's been moved.'

'Where to?'

'That's not information I'm in a position to disclose.'

Another glassy flutter was sufficient to march Arthur down the corridor and open Sylvie's door to find no Sylvie but an elderly woman sitting in the chair at the end of her bed, reading to the little boy on her lap. The little boy looked up at the woman and the woman looked at Arthur. There was a vase of yellow flowers on the bedside table. Bright yellow. Horribly bright.

'Sorry. Wrong—'

Wrong what? The little boy's lashed marble black eyes were on him, they wanted to know –

'Who's that?'

'I'm—'

*Sorry* didn't quite make it aloud. Arthur turned, hearing the little boy still asking 'Who's that, who's that?' 'I don't know, dear,' and the pages turn and the storyteller voice start again… Once upon a… 'But who's—'

It was absolutely no one and absolutely no one was leaving, going back to the Holloway Road, going to put his grubby robe back on and listen to the rustle and shuffle and eat the consequences of the caretaker's inability not to make too much and wait until Lydia, hatted and dressed as whoever she damn well liked, came back with nothing more than a kissed hand and a new store of unspilt smiles ready to deal out like cards while they all sat in the caretaker's room not mentioning a thing, playing along with their meticulously dealt hands as though they'd all just suppered on pickle sandwiches together and Keith wasn't wearing that absurd purple bowtie and Lydia wasn't still in her hat and that none of them were knocking back the whiskey.

But unhatted, undressed, Lydia was sitting on the mattress.

'I wanted to wait till you got back,' Lydia said. 'I didn't want to leave before you'd said goodbye.'

'Well I won't be, I'm not going anywhere.'

'Neither am I.'

'Aren't you cold?'

'No.'

Arthur picked up his robe and put it round her and, catching his sigh before it slipped, sat down, ready to tell and tell and would have done – told and told for as long as she wanted – but she didn't want any more of his telling –

'Milly,' Lydia said. 'That's what she'd be called.'

'Who?'

'It's a pretty little name don't you think.'

'Quite. Yes. I suppose.'

'You suppose. It's not something you suppose, Arthur. Either you do or you don't.'

'What?'

'Oh never mind. It doesn't matter.'

No – the Grande Dame's good clean job had seen to that. Oh. Right. Yes. Arthur pulled the robe a little more round Lydia, she'd get cold – she would.

'Milly.'

'It mightn't have been a girl,' Arthur pointed out, relieved to have found a consolation.

'Don't be stupid, Arthur, of course it would have been a girl.'

'You don't know that.'

'Yes I do. Shut up Arthur. Yes I do.'

Well if she wanted to go upsetting herself –

'I am not *upsetting myself!*'

'You're upset—'

'Yes I'm *upset*. There is a difference,' she informed him as she got up, leaving the robe on the bed, getting her hat, her dress –

'I'm sorry Lydia, I didn't mean—'

'Yes you did. You really do want to get rid of me – won't say goodbye, won't let me meet your mother when all I wanted to do was say nice things, brush her hair, make her better – was that really so much to ask?'

Apparently so.

'Make the twins all pretty for their nanna – Do you think the twins still miss me? They must. Oh I know you should never have favourites but—' she glazed for a moment, the hat falling from her hand. She picked it up and brushed it off, 'anyway, I'll bet Mrs Simons gets the stories all wrong. I'll bet they never get off to sleep. I'll bet she's wishing right now—'

'A cat!' Arthur erupted from the mattress.

'A what?' Lydia dropped the hat.

'I'll get you a cat!' Arthur's capacity to contain the uncontainable had once again deserted him – the branch of veins on his forehead found itself enjoying a premature spring.

'But I don't want a bloody cat.'

'Oh.' No, of course she didn't want a cat. She wanted the twins, she wanted them to have a nanna to be all pretty for… Arthur watched as Lydia laid the hat down. No, she didn't want the twins or a nanna for them to be all pretty for – she wanted Milly. That was all. Arthur hoped the mattress would have him back.

'What kind of cat?'

*September 1968*

Suggesting the insurmountable might be surmounted with a cat had meant that Lydia's occasions out with Keith had become considerably more than occasional. The better part of each evening now saw Arthur in the singular company of a pickle sandwich.

Making her departure in a twirling shower of freely spilt smiles, Lydia looked forward to seeing him later –

'Oh and Arthur—'

'What?'

'Don't sigh.'

The sigh – and a number of its siblings – reserved itself until Lydia was on her way down the stairs with Keith. She might at least close the door properly. The procedure had become no less hopelessly inevitable than the one that followed: without fail, there would be the pause of the rustle and shuffle, the caretaker's door would open and Arthur would hear the muffled crackle that announced the arrival of yet another paper-wrapped parcel. The rustle and shuffle would then fall again into its arrhythmic persistence, telling Arthur the caretaker was safely back on the other side of the wall and the parcel could be retrieved, considered, consumed – a discreet operation that kept both benefactor and recipient supposedly anonymous; a pact that, if broken, would make an intrusion out of benevolence and a charity case out of Arthur – and Arthur was most certainly not a charity case. Not the caretaker's. Not Keith's. Not Lydia's –

Arthur eyed the vacancy where the paper-wrapped parcel would shortly be laid… or not – why should he go on allowing this absurd ritual? He would put an end to this: no more pickle sandwiches. He would rather starve.

'Oh, you do not like?'

Like? It wasn't a matter of liking or not liking.

'We make something else?' The caretaker's half-moon eyes vanished and reappeared.

*We?* There was no *we* about this.

'Today,' the caretaker began, that quiet glimmer in his eyes again as he nodded towards the door left ajar, 'I find one two three crates – full full full with apples.'

The glimmer settled on Arthur – but he did not want – he wanted – what did he want? A simple absence of consciousness wouldn't have been unwelcome.

'Please then,' the caretaker said, his hand opening towards Arthur, 'to sit only.'

Arthur eyed the caretaker's door, his own – alright then, to sit.

The one two three crates were waiting patiently by the sink and the chair was waiting patiently for Arthur.

'If you except – except? No, excuse – forgive my speaking—' His eyes were flashing round Arthur, catching the room in snatches as though chasing the words dodging and hiding – 'England – it ruins my English! In Polish my English always speak perfect.'

'Perfectly.'

Hateful to be corrected!

'Perfectly,' the caretaker was delighted. 'Yes perfectly. In Polish always.'

'Poland,' Arthur suggested, confident of another escalation of delight.

'No,' the caretaker didn't want correcting. 'No, in Polish. Not Poland.'

'You're from Poland.'

The caretaker alternated slight nods with slight shakes of his head. 'It depends,' he said, untying the string and the pocket dictionary, 'depends on border. Borders.'

'Borders.'

The caretaker went to the trunk and took out fresh sheets of paper and pencils, laying them over the table, and began sketching maps. Urgency snapped the neat sharp nib off. The caretaker stretched across for another, his sleeve rising with his reach. It was only when the bare forearm was snatched back and the caretaker tugged his sleeve down, buttoning the cuff, that the exposed numbers imprinted their indelibility on Arthur: no he was not the Jack he had been named on arrival, not the Professor Keith insisted he was or the clown Lydia wanted him to be –

*Oh do be! I just know you'd make the perfect clown!*

*No!* –

But nor was he the caretaker – he was number –

Half-moons set in a skyless night. Arthur waited for them to rise but when they didn't he got up and pushed his chair in with the care he might have taken to avoid waking a sleeping child –

'Please to sit.'

To sit, yes. Arthur's eyes matched the set half-moons until he felt a hand touch and leave his shoulder. The caretaker opened the cover of the pocket dictionary, moving it towards Arthur, his fingers just above the photograph taped inside, 'He is a clown – was a clown. *Professional.* But his number is not lucky,' the caretaker said and put the dictionary in the trunk. 'Professor,' he said, shaking his head, 'what good is professor? What good is truth?'

Arthur opened and closed his mouth, the two faces in the picture taking his words away. But, already behind him, standing at the sink, the caretaker was again the caretaker, approving apples. He held one in each of his upturned palms as though weighing them before throwing each in opposite arcs. 'Now for to juggle,' he said, his smile frail then fierce. 'And so we will make.'

We.

The caretaker put an apple in Arthur's hand, and began peeling the one in his own, nodding at Arthur to do the same, slicing them into a pot.

'Too much,' the caretaker was saying as he lit the stove, 'always too much.'

The front door opened – Keith would be kissing Lydia's hand now – and shut. Keith's steps were slow to catch up with Lydia's. A bubble of laughter fell.

'I think,' the caretaker said, turning the fire under the stove down until it was almost out, 'I think she is very sad.'

*

On everything under and over the sun that was still a good hour away from getting up Arthur swore – swore! – he did not dream. But on this someone else's little someone went, mud-caked, earth-caked, digging through the night, digging himself in to dig that other little Arthur out, digging and digging while Sylvie, tottering on toy stilts fell, broken-toothed, smiling: smiling, falling; stones sinking, wreaths unravelling.

Someone else's dreams. Someone else's little someone. They were keeping him awake. He had to find a reason to get up, but Lydia was just then slipping into sleep, the spell was still too weak, her own dreams were threat enough. Instead he had to watch Sylvie, watch himself, watch that other little Arthur. Lydia reached a hand over, blending into the scene – it was as though she'd been watching Sylvie and that other little Arthur too – *her* Arthur – coming into their dream again. No more than a flicker from the bulb, but enough to catch him while that other little Arthur flickered out, letting him sleep until the bang of a car outside set the guns off in his head. His eyes were open but he couldn't see anything, smoke had made the world invisible. He could hear Lydia's voice, feel her shaking him –

'Stop it Arthur, stop it.'

But he couldn't speak, his mouth was filled with the decomposing flesh of unburied corpses, he couldn't move. There was no choice but to give into their weight.

Awake. Was he awake? Lydia wrapped tight around him. He pulled himself free, couldn't stand the feel of flesh against flesh, not even Lydia's. She tried to kiss him but he couldn't let her taste the rot that filled his mouth. All he wanted was for his chest to let him breathe. She came towards him as he got up to dress but he wouldn't look at her, wouldn't hear her, the sound of her bringing back the touch of her, which brought back the night and the smoke and the guns and the corpses. His clothes made him flinch from himself, reminding him he had a body.

'Where did you go last night?' she asked him.

'Don't start, Lydia, you know I was right here.'

'No you weren't. Tell me where you went, take me with you, Arthur. Please take me. You can't keep leaving like that without me.' She tried to split her red heart of a mouth against his again, but his tongue went slack, dead, thickness stuffing his throat while she spilled all the smiles she had into him. She stood back a bit but stretched out her fingers, looking up in fractions, dividing him into slivers. Arthur watched her hand, concentrating on it until he couldn't be sure whether it was his eyes blurring that made it seem unsteady or whether it was shaking. He took it and remembered the comfort he found in unscarred palms.

'I'll come with you,' she said.

'You can't,' Arthur said. 'I don't know where it was I went.'

'Then you must promise never to go again without me – what if you never found your way back?'

'Don't be silly, don't be…' Couldn't look at her. He tried to blink his eyes into sight but the smoke was clouding dense again. He groped round the table for his keys.

'Where are you going?'

Nowhere. He wasn't going – he was –

'Please let me come with you, Arthur, don't leave – not at least without saying—'

*

The end of the night and the start of the day were crossing one another's path on the Finchley Road. Arthur was caught there in a musty lull of just skimmed sleep and it wasn't until he put his key in the door that his eyes started to clear a little, the silhouette of that someone else's little someone, beginning to slip back and fade, dulled without the night, but digging, still digging –

*He's not there, Arthur, he's –*

*Not there –*

'What are you doing here?' Gerald was at the foot of the stairs.

'You're up,' Arthur said, slack tongue drugging his voice. What was he doing there? He didn't know. Arthur looked at the key in his hand, at the door behind him. He bit into his tongue but he could hardly feel it.

'Do you have any idea what time it is?'

'No.'

'Don't give me that.'

'I'm not giving you anything.'

Gerald's chuckle failed him. He walked into the kitchen. 'Make yourself at home, won't you,' he said. Arthur went as far as the end of the hall and looked up. Too long practised in avoiding Sylvie's half-closed eyes. Not there now. Not there just as he wanted to see them, wanted to meet them.

'Don't bloody hover like that,' Gerald said. 'Sit down or bugger off.'

Arthur stepped inside the kitchen. Days had built up in the sink and across the table.

Gerald cleared a space in front of him, 'I thought I just told you to sit down or bugger off.'

Arthur moved towards the chair across from Gerald, stopped, stepped back.

'What have they done with her?'

'No one's done bloody anything with her.'

'If I can't see her you can at least—'

'No one's done bloody anything. No one's doing bloody anything – that's the whole bloody problem, chum and if you don't sit down you can bloody well—'

Bugger off. Alright he would. Bugger off back to the Holloway Road.

'Dad?'

'What?'

'Nothing.'

A cat jumped through the open window onto the front lawn of Mrs Cohen's old house. Never did find out what they did with Mrs Cohen.

*November 1953*

'Don't you want to see what Aunt Cynthia's sent you, Arthur?' Sylvie took Harry's parcel back from him, 'Wait for Arthur.'

'Dad says we don't do Christmas,' Harry said.

'It's not Christmas yet, darling.'

'But the card says, Dearest Harry—'

'What's this about Christmas?' Gerald asked, coming in, 'Sit down, Arthur, the neighbours will start to think you're a spy,' he took a breath to recalibrate. 'Are you alright, Sylvie? Do you want to go back to bed?'

'No thank you.'

'I think you should.'

Arthur turned round, 'No.'

'I beg your pardon,' Gerald got up, stopped and looked back at Sylvie. *Leave it,* she mouthed. 'I will not leave anything.' His voice was quiet but Arthur heard a roar and dropped to the floor, head between his knees.

'Well done, Gerald,' Sylvie said.

'Ma,' Harry started.

'Go and get on with your prep, Harry,' Sylvie said.

'I told you, I can't do it.'

'What did your father say about that?'

'No such thing as can't!' Gerald bellowed.

'I don't want a present anyway,' Harry said.

'I thought I told you to tell that Aunt Cynthia that we do not do Christmas,' Gerald said, tearing the wrapping open.

'It's not Christmas.'

'Don't mock me.'

Sylvie picked up the knitted elf and handed it to Harry.

'I don't want it,' Harry said, going upstairs.

Sylvie went over to Arthur. 'It's alright,' she said, rubbing his back until his head came up. 'Shall we have a look at what Aunt Cynthia sent?'

Arthur shook his head and looked out the window at Mrs Cohen's old house, 'What did they do with her, Ma? Won't she ever come back?'

'Ones like that,' Gerald said, 'get put away for good, isn't that right, Sylvie? Put my old man away in the end, didn't we? What else can you do with a vegetable?'

'He wasn't a vegetable,' Sylvie said. 'Mrs Cohen wasn't and your father wasn't either.'

Gerald pushed past Sylvie and went up to Arthur, 'Tell your mother that the old man. Was. A. Vegetable.'

'Will the new people be as nice as Mrs Cohen?' Arthur asked Sylvie.

'Of course they will.'

'A vegetable! Just like the old man! Arthur, you get back—'

'I have to find out if they killed Mrs Cohen.'

'Oh darling,' Sylvie said, 'we told you no one killed Mrs Cohen, she just wasn't very well.'

'Did she die?'

'No, she… I don't know.'

'All a lot of vegetables! I could have started another bloody allotment. Give the two of you something proper to damn well dig for.'

'Your father used to sing for us,' Sylvie said to Gerald.

'Sing! Christ, woman, you're as mad as he was!'

Sylvie started a tune then, smiling, 'He liked to give a little concert.'

'All a lot of gibberish! The way you used to talk to him as if he – well, as if he was normal. He couldn't have understood a word you said, you know.'

Arthur put his hands over his ears. Gerald's voice did horrible things to Sylvie's face – it took her smile away. He needed her smile to come back and her face to stay still. If her face was still it was all OK. He felt her hand on his head and looked up as she eased one of his hands down.

'Why don't you go and say hello,' she said, nodding towards Mrs Cohen's old house.

'Singing in his bloody Polish,' Gerald muttered. 'You won't test my nerve. I won't lose my nerve…'

*October 1968*

The caretaker had found it – whatever it was – in one of the bins behind the college. Keith raised his eyebrows – the professor was having them on –

'Having on?' The caretaker's eyebrows mirrored Keith's.

'No he's not,' Lydia said. 'You couldn't find a thing like that anywhere else.' Lydia bent down, a delicate nose leading the way, and was answered with a hiss. 'I don't know what it is,' she said, 'but it's not a cat.'

Keith folded his arms and nodded, 'It's not.'

'We nearly finish,' the caretaker said, painting ointment on the sores welling from a hairless patch above a paw. A skeleton barely sheathed in matted fur seized and curled against the caretaker, he set it down and watched it limp.

'Well you can't have a thing like that in here,' Keith said. 'It's a feral creature, it needs to hunt – in any case, where would it do its business?'

The caretaker lifted the cat up and brought it over towards Keith, stroking its head. 'She is very good.'

'It's not a she,' Lydia said. The caretaker held the cat up under its front legs. Lydia said she didn't know what she was supposed to be looking at.

'Aha, yes!' The caretaker was triumphant. 'Now you take, now you see.'

'No – it's not… hygienic.'

The cat lifted its head into Lydia's palm hovering over it. 'Well I suppose it's quite sweet. Arthur, do you think it's sweet?'

How was he supposed to know? Four pairs of eyes asked again.

'Yes, yes, alright, I think it's sweet,' Arthur said with the urgency of a convicted man. But it was. He supposed. Quite.

'Well that's that then,' Lydia said. 'We'll call it Milly.'

*

'Please Arthur, you know I hate being late.'

Crouching on all fours, Arthur had braced himself with a sponge, a sigh and a scrunched brow: a pool of vomit had been delivered at his bedside. Maybe he could just get a rug. The cat, shivering on the pillow, couldn't watch.

'Arthur!'

No, he was busy – he was attending to cat vomit, he was considering how best to acquire a rug, he was waiting for Lydia to go off in her hat and her dress so that he could get on with clearing up this mess and get back to Llanvanor Road and demand – yes he would demand! – to be told what the hell they'd gone and done with his Ma and the last thing he needed was another showering of smiles or swarm of kisses and he most certainly didn't need another nice goodbye –

'Please!'

Arthur looked up. Lydia was rubbing the brim of the hat in her hand between her thumb and forefinger.

'Don't you want to come?' Lydia asked – her eyes blinking before him and the cat's eyes behind him pushed, prodded –

No. Let them find someone else to make a joke out of. What was he going to do? Be dogsbody all over again? He'd resigned from that post the day he left Llanvanor Road so if she thought he was going to stand there holding the coats and keeping the table while she and Keith –

'I've been looking forward to it all week,' Lydia said. 'I thought you'd like to.'

'Like to!'

'I just thought – I mean by now – wouldn't you? It is your turn after all.'

Cab for seven, table for seven-thirty – the one in the corner – no, not by the peacocks – the other corner. All booked and paid for without a fairy godmother in sight – she was upstairs appearing in the guise of Keith who was doing a frighteningly convincing impression of a seventeenth-century invalid –

'Eighteenth-century,' Keith amended. 'Oh Arthur, don't get all precious about it, just go – you can't keep our lady waiting.'

Our? *His* Lydia was not communal property. No alright, alright, not his Lydia at all – not between the hat and the dress and –

'And get me my wallet out the drawer,' Keith said. 'I don't want you going short.'

Arthur's pocketed hands and rebelliously inert feet sat Keith up. 'Christ almighty,' Keith said, throwing out a hand, 'you know I'm about to peg it any minute.'

'You are not about to peg it,' Arthur said, his head tipping back, eyes up at the ceiling. The damp had crept up each of Keith's walls too. To his credit he refused to indulge himself whilst his tenants lived in squalor. Arthur surveyed its progress: the whole place was going to cave in – they'd all be under a heap of plaster and rubble and it would be days, months, years before anyone found them, everyone just stomping along the Holloway Road, blind, deaf –

'You have to give it a good pull,' Keith said, walking Arthur to the drawer.

Why couldn't he have just stuck to Shelley and whiskey and leave whoever's Lydia she was or wasn't be? Leave her alone, leave him alone, go and take the table in the corner himself and stop making an Oliver Twist out of Arthur – Cinders and Goldilocks were enough. Arthur handed Keith his wallet, took the note.

'I'd sooner you spent it on sorting the place out,' Arthur said.

'Oh Arthur, you do make me laugh!'

Arthur closed Keith's door on his way out –

'Leave it! I don't want to be banged up!'

The cab was waiting, the table was waiting, Lydia – holding the suit towards Arthur – was waiting.

'It's been sick again,' she said, patting a lapel. Arthur swallowed: he had reached the summit of Arthurian nobility.

*

The table in the corner was taken –

'Would Sir, Madam, care to wait in the bar?'

Why not? Why not prolong the agony?

'You don't want to be here,' Lydia said as the waiter went to clear the table where a man was getting up to help a woman with her coat, squeezing her hand, covering her face in kisses.

'I do.'

'No you don't. I can tell.'

The man added to the tip left on the metal dish and the waiter nodded without smiling, whisked the tip up and brushed the tablecloth down. The cat's vomit would be drying on his pillow now.

'Arthur!'

'What?'

'Can't you say something?'

'Like what?'

'Something nice.'

No. No he couldn't. He wanted to – he wanted to do anything but sigh and clench his jaw and pocket his hands but sighing and clenching and pocketing were not negotiable.

'Please, Arthur.'

He unpocketed a hand and urged a stiffened arm round Lydia's waist. The waiter was ushering them into place, waving out fanned napkins, spouting something in – French was it? – perhaps fairy-godmother Keith could translate – uncorking wine –

'Do like it here,' Lydia said, a flattened hand shading her eyes.

'I do, it's fine – it's—'

The menu was indenting lines across the pristine wax of Lydia's forehead. 'I hate olives,' she said, putting one into her mouth as she got up. 'Order for me, would you?'

Arthur looked up but already she had disappeared behind a gold-plated procession of ladies and now all that was in Arthur's eye line was a pen poised –

'To start?'

The gold-plated procession had been seated, their fizz and tinkle of giggles nothing like the soft pop of Lydia's laughing bubbles.

'Sir, might I suggest?'

Arthur leaned back, forward – the pen was scribbling – he couldn't see.

'I'm sorry but my—' *His* what?

'Your?'

'No. Thank you. No.'

The pen hovered, withdrew – 'Sir would like a few more minutes?' Arthur's head sank into his neck. She would be back in a minute. She would be back and he would have something nice to say – yes, he would say – what had that man said to the woman while he was helping her into her coat? Arthur considered an olive but opted for rolling and re-rolling the napkin in his lap, listening to the gold-plated chorus.

'I don't feel right,' Lydia said, sliding into her chair, eyes too bright.

'What's wrong? Do you want to go? We don't have to stay.'

'No. I don't know.'

'Do you need to lie down – you should lie down.'

She stabbed an olive with a toothpick and dropped it back into the dish, 'Oh so you're a doctor now, are you?'

Arthur returned to rolling and re-rolling the napkin – no, he never said he was a doctor, he was just –

'Can we go for a walk? I'd like to go for a walk.'

'Of course, of—'

Plates were being set in front of them but Lydia was pushing herself back in her chair, picking her bag up – she didn't feel right – not right – she didn't feel – what did she – she didn't know, she just –

'Sir! Sir! This hasn't been – sorry Sir, my mistake, have a lovely evening.'

She just wanted to walk – along the canal – along the canal walking was all she wanted – but they weren't anywhere near – then walk till they got there –

The lights on the waterbus flashed over dangling legs and reaching arms, switching on hands and faces in turn.

'Walk on the other side of me, Arthur,' Lydia said. 'I might fall in.'

'No you won't,' he said, crossing behind her as a head from a stuffed sleeping bag emerged.

'I might,' she said. 'How would you fish me out?'

'I won't need to fish you out – you're not going to—'

'But what if I did? Me and all the dead cats along the bottom. What a lot of lost treasure. Must be a million Millys down there.'

'I doubt it.'

'I'll bet there are. That's what gives the canal its colour. Or if you pushed me?'

'What! Lydia! Don't talk like that.'

'You could – who's to say what you might do.'

'I'll go and get that cat and the canal can have another bloody Milly if you go on like that.'

'Arthur! How can you say such a thing?'

'Sorry.'

'So you should be! Arthur, I never thought you'd say a thing like that – I wouldn't be surprised if you did push me in. I'll bet you'd like to. You would, wouldn't you?'

'No!'

'I think you would. Go on then.'

'Stop it Lydia, stop it.'

'What a way to go.'

'One more word, Lydia and I'll throw that cat in the canal.'

'Bet—'

Word enough.

*

'What will we tell Jack?'

Cheeks hot, eyes hot but no she was not – she was not –

'Please don't, Lydia – don't—'

Not –

'Cry—'

'I'm—'

'We'll get another – I'll get you another—'

'Oh shut up Arthur. Shut up. As if I cared about the cat.'

*

There was no need to sit round not mentioning anything because it seemed there was nothing much left not to mention – not now that Lydia had said everything her too-bright eyes were saying again –

'Wanted to chuck me in so he chucked the cat in instead!' She reached round Arthur's back and ran a splayed hand from the base of his neck, drawing her fingers up the back of his head, 'Isn't that right – darling?' She had never used the endearment before this evening and she stretched it out like a rubber band until it pinged back on Arthur's cheek. Arthur pulled back in his chair – no it was not right – he looked at Keith – at the caretaker – could they not see that it – that she – she who was kissing Arthur's pinged cheek better with a kiss-it-better kiss – was not right – she'd said so herself – not right, she'd said – not right, not well. Keith was chewing a lip, taking slow, congested inhalations, thick in, thick out. The caretaker didn't seem to hear – his thumb held the pocket dictionary open but he was staring just over it. A flash across his face then and he jolted, blinking as he slid his thumb down, inserted a scrap of paper and left the pocket dictionary on the table.

Arthur slouched over the stew in front of him, picked up his spoon and began crushing already disintegrated cubes along the bottom.

'For later,' the caretaker said, permitting Arthur to let his spoon sink into the pale brown slush.

'Well I thought it was delicious,' Lydia said, licking her spoon as she handed the caretaker her empty bowl.

'Off his food,' Keith lamented.

'Later,' the caretaker repeated, 'later later,' he told the full bowl, 'we make hot again.'

'We make *it* hot again,' Lydia said. 'It. It. We make it.'

'We make it…' The caretaker let the water run and then turned back round to Lydia. 'We taked the train?'

'Took. We *took* the train.' Lydia's raised hands clapped then plunged. 'I love trains! Journeys – I love – so long as you're on the train you might be… anywhere… always going…'

'Somewhere?' It might have been the caretaker's turn to repay Lydia's tutelage but the question was for Arthur who, having made no effort to withhold his sigh was knocking the heel of his palm against his forehead.

'We took the train. Me, my friend. Me and my friend we took the train. Everyone say go go, we see you there. But we do not see – they are gone, everyone is gone – where? I ask, where? And no one can say. Only the smoke say—'

'Now hang on a sec, Prof – I'm not sure I get your meaning,' Keith was rubbing his eyes, his nose.

The caretaker let a vague smile fall, shrugged, held up the pocket dictionary. 'No meaning, no.'

'Arthur,' Lydia was leaning towards him, too-bright eyes glinting through slits, 'you don't look – are you—'

'No you don't—' Keith was leaning in towards him now.

Didn't look *what*? Arthur got up. Two pairs of narrowed eyes agreed on a diagnosis: not right.

Not right?

'Oh dear Arthur,' Lydia said, 'perhaps you'd better lie down.'

Lie down? Oh very clever. Alright Lydia, alright, so he shouldn't have said that but there was no need to – absolutely no need to –

'You ought to, Arthur,' Keith said.

'I do not need to lie down!' This was worse than Harry and his father, next they'd be calling him Goldilocks.

'Go on, darling,' Lydia said, blinking thoughtfully dimmed eyes for the sick man's benefit. Darling. A soft soft ping. The softest. He would rather be Goldilocks. Lydia played a musical set of fingers under her jaw line. *Oh darling*. The voice that had called out that it was time to go would never – never have said –

'Bit touchy.'

'Touchy?' The caretaker picked up his pocket dictionary and handed it to Lydia.

'Sensitive,' Lydia said, taking the pocket dictionary without opening it. The caretaker's brow creased, his hand opening towards the pocket dictionary, nodding as he found the page *sens-it-ive... sens—*

'Delicate. On edge,' Lydia said sharply.

'Wants the kid gloves,' Keith said, holding his hands up. The caretaker studied Arthur for the best source of translation until Arthur stood up and the caretaker saw his object of enquiry was on his way to the door –

'Please to stay—'

An object that could therefore not be in the least bit touchy – kid gloves! – why couldn't Keith just have taken her out – his turn? – whose idea was that then? If he'd just taken her out then Arthur would have gone straight to Llanvanor Road, had it all out, demanded to be told and the cat would have been left to vomit as it pleased – Arthur wouldn't have been anywhere near the canal – the perfect alibi! Maybe the caretaker was in on the joke – maybe it was the caretaker who organised the whole set-up – if he hadn't brought the cat back in the first place there wouldn't have been any cat to throw in the canal – he'd be innocent! – the perfect alibi was the need for no alibi at all – no cat and no table in the corner and he would have just gone to Llanvanor Road and –

'Going? No, please—'

'Please, Arthur.'

'Don't get all—'

*November 1968*

The car wasn't there and the lights were out. The lights were out in Mrs Cohen's old house too. Four different families had moved in and sold up since she'd gone. All kept themselves to themselves, Gerald had been pleased to observe – except the second, the husband always wanting Gerald to come and have a friendly at the cricket club and the wife unable to help herself making the mistake of inviting Sylvie round or getting her to join some committee or other – you could always hear the youngest practising the recorder – they could shut the window, Gerald suggested. Closed now. Another woman living there these last two years – nothing like Mrs Cohen – wiry, brisk, spectacles, the cat quick, green-eyed, black – nothing like the tabby – and yes, this woman knew to keep herself to herself. Mrs Cohen might have known to do the same – if she had Arthur might always have just been a dirty little sea mite rather than a dirty little Semite.

Dirty. Little. Jew.

'Ma, I'm not dirty am I?'

'Don't be silly, Arthur!'

'Am I a Semite?'

Sylvie twitched. 'A what?'

'Mrs Cohen says it's a Jew. What's Jew?'

'A Jew. A Jew's a—'

'Mrs Cohen said it's someone who's a jewish. What's a jewish? Am I a jewish.'

'Jewish. Not a jewish – I thought your father said no more talking to Mrs Cohen.'

'Is Harry? Are you? Is Dad?'

A different sort. The good sort, the clean sort – the English sort. Gerald had been born here, his mother had been born here, his father – well his father was another matter altogether but he had joined up, hadn't he? Done his bit? Done his bit and lost his nerve – if Gerald had only known that letting them bring Arthur – or what, with sufficient training and shaping and enough dedication on his part, might become Arthur – back would mean another bedwetting mute on his hands –

Dirty. Little – hadn't said it again since that day – though he punctuated it with a translation Arthur didn't understand – didn't understand but knew. A chant that rang in and out of hearing, fading into silence at some indefinable point – clear again now: Dirty. Little. Jew. Sticks and stones, sticks and stones. Stones too. Gerald wasn't sure how he managed to stand even looking at the boy. Should never have let them – but he did. Someone else's little someone dug up and brought back to make a proper little Englishman, a proper little soldier and a proper little Arthur.

*

The caretaker picked the pocket dictionary up off the floor, turned as he slid it up his sleeve and tied it with the string. Arthur hadn't meant to knock it on the floor – or the tumblers – or the whiskey for that matter – but then he hadn't meant to kick the table over onto its side either. Two of its legs made pointed daggers across the room at Arthur. The caretaker intervened and pulled them down while Arthur watched the amber disappear into the carpet.

'Least it wasn't full,' Keith offered.

'And everyone has his bones,' the caretaker said, picking the tumblers and the whiskey bottle up.

'Bang on, Professor. Nothing broken.'

Oh on the contrary: *everything* was broken. Arthur checked their placidity: unbreakable as the tumblers. He tried to compensate for it by mustering a little horror at his own performance only to find he'd spent all the horror he had on the performance itself. All he could do was drink in the green darkening under their feet.

'To clean with?' the caretaker was asking the cupboards as he opened them.

'Think I'm going to turn in,' Keith said, hands under his arms, a nod for the caretaker, another for Arthur. Turn in? Clean? Lydia was out, roaming the streets – that is, if she was still roaming – if she hadn't been kidnapped or shot or – couldn't he have left her with them for five minutes? The short answer was useless and the longer ones weren't much better – one that involved absolution for Keith on account of the fact he wasn't anyone's babysitter and another – implausible to the point of incomprehensibility – that found *him, Arthur,* responsible for Lydia's disappearance.

'She didn't disappear,' Keith assured Arthur. 'She went to check you weren't throwing any more cats in the canal.'

'Don't go on about it – that was weeks ago!'

'I think she like the cat very much,' the caretaker said – his English was improving at an intolerable rate. Well others might have the luxury of turning in and cleaning up but Noble Honourable Arthur would stand vigil at the top of the stairs until a miracle opened the door and bubbles of unpopped laughter floated up to meet him. Closed eyes reversed Lydia's steps to the canal and brought her back to the Holloway Road, put her hand on his arm, his shoulder –

'Better to sleep,' the caretaker said, his hand on Arthur's shoulder a moment longer before the caretaker went back into his room. Arthur opened his eyes. Not Lydia's hand. His shoulder tried to shake out the impression the hand had left and the one it had not.

Opened or closed Arthur's eyes saw the same hat floating up the canal. Better to sleep, yes – he'd fallen out of the habit of waiting for the morning to have a good laugh at him in exchange for returning Lydia to the Holloway Road. He sat on the top step and let himself fall against the wall and watched the hat float up and up a never-ending canal. Up to number sixty-three tomorrow and past the park, down to the corner – familiar now unfamiliar would be familiar as soon as it was light – if she wasn't already back – which she might be – she would be – yes, and the morning could have its laugh – and he could have his Lydia.

*

Since Arthur did not dream, a night spent watching the hat drifting, a dress and a mix of limbs following, a head shaven of brown curls left bobbing behind could only confirm the mumblings dull nausea made – he had not slept. But he hadn't heard anyone come and leave the blanket that was next to him on the top step. Arthur picked it up and put it outside the caretaker's door. The morning wasn't laughing. There was no Lydia. Too early to make the unfamiliar familiar again, perhaps, but he might as well make a start. Wait outside number sixty-three till it was up.

But number sixty-three was an early riser and it seemed to have been up before Arthur had even left the Holloway Road – the absence of the rustle and shuffle had failed to signal the beginning of the day – the windows at number sixty-three were being cleaned, the front step swept –

The broom stopped as Arthur opened the front gate and a starched face prompted Lydia's name out of Arthur.

'Who?'

'Lydia – is she—' Arthur stopped, his eyes climbing to check the windows of each floor. 'She used to live here – Lydia…' The broom was sweeping again, back it went over the same clear step, 'Before my time, before my time,' muttered over it, 'and I've been here since time began.'

'This *is* Mrs Simons's house? – Mrs Simons, she—'

Broom in hand, the starched-faced housekeeper came towards Arthur, sending him a step back with each of hers ahead. 'There's no Mrs Simons here.'

'But Lydia—'

'Go on, get off, it's too early for this sort of trouble.'

Arthur's eyes made their way back up the windows again from behind the gate – but she must be, that night, he'd seen her here, number sixty-three, he'd seen her go in – number sixty-three, Mrs Simons –

No. No Mrs Simons. No Lydia. Not his or anyone else's. None to be anyone's – none except the one who might still have been Lydia, before he'd had the name –

*No harm in you having that I suppose –*

When she was still just a voice calling out that it was time to go –

The head and the dress, the limbs and the head –

Number sixty-three closed, number sixty-five opened and a hand reached down to pick up a milk bottle.

'I don't want to trouble you,' Arthur began but his beginning was ended by a shout from inside and the second starched face of the morning was gone, leaving the eyes narrowing in it to peer down the gravel path –

'Coming!'

Before Arthur could be the trouble he sincerely did not want to be. And he wouldn't be, not at number sixty-three, not at number sixty-five, not on his park bench where he would sit and wait for no one, his park bench which, at just past eight on a Friday morning, would be his alone, the young man would not be there with a briefcase on his lap sitting next to a woman twirling brown curls, pressing her finger against her red heart of a mouth before she spilt a smile and her name, letting the young man have them both –

Good luck to him –

To her –

Lydia. His Lydia.

The head and the dress –

Arthur cut the corner and redirected to the canal –

The limbs and the head –

To find nothing more than chucked cans and leaves bobbing, floating, implausibly beautiful in the white gold of a cold sun.

*

Number sixty-three, the park, the corner, the absence of Lydia at each coordinate projected her onto the next, pushing Arthur on. It didn't matter whether she was no more Lydia than Old Mother Hubbard or the Lady of Shallot, it would take more than a starched face to unmake the Lydia she had made and, as Arthur repeated the route, Lydia's repeated absence consolidated her – he could see her so clearly without her face obscuring the sight, hear her so much better without bubbles of laughter popping round the fulcrum of her voice turning from hiss to trill to scold –

*Daddy wants, Daddy wants, Say goodbye nicely, anyone would think you were in some sort of –*

He was not in any pain –

*Daddy wants, Daddy wants –*

Why did she say that? He did not want to get rid of her – a ludicrous – he adored – adored! – Lydia, his Lydia –

The hat and the dress –

Walk it out of sight and hearing to see and hear her – his Lydia – repeating until everything else was the blur of a shuffled deck so that when the interruption came – as it did, on the corner of the Finchley Road – Arthur swerved off balance and the hat and the dress, the limbs and the head, all came back into view while the face and figure of next door began to materialise in front of him –

'Steady as you go,' next door was holding onto Arthur's arm – next door here on the corner when next door should be where next door belonged, not taking liberties with Arthur's arm – or with his laces –

'Mind you don't have a nasty fall. You could do with a new set of laces if you don't mind me saying.'

Yes Arthur did mind. Very much – and he minded this looking up and down –

'Bit worse for wear, if you don't mind me saying.'

Well he might also be a bit worse for wear if he'd traipsed for… the day – what day was it? How many days had he – five? Fifteen? – could be anything either side or between – could be fifty, a hundred – no it couldn't – he'd be dead – but then he didn't feel far off – bastard next door, if he hadn't been interrupted he'd still be on his route, not seeing or hearing anything but –

'So you'll have a word with your father for me, then?'

What? His what? Next door was nodding a nod so pronounced it initiated one from Arthur – how did people always do this to him? –

'I don't want to be a bother but that tree really does need cutting back – it's blocking all my light. You'll have to see it gets done. I've been round every day last week and every day this and never any answer which is all a bit odd – if you don't mind me saying. Gone away have they? Business is it?'

'Yes. Business.'

# Part Three

*December 1968*

Harry opened the door and went back down the hall. No thump on the back, no Hello there Goldilocks. Arthur could hear Harry mumbling something about a key – what might have been a bite of sarcasm if he'd had the strength for an easy snipe, but his flattened tone couldn't carry it and the words sank.

'Dad in?'

Arthur left a space for the reply to shed its reluctance and, when it didn't, made what he could of next door's wanting to know – the tree, the light – he shook it off, Harry wasn't listening, he was sitting where Arthur had last left Gerald, the same days still piled up over the table and in the sink. It was the dank sheen of Harry's hair and face and the black under his nails that made Arthur see what next door had seen in him – over twenty years late, perhaps but, unwashed, unfed, sleepless, the boys were beginning to match up.

'Taken Ma back,' Harry said, picking up a plate which defeated him. It took a moment for Arthur to bridge the delay and tag Harry's answer to his question while Harry began puncturing Arthur's bewilderment: Essex. Maldon. Back to where she came from, Gerald had told Harry, back where she belonged – a small, dark pressure gathered a quiet density in Arthur's ears, behind his eyes – Gerald liked things back where they belonged and that's just where Arthur, caught on his way to dig and dig would find himself if this digging business didn't stop once and for all.

'Taken Ma?'

'Yes, and to tell you if you give a damn at all—'

'I do – of course I do! – it was Dad who—'

'Shut it, Arthur—'

Arthur tried a plate but found he was no more capable than Harry. He put it back down. Of course he gave a damn – Arthur felt Gerald's eyes on him courtesy of Harry – Gave a damn, did he? Well if that meant disappearing off while his mother was stabbing and jabbing her legs with a pair of nail scissors of all things then yes, he gave a damn –

'Nail scissors!'

'Dad couldn't leave her in that place after that. Said they couldn't tolerate that sort of behaviour. So Dad took her—'

'Back to where she came from?'

'Back where she belongs.'

'And what does that mean?'

'Like I already said – Maldon, Essex. Taking her to Cynthia's, Dad said it would be good for her.'

'Cynthia's!'

'*Aunt* Cynthia,' Harry reminded Arthur –

Well Arthur didn't want reminding, he wanted to know why the hell anyone –

'Because he can keep a proper eye on her there – he didn't want to call and be a nuisance but if I don't give a damn and you don't give –'

'But I do! Harry!—'

'And you think I don't? Look, I'm only saying what Dad—'

Well he did – gave more than a damn, Arthur who, still unwashed, unfed, sleepless, swerved off course by next door and swerved onto another by Harry, found himself on a train, the hat and the dress floating up to the surface of the canal at every stop, limbs drifting, head bobbing, all sinking back down again as the whistle went and the wheels turned, making his way to Cynthia's – or rather, *Aunt* Cynthia's if Arthur wanted to make it inside the door –

'No! It isn't! It is! Oh little Arthur – to think the last time I – now let me see – how long must it have been—'

Arthur and Harry had tried to work it out, plucking numbers that meant nothing to either of them, Arthur just about to go, standing there just that bit too long, finding something to say while the hands neither of them reached out pocketed themselves –

'Could let them know you're on your way,' Harry had said as Arthur nodded a goodbye. Hadn't thought – of course, yes –

'Thanks, Harry.'

Arthur hadn't made it much more than a couple of doors along when he turned back to ask Harry if he didn't want to come with –

'Rather stick needles in my eyes, thanks.'

Harry had had it with Maldon after a week – well alright so maybe he hadn't lasted a week but who would?

'Besides someone had go to into the office at some point and tidy things up, though truth is I'm not sure I can stand it here much longer either—'

'Why not?'

'What does it matter why?'

'Alright! Was only—'

'Well don't – oh look, go on or you'll miss the four-thirty and the whole thing only gets worse as the day goes on – you're better off getting there before they start with the bloody blancmange or whatever it is – I swear to God I'll never be about to touch blancmange again—'

It had gone seven by the time Aunt Cynthia – the most perfectly formed of dumplings who had never been anyone's aunt – squeezed her doughy arms round Arthur. Standing back to re-dimple her shape, Aunt Cynthia assessed Arthur's size against a hand held out at her waist –

'This big!' –

Arthur's face was caught in a horrified grin –

'And little Harry too!' –

Clearly, the transformation in Harry had done little to prepare Aunt Cynthia –

'Oh the two of you!'

Though Arthur might not have looked forward to this reunion, he couldn't help but feel at least some degree of warmth for one who shared his inability to contain the uncontainable – particularly when he was containing it so successfully, no less particularly when there was possibly no one but Aunt Cynthia who had been quite so thrilled –

'Thrilled!' –

To see him – and though her kisses were no less sticky than Arthur remembered and her hands no less damp – not that Arthur was entirely confident his were dry – the delay Aunt Cynthia provided was not unwelcome. Once next door had swerved him off course the imperative of his route was displaced by the imperative that he see Sylvie, but, now that he was here, all will abandoned him –

*Not my Arthur* –

Aunt Cynthia offered her doughy arms and Arthur's maniac grin eased. He was not in a position to refuse.

'It really is lovely to see you, Aunt Cynthia.' Blanketed by the sight of Aunt Cynthia's well-floured pudgy cheeks, Arthur graciously complied with the impression Aunt Cynthia constructed as she offered him the chair reserved for her most special visitor –

'Did you really come all that way?'

'It really isn't far—'

'Just to see me! And is it all just as you remember?'

'Oh yes.'

Arthur had to admire his effortless nostalgia for the cottage he'd never seen before.

'You boys were always so thoughtful,' she said, lips and cheeks besides themselves, 'of course I kept them all, every card you boys sent.' She put a hand over her uncontainable mouth, dipped her eyes and chin, whispered, 'You know, Arthur, you were always my favourite – but you mustn't tell Harry – promise?'

'I promise, Aunt Cynthia,' Arthur said, impressed by the sincerity of the thank-you note written in his nine or ten-year-old hand. There was only one year Sylvie had to insist he write it, but every other year he had sat at the table with Harry, pencil gripped between his thumb and fingers, rubbing out the first letter again and again until it was perfect. He'd never met Aunt Cynthia but he had to get it right. That moment when the parcels from her arrived was the closest Llanvanor ever came to doing Christmas. She always sent them at least a month in advance, always hand-knitted elves. Every bloody year. Gerald said the elves were ghastly – and they were. Still, Arthur looked forward to them – or looked forward to Sylvie looking over his shoulders, spelling out C-Y-N-T-H-I-A, dictating the boys' gratitude, a task she was scrupulous about until one of her 'little spells', as she called them, outgrew its euphemism, beginning in autumn and eating its way into Advent. Aunt Cynthia waited patiently for the thank-you that didn't come but while one could accept the absence of French hens and turtle doves, one might at least be sustained by the adoring appreciation of the nephews she hadn't been allowed to fuss over and spoil. Sylvie might have invited her at least once. Only London could do that to a sweet girl like Sylvie. There was only one thing for it: Aunt Cynthia put a night bag together on Christmas Eve and looked forward to receiving the goodwill she was due in person. Her chief anxiety (Sylvie, sweet Sylvie!) was temporarily drowned by the thought that the knitted elves might have been left to languish with the comics under one of the boys' beds.

They couldn't very well let her stay, Gerald had said, they didn't have anywhere to put her – Sylvie, trying to rub sensation into her arms, half-mouthed half-whispered that they couldn't very well send her back either – oh Gerald, refusing to halve anything, rather thought they could, he also thought it was a pity Sylvie hadn't spared some of the lashings of sympathy she had for this so-called Aunt Cynthia for him when he was the one being put through hell by a wife that as good as disappeared into thin air for months on end – what the hell was the matter with her?

'Nothing, Gerald, nothing.'

'Clearly not if you can be so bright and breezy just like that, all for the sake of some *aunt*. It's enough to make a man lose his—'

'Ssshh, please, the boys, Aunt Cynthia, they'll—'

'Do tell me, dear, where are the stockings to put out?'

With one arm round Arthur and one round Harry, Aunt Cynthia and her own two proper little soldiers were standing at Gerald and Sylvie's door –

'We don't do stockings,' Sylvie said.

'And we don't do Christmas.' Gerald flicked his eyes onto Harry who pulled first himself then Arthur out of Aunt Cynthia's clasp.

So-called. Whatever else Gerald had said, he shouldn't have said that. But Aunt Cynthia would let bygones be bygones –

'Besides you've enough troubles now,' Aunt Cynthia said to Arthur. 'Breaks your heart, doesn't it? But your grandmother was prone to spells too if you want to know the truth.'

No, he didn't, he was quite content watching so-called Aunt Cynthia construct her house of cards, which brought him all that way just to visit –

'Ever since the day Sylvie was born I only wanted what was best for her,' she said, a misshapen dumpling as she plopped into the chair. 'I felt a duty when her mother died to see she wasn't left with only grief and guilt for company – and there were these… intimations you might say, you know, from what they call the other side. Of course it was no surprise really, I've always had a sensitivity and considering how close your grandmother and I had always been. Two peas in a pod, as I told Sylvie, we might have been sisters!'

Couldn't she be an Aunt Cynthia to Sylvie then? she'd asked. At least until the shock had passed.

'She really was such a dear,' Cynthia said, putting the shoebox back on the shelf. 'You will excuse me while I spend a penny.'

*

'Just like you used to do for my old man,' Gerald was saying as he brought the spoon up to Sylvie's lips. 'He liked you, my old man. Mother always said he liked you. Never sang for anyone else, only sang for you. Remember what it was?' Gerald tried a note, grasping a word of the song before he gave up on it. 'Sing it for me, Sylvie. Such a pretty voice you had.'

There was a fog round Gerald's voice and, as Arthur saw him there, head bent and shoulders hunched, holding the spoon towards Sylvie, Arthur felt as though he were watching him from an ever increasing distance, straining to make out this diminishing man, no more than a cipher, bearing less and less relation to the General. It was as if Gerald was being scaled down to meet the proportions of the other figure in the picture – two dots on the horizon that didn't know Arthur was there – the picture couldn't accommodate Arthur, made him monstrous beside it – would Harry have made it into that picture? Could that other little Arthur have been sketched on?

'No more, love?' Gerald asked, putting the spoon down, sighing Arthur's old-man sigh. Sighing one for himself, Arthur heard what had been inaudible to him – what Lydia must have heard: it was Gerald's sigh, not his.

Sylvie's hand came up and fell. Her eyes closed, a slight flutter in the lids as Arthur came towards the bed, he didn't want them to open, he didn't want her to see him see her.

'I don't know,' Gerald said as he and Arthur took turns not to look at Sylvie, at each other. Gerald took Sylvie's hand and gave it a stiff pat before he stroked it, 'I don't know.' Gerald flattened his hands over his thighs and got up, 'Good of you to—' he began.

'No, really, it's—'

'You should have a wash or something, you look—'

'I know, yes, sorry, all been a bit—'

'Yes. I'll go and get you some towels. Keep an eye.'

Sylvie was digging her nails into the tops of her legs, pulling at the blankets, her breath shortening and eyes squeezing.

'It's OK, Ma,' Arthur said, 'we'll just take the blankets off.'

Her breath eased and she blinked at Arthur, quiet, unstaring eyes meeting his. The sheet over her was stained yellow, orange and pink, sunset patches bleeding into dirty white over the top of her legs. She was pulling at the sheet now.

'No, Ma, you'll get cold without that – alright Ma, alright.'

The sheet stuck as he drew it down, pulling at the gauze and tape and soiled cotton, giving away the septic nests Sylvie had etched into her thighs.

'Oh Ma, don't do that, please don't do—' Arthur turned away from her and followed Gerald into the hall.

'I thought I told you to keep an—' Gerald began, going back towards Sylvie's room.

'What did she go and do that for?'

'Do what?' Gerald's eyes were switching between Arthur and the door.

'The scissors. Harry said—'

'Don't be ridiculous – they've been taken away from her,' Gerald said, pulling his hand through his hair.

'You've got to put something on those cuts.'

'A doctor, are you?'

Oh Christ, first Lydia, now him.

'Please Dad, she's obviously—'

'Have your bath. I'll have a word with Cynthia about making up the spare room for you when you're done.'

'No, it's alright, I can't stay.'

Gerald regained his lost stature and set his eyes on Arthur. Yes he could. He was the only thing Gerald had been able to get her to talk about – '*My little Arthur*, she says.'

Arthur took the towels, 'I don't think she means me.'

'I haven't got time for all this nonsense. You're staying and that's all there is to it—' Sylvie's voice halted Gerald's.

'They won't work,' she was saying. 'My legs – why won't they work?' She went on digging her nails in.

'Don't do that, love,' Gerald said, taking her hand. She looked up at him and smacked her leg with the back of her other hand. Gerald grasped her wrist – 'Don't love, you mustn't—' his voice unable to hold as he pressed his hands round both of hers.

'But they don't work—' she stopped, eyes darting for Arthur – 'they don't work – how can we go to the park if—'

'But we can't go to the park now—'

'Have to go to the—' she was nodding, her eyes trying to steady on Arthur – 'remember – you do remember—'

'Yes, I remember, Ma.'

'Arthur… my Arthur…' But she wasn't looking at him, her eyes were drifting, a feverish light in them that died almost as soon as it glowed. 'Big enough and strong enough…'

Gerald's eyes fell to the backs of his hands and Sylvie looked towards him, at the hands she had been exchanged for, reaching for the spoon as though trying to bring Gerald back to her, to see her as she raised it, pushing it to the back of her mouth before she dropped it. She swallowed and looked again at Gerald. She had taken that spoonful for him and he hadn't seen it.

'Put your suit in the basket, Arthur,' Gerald said. 'I'll leave you something of mine to wear outside.'

*

Now that the bed was no longer cold, Arthur couldn't feel it – just as he felt it start to warm it disappeared beneath him, and himself with it – there was nothing to tell him that he was there. He had to open his eyes. It was the quiet – the way it was here – it was different, this quiet. And the dark. Solid – nothing to break them. The Holloway

Road was never so cruel – always some flash or screech. That must be what it was that drove people to London where there was no dark or quiet so total it would swallow you up. Not like this. London ate you in a different way – and Arthur never doubted it would spit him out again. Or almost never. But here, once you were gone you were gone. At least that awful moaning every night had told him something was alive – that he was alive, there, hearing it – awful! – how could Lydia have said he moaned like that?

*Anyone would think –*

Well he didn't and he wasn't. Arthur got up. Standing allowed the dark shades. Yes, he was still here – feet on the carpet – wondrously itchy! – a step creaked a board – even better! – he had to make it creak again – well that decided it once and for all – both he and the creaking board were absolutely, irrevocably real and no dark or quiet could tell him otherwise – the light would make his defence: switch, floor, bed, blankets – even if everything else since he'd arrived in Maldon had been drained of all substance, all this here – himself included – was absolutely, irrevocably –

But the hat and the dress hadn't seemed any less so. The hat, the dress, the limbs, the head. None any less real than the spoon Gerald had brought to Sylvie's lips – even if the man who appeared to hold it had no basis in any reality Arthur had ever known – not least the one built and conserved for so many years at Llanvanor Road who had let them bring Arthur back, who would make a proper little Englishman out of him, who knew that no one liked peas and chuckled over Goldilocks and crunched fistfuls of nuts and wondered –

*Have you seen –*

Where his Sylvie's smile had gone –

*My Sylvie had a nice smile –*

Arthur had to get out of his room, out of the cottage – go back to London, to Lydia – no, no he couldn't. He would just go downstairs, sit in the front room with the light on – sit until he was absolutely sure that he, Arthur, was there.

He went out into the hall – the light was already on, coming through from under the door to the front room. He wouldn't have risked it if he'd been at Llanvanor where the light could only mean Gerald was up. Gerald could never stand being caught in the middle of the night, seen holding onto his nerve. Sylvie didn't put the light on at Llanvanor when she went down, she'd still be visible in the half dark but somehow it was alright – she didn't seem to sense herself seen – or else it was just as easy to pretend that she hadn't been seen – she was so still – but Gerald, holding onto his nerve, would never have been more than a second away from sending that dirty little Semite back where he belonged – no, he hadn't called him that the last time, but Arthur had heard it anyway and the dirty little Semite had gone back upstairs before he could be sent back to wherever this unknowable, unnameable place was –

*And if you say a word of this to anyone*, Gerald had told Arthur, *I swear I'll bloody* –

But this wasn't Llanvanor and the Gerald downstairs now – it was Gerald down there, it must be – wasn't the Gerald drawn in the broad black strokes Arthur had known so well. If nothing else, Arthur could always depend on Gerald not to fade close up – but seeing him that evening – chalk edges rubbed out – maybe it was being here, this cottage that housed Aunt Cynthia's invention of herself and them with it – or else too many nights being swallowed up by the dark and the quiet and what was left was a Gerald Arthur never thought he'd meet and still couldn't quite believe, hunched and bent, holding a spoon up –

It took Arthur a moment to be convinced of the hand stitching a second holly leaf to a stocking, the green felt trimmings round tiny satin slippered feet.

'Cynthia?'

She didn't look up but went on stitching, humming a carol – Arthur knew it, but something kept words from being fitted to the tune –

'Aunt Cynthia?'

The needle and the quick thimbled finger paused, then the hum. Aunt Cynthia laid the stocking on the arm of the chair and bent to gather up the trimmings at her feet.

'I can make one for you too if you like,' she said. 'We've still time.'

Three weeks – more – yesterday's train ticket had at last anchored Arthur in a time and a place so securely it was almost disorientating – a disorientation he'd have gladly extended –

'What day is it today?'

Aunt Cynthia smiled and started humming something else – he did know this one – sung it himself with Sylvie and Harry and the others outside the Tube, raising money for something or other – song sheets soggy in the snow – it didn't matter that he didn't know what he was singing about or what a manger was – only that it was cold and the singing was warm and Sylvie and Harry and being huddled with everyone else was warm and so long as he was singing he was just like them and not a dirty little anything – best not tell their father, Sylvie had said – and that was the real magic of it – the silence of secrets and snow –

'Your mother was always asking the same thing when they first got here – Sylvie dear, I said, it's the day after yesterday.'

Why couldn't she just tell him what the damn day was? Why couldn't she have just told Sylvie? Well fine, he would work it out himself –

'Dear dear Sylvie, dear dear Arthur—'

He didn't want to be a dear, he wanted to know what day it was – the second – or no, the third – the second was yesterday now – would she stop that stitching and humming – three weeks! – he wouldn't still be here in three weeks – he'd go mad! – besides, they didn't do stockings –

*

'Go up to your mother, will you?'

Arthur had fallen asleep downstairs and now Gerald was sitting where Aunt Cynthia must have sat all night, humming and stitching. Gerald's elbows were on his knees, fingers pressed into a bridge. 'Go on, Arthur,' he said, 'she's been asking after you all morning.'

Arthur rubbed his face, got up and, still half submerged in Aunt Cynthia's hum, found himself reminded by Sylvie's speckled eyes staring through him, past him, staring all the way to that other little Arthur, that no, she hadn't meant him. Arthur wanted Gerald to come up – no, he wanted to leave – just leave – before Sylvie's eyes switched and flared and saw Arthur – her Arthur! – who would take her to the park – take her –

*Back back back* –

'No Ma, please, Ma—'

'They don't work – my legs – why don't they – Arthur, my—'

The limbs floating up the canal caught Arthur, showing themselves and the head bobbing behind, the surface of the canal dancing with sun and rain. Oh Lydia-not-his-Lydia. He had to get back – had to make sure – not stay here with this, this and Aunt Cynthia and her needle; so quick that needle – invisible thread licked through the eye, the eye of that needle threaded with her happy happy hum –

Three weeks. He couldn't – it was more – yes, Aunt Cynthia had insisted he open the advent calendar – three was lucky, she said and Arthur heard another Gerald's voice in his head, the voice of General Gerald, saying they didn't do advent calendars while Gerald coming in to tell Arthur to go up to his mother said it was his turn tomorrow because, here, this Gerald did do advent calendars and stockings and liked peas and never wondered where his Sylvie's smile had gone. Arthur would stay until lunchtime. Go while he was still quite firm about it. He didn't need to explain himself. He simply had things he had to get back to –

'What things?'

Alright then – but just that night, then he really did have to get –

In the end he outdid Harry and lasted six days of changing places with Gerald, six evenings of trying to keep Sylvie from tugging off the mittens Aunt Cynthia had made for her. Nothing was said about the mittens, one red, one red and white, only the instructions that under no circumstances should they or the blankets be removed –

'I'm sorry dear,' Cynthia had said, handing the mismatched mittens to Gerald, 'I ran out of red wool.'

Arthur watched Sylvie make floppy jabs with the spoon into the blancmange before going back into another night of that same dark and quiet, waking to find himself and the bed and blankets still there, absolutely and irrevocably real as Christmas miracles.

Sylvie didn't seem to register his goodbye. She'd miss him, Gerald said, said it was a shame he couldn't stay a little longer, must get Harry up here again too, having both of them might do the trick and the four of them could go out for a knickerbocker glory one afternoon like they used to. Gerald had encouraged his eyes towards Sylvie then. 'Remember that? he asked her. 'You do remember that, don't you love?'

'Think they still serve them up in those sundae glasses? You boys in your army caps. You used to like the long spoons they came with. Now that's not something I could ever forget. You haven't forgotten, have you Arthur?'

Gerald was patting Sylvie's mittened palm but his eyes were on Arthur.

'No Dad, of course I haven't.'

*

Back. He had to get back. Away from there. From Maldon. From Sylvie who wanted Arthur, her Arthur, the little Arthur he never was and never could be; away from this Gerald who liked peas and did Christmas and remembered the knickerbocker glories they'd never had; away from Cynthia who'd never been anyone's aunt – that humming and stitching, it was relentless – enough to unleash the uncontainable –

'London. Didn't I just say – thank you,' Arthur managed as he took his ticket – yes, he would contain himself. It was simply a matter of getting away from blancmange and back to Lydia –

Lydia-his-not-his –

The hat and the dress, the limbs and the head – again at each stop they floated up the canal. On the seat opposite a woman twirled a brown curl.

Lydia!

He mightn't have said her name aloud but the lurch of breath and head and drug-wide eyes were voluble enough. The woman got up and went into the next carriage. Several pairs of eyes checked Arthur. *What?* Arthur turned to the window – he would keep his own eyes on the blur of fields racing backwards. Lydia would be there, of course she would – but the mix of floating limbs objected, the head, bobbing, followed, the hat and the dress right behind – no… Arthur fished out the limbs and head, attached them to a body, dressed it, put on the hat – better without the hat, have her, his Lydia, just as she was in the moment when he found the very best Arthur he could possibly be was Lydia's Arthur – she needn't even be *his* Lydia – unless she suggested it, in which case he would be gracious enough to oblige – yes, all pieced up and back on course – it had just been that business with the cat and that was weeks ago now – not that any of it had been his fault, winding him up like that – well, it was alright, he wouldn't press the point, honour and nobility wouldn't allow it and he, Noble, Honourable Arthur, would let her have a go about his leaving without saying goodbye nicely or otherwise and let her spill smiles and twirl brown curls while she hatted and dressed herself for whatever evening out might be lined up with Keith – well how was she to know when he might be back, she'd say, turning round to ask where Arthur managed to get that suit, unable to help noticing that it did fit terribly well – and there wouldn't be any point in denying it – it shouldn't have, though; General Gerald was a giant, enormous, he had towered over Arthur, loomed – but then that was General Gerald –

Back. He had to get – he'd even plait the twins' hair and eat pickle sandwiches – oh the caretaker, the dear dearest caretaker, the caretaker and his pickle sandwiches – he could rustle and shuffle and moan with pleasure – the greatest pleasure! And Keith! Dearest Keith, of course he could take her out – a dinner? A concert? Well if that's what his – no, he wouldn't presume anything, not yet – if that was what *Lydia* wanted then, of course –

No, for God's sake he did not want milk in his coffee, if he had wanted milk he would have –

'Thank you, that's grand.' Noble Honourable Arthur smiles and, without squandering the last scrap of will he had managed to preserve, accepts, without comment, a perfectly decent coffee ruined with milk.

The urgency that prolonged the journey was met with one hall of mirrors after another on arrival – yet what could possibly be more urgent than getting back to his Lydia? Yes: why not *his*? There was no way of knowing what metamorphosis might have occurred during this interim – perhaps that wasn't such a helpful thought, anything – anything! – might have happened – no, no, he, like everything and everyone else, was back on course and now, having been washed and fed for six consecutive days and fitted in Gerald's horribly well-fitting suit Arthur found himself just as he should: unseen, unquestioned, camouflaged without reservation: here was a young man simply on his way – if only he'd had his briefcase.

The Holloway Road was too easily going about eleven o'clock for Arthur to have any part in it. He manufactured a due air of annoyance at the key's failure to open the door. Repeatedly ramming the key against the lock, however, did not seem to be bringing him any closer to getting the hell off the Holloway Road and up to his room and his Lydia. Arthur raised the key for a final stab and found himself aiming it at an obscenely necessary young man, briefcase in hand –

'Yes?'

Could this necessary young man opening the door, standing inside the house, not at least *appear* a little bemused? Could he not conjure *some* degree of embarrassment? Arthur gave the young man a moment to modify his face – imposter!

'What are you doing here?' Arthur was forced to ask, unimpressed by this necessary young man's peachy-cheeked composure while he himself fought to contain the uncontainable.

'I might ask you the same thing.'

Oh might he? Oh might – the necessary young man considered Arthur's key as it threatened skyward.

'I live here,' the young man explained with the matter-of-fact calm and kindness reserved for the infirm.

'Who's that?' A woman receded just as she came into view.

'No one.'

No one? How –

'Will you be back by six?' the woman asked.

'Six-thirty,' the young man said, his step out stepping Arthur back.

Arthur readied himself with a tightened grip round his key, General Gerald's suit lending him General Gerald's tone and stride but the necessary young man with his necessary briefcase and peachy-cheeked smile was already off down the Holloway Road. Obscene! Arthur took a stride voided of any potential militancy: it was the wrong door. Arthur cupped his hands into a cradle and rocked his key, recovering the distance back to the irredeemably wrong door where, containing the uncontainable, he restrained his toe from administering the punishment the door was surely due. At least he had been prevented from going directly to his room that, in Lydia's absence, would readily gape at him. Hadn't it gaped enough? Well he wouldn't let it. And the last thing he needed right now was the caretaker peeping out his door with a pickle sandwich and Keith crashing overhead, thundering down, welcoming him home – the door was a blessing. The door – was he even on the right street? Arthur took two quarter turns – wasn't that Shel? – blue-lipped Shel from the café – yes, this was, without any cause for doubt, the Holloway Road. Shel, approaching, must be awarded a smile for this confirmation. She sped past. But she had been so kind. She had called him sweetheart, had she not? She had given him pickle. The irredeemably right door was coming towards him a little too soon – Bench Time was needed, time to Work It All Out.

His bench was taken, of course, but the young man sitting there in his brown three-piece with crusts at his feet was amenable to sharing. He may have had the advantage of a briefcase, but Arthur found the uncontainable satisfactorily contained by the thought that lacking a briefcase removed the concern of how one might conceal the emptiness of such a case. Nevertheless, Arthur could not deny a slight twinge when the young man popped open the gold locks. He would not humiliate the young man – he would avert his eyes. At least this young man was not guilty of obscenely peachy cheeks, at least this young man appeared no more necessary than Arthur felt. The consolation held then disintegrated as the image of Arthur's double disclosed the shape and measure of redundancy: if he couldn't be what he was meant to be, he may as well have not been at all.

Webs of black nerves had been stretched up from the tops of the trees and petrified against the sky. Arthur didn't want to intrude but he wondered if the young man might have happened to see a young woman twirling brown curls, with or without twins. The young man was not in a position to divulge. It would have been yesterday, Arthur explained, yesterday being a Thursday. The young man got up – Wait! He hadn't finished! – fading as he went towards the bandstand. No more digging, Arthur might have warned him – he's not there, no more other little –

*No, Ma, no more other little Arthur.*

Arthur heard again what he'd tried to say on his third night in Maldon, the untouched blancmange shining absurdly pink –

*Little Arthur, my Arthur –*

*No, Ma.*

The sliver of glass framed by the gap in the curtains had caught the light. Was that what she was looking at? He should close them properly, the night would come in. A delighted twinkle trebled on the window and bounced back into the room. Arthur's hand on Sylvie didn't turn her towards him. He went round to the other side of the bed to find her eyes, to take her in. But there was no one to take in. Not all there, Gerald had said before Arthur had gone to see her in that place – no, gone after that other little Arthur and still hadn't come back and the eyes he'd spent so long trying to avoid catching wouldn't be caught – couldn't be; they weren't set in her face. She wasn't even looking through him or past him, what she saw played out inside her eye: another Sylvie, one with legs that would take her –

*No, Ma – he's not –*

But she went on seeing and Arthur saw with her, himself again beside her, both forgetting the legs, sliding, iced rigid, until the stroke of a puckered palm recalled them.

'Out,' Sylvie mouthed.

'Tomorrow – it's late now, it's cold. Tomorrow—'

'Out!'

It was Sylvie speaking but not her voice. Arthur bent towards her, but her mouth, twitching to call out again, sent him back. It was OK, tomorrow he would get her up and dressed and out – if she wanted to get –

'Out!'

'Yes Ma, out.'

She seemed to see him now. 'Out,' she whispered and he leaned towards her again, stroking the puckered palm to say he'd seen what she'd seen. Tomorrow, yes.

Gerald was standing sentry behind what had become his chair, not at the head of the table, but opposite Aunt Cynthia's chair. Aunt Cynthia had encouraged Arthur to take the seat next to her, making him give his scout's honour not to tell Harry. Gerald indicated just enough of a nod to acknowledge Arthur without either inviting or dismissing him.

'Do you think we might try and get Ma out tomorrow? I think she wants to go out.' Arthur's question was sufficient to rouse a touch of the General Gerald Arthur had thought was still behind the barracks at Llanvanor. The general lifted his head out of his neck, pulled his shoulders back.

'Out?'

'Yes, Dad.'

Gerald shook his head and the general imitated the General's chuckle, throwing a hand up.

'Mad!' he said, 'absolutely—' he broke off with the General's stride to the back of the kitchen. 'Out! How the bloody hell do you suggest we get her out? Got new legs for her, have you?' The General shot up to his former stature as he marched back to Arthur. 'Well do you know what I think? I think if anyone should be getting out it's you.'

Fine then, he would. Three nights of this had been enough. Harry was right about all of it – especially the blancmange. He'd go straight back to London – but then Gerald had squeezed his eyes and Arthur strained to see the General, seeing instead only a man struggling to fill the outlines that had been drawn, his head sinking, thumbs pressing into his palms. He cleared his throat, rubbed his forehead, 'Arthur?'

'Yes.'

'Stay a little longer, would you?'

*

It might not have been a Thursday but when the bells chimed the half hour both Arthur and the young man listened for the voice that would not call out that it was time to go. It was time nevertheless: the young man would have to get back to Llanvanor, Arthur to the Holloway Road – the Holloway Road where the room would gape and the doll would scold. The young man was first to the gate – but then he had no cause to delay: his briefcase didn't require explanation, there were no half-closing eyes to avoid catching – those eyes were in Maldon, following a path all the way back to that other little Arthur –

*Sssh Gerald is sleeping, the boys are sleeping –*

Her handful of buds, going to dig and dig –

*No, Ma –*

In Maldon those eyes.

Arthur followed the young man down towards the station. It wasn't just dread of the Holloway Road that prompted him – he couldn't go back before he'd seen Harry. Not since they'd sat in the park together, two brave, soon to be blue and shivering soldiers, waiting for Sylvie, had Arthur felt uneven without Harry beside him. They hadn't ever matched up – they couldn't and never would, but he had to see Harry all the same because matched up or not, it was only Harry who understood that the true meaning of hell was blancmange.

*

If it had been the Holloway Road, the sight of Lydia would have fished out the mix of floating limbs and bobbing head, never to float up that canal again. But, standing there, in Sylvie's clothes, finding just the right face and just the right tone, giving him the gentlest of kisses and this smile that didn't spill from a red heart of a mouth but slipped up quietly through uncoloured cheeks, saying how nice it was for her Arthur to pop by, this Lydia could not be assimilated – so on they floated, the limbs and the head, the hat and the dress –

This all too strange all too familiar Lydia going down the hall until, stopping to tell Harry not to pick or he'd spoil his dinner, both strangeness and familiarity were lost. Nothing like Lydia, nothing like Sylvie, just an insipid tea-time show with unconvincing but recognisable characters. It was from a distance that Arthur knew them all best, far enough away to keep them clear cut. Proximity multiplied them – each of them revealed as an unintelligible configuration that rendered them invisible. And yet it wasn't just from that distance that he knew them best, but that they were best – at least his Lydia was, his Lydia who could only be his when he saw her from wherever that there was, not when she was settling onto the sofa in the front room, not twirling brown curls, keeping the limbs and the head, the hat and the dress –

Arthur checked Harry – washed, fed, but more or less the Harry he'd left a week before. 'What's she doing in Ma's clothes?' Arthur spoke as though Lydia couldn't hear him and she assisted him by not turning round.

Harry answered Arthur by asking what he was doing in their father's suit and wandered into the kitchen. The table had been dressed with the contents of the case that never did go back: Mr and Mrs Simons, in their plastic covers, were each folded over a chair, the tablecloth, the plastic fruit – only the dried lilacs showed symptoms of new life –

'She came with those, said they were for Ma – fancy bringing a bunch of dead flowers.'

'Dried! Dried!' Arthur, defeated by the uncontainable, pulled the vase off the table.

'What are you, some horticulturist now? Careful with that, your girl is very fond of them, said they make her feel more at home.'

'For Christ's sake, Harry!'

'What?' Harry dipped his finger into a bowl of blancmange. 'Your girl asked me what Ma liked so—'

'Ma hates blancmange. I hate blancmange. *You*—'

'Can't stand the stuff.'

'Said you'd never be able to look at it again.'

'Alright Arthur, don't get y'knick-knacks in a twist.'

'And anyway she's not *my* girl.'

'She certainly seems to think she is.'

'She probably told you she was Mrs Simons too.'

'Mrs who?'

'Never mind – just get rid of the blancmange and I'll get rid of –'

*Daddy wants, Daddy wants, Daddy wants to get rid of us –*

*Wanted to throw me in the canal so he chucked the cat in instead!*

No, he didn't want to get rid of her – how could she have said that?

*Milly, that's what she would have been called –*

'Leave her, Arthur,' Harry said, 'she's been upset.'

*I'm not trouble – you do believe me, don't you, Arthur? –*

She'd been upset! How dare he – Harry the gentleman, Noble Honourable Harry –

'She wasn't in a good way when she got here,' Harry went on. 'Kept thinking she was going to sort of cry or something, hadn't slept for she didn't know how long, she said, asked if she couldn't wait a bit for you – told her you didn't live here, of course, but she just said she knew perfectly well where you lived.' Harry tipped the blancmange into the sink, keeping his back to Arthur to facilitate the remainder of the story: Lydia had arrived the day before yesterday, out of her mind about where Arthur was since he'd left without saying goodbye and out of her head since she hadn't slept and wasn't there somewhere she could lie down and that no she wouldn't sleep in the front room or the spare room or the boys' room – is that where their Ma had told them stories? – what stories Lydia meant Harry hadn't a clue since his Ma had never told him a story his whole life – she really did look like she was going to cry then and asked if she could see Ma's room – couldn't she sleep in there? It was such a lovely room! She'd sat on the bed then and said – you'll love this, Goldilocks – that it was just right – so I told her it wasn't baby bear's bed – get it? – Anyway next morning I come down and she's in Ma's clothes and I don't like to say too much because at least she doesn't look like she's going to cry and wants to make something special for Ma for when she gets home –'

Harry turned back round to Arthur, 'She's not coming back, is she?'

'Dad wanted the two of us up there, thought it might help, all go out for knickerbocker glories like we used to.'

'We never went out for – at least you and Ma never did – I had to sit there with Dad glaring right over me, timing me, every spoonful on my conduct sheet—'

'Oh come off it Harry.'

'He did – anyway I hate knickerbocker glories – more than blancmange.'

'Arthur.' Lydia was just inside the kitchen, face blotching, neck blotching – but no she was not, was not –

'Please don't, Lydia.'

'Not—' Her face settled, open eyes landing neatly and surely on Arthur. 'I'd like to go home now.'

Arthur stopped to check the pot meant for the spare key – Sylvie's last handful had been replenished. He knew the Holloway Road wasn't what Lydia meant by home but it was the closest he could get. They'd left the contents of the case that never did go back at Llanvanor – in case your Ma – she'd like all this, don't you think? Something for her to come back to – if you'd let me come with you I could have given it all to her myself, then she'd like me, then she'd help me –

Lydia, please, you don't –

Why couldn't she have come? Hadn't she said she'd make her all better? Hadn't she? And what did he mean about her legs not working? Well what did that matter? Lydia would help her, of course she would – she would help Sylvie and Sylvie would help Lydia and with a last handful they'd go – go together, a handful, yes, she'd take her to the park, scatter the buds, take Sylvie back – back to that other little Arthur, her Arthur –

Oh stop it – would she just stop! She knew there was no such –

Big enough and strong enough now, must be – dig and dig, they'd go –

No such –

Oh no, she wasn't, not, please not, don't –

But she wasn't. She was adding colour to another face that would also be just right, spilling a smile, twirling a curl, 'you know what, Arthur, when she's dead you might be just a little sorry you didn't take me. I would have made her better.'

*

Keith gave his chest its obligatory thwack. Arthur was grateful not only for Keith's sense of a need for continuity but also for interrupting the hiatus that had been extending since the caretaker had wondered for to where did Arthur go, for so to miss. What Arthur was considerably less grateful for, however, was Keith's wordless initiation of a conspiracy theory, speculating on Arthur's former absence and present silence, by way of throat clearing, coughs and pantomime nods. Lydia's unchanging face had already been cast but the caretaker's was hidden, bent over a piece of paper that had been tucked into his pocket dictionary. He rubbed out a line and looked up at Arthur before picking up a pencil, nodding as he muttered, 'but he is here, he is safe. Back safe, home safe.' He laid the pencil down, folded the piece of paper and tucked it back into the dictionary.

'We all thought,' Keith said, turning to face Arthur, 'you'd done a bunk.'

'A bun-kah?' the caretaker asked, eyes moving from Keith to Arthur.

'A bunk, a runner – pass over that dictionary of yours.'

'Escaped,' Lydia said blandly, eyes on the bubbling pot which was beginning to rock and sputter on the stove. 'I think you should turn that off.'

The caretaker bumped and scurried to the pot's rescue, a glance back at Keith dropping the dictionary. Arthur picked it up, focusing his eyes on the alien script which made no more sense to Arthur than the English that supposedly translated it. Escaped. Why hadn't he? Why hadn't he just *done a bunk*? But then where would he have done this bunk to? He didn't even have his park bench anymore now that that equally unnecessary young man had hijacked it.

'All better,' the caretaker assured the settled pot, opening then closing the cupboard. 'But to wait.'

'Oh go on, Professor, before I keel over,' Keith was patting his growing belly, eyes inclined towards Lydia.

Arthur might need to give this bunk more consideration. He had to get hold of Harry first. He couldn't do any sort of bunk without tidying things up and tidying up meant getting back to Maldon – the pre-bunk bunk. Even blancmange wasn't so awful if there was someone else there who knew just how bloody awful it was. And that someone was Harry.

A bowlful of something unidentifiable had been placed in front of Arthur; he poured a spoonful, greenish brown, from a height back into the bowl. Keith remembered his chest and spluttered a mouthful. Arthur consented to a sip. At least it wasn't blancmange. At least between Keith's chest and dinner his eyes might perhaps be a little less inclined towards Lydia who was taking silent methodical spoonfuls. Arthur, to the caretaker's approval, adopted her method, finding comfort in the efficiency of repetition if not the spoonfuls themselves. Keith puffed his cheeks and stared into his empty bowl, prompting the caretaker to refill it. Keith pronounced the end of this second helping not only by slapping his own belly, but slapping Arthur's too. Arthur's cheeks and hands began to prickle. The caretaker caught his eye, turning his palms up as he shrugged and gave the nod that said he understood. Arthur pulled in his lips, returned the nod, let a breath go.

'It's alright, Professor, our man Arthur is recovering from the trip,' Keith said. 'Our Lydia was besides herself.'

*Our* Arthur? *Our* Lydia? No one's Arthur glanced at no one's Lydia as she got up, put her bowl in the sink and went to the trunk. Her eyes sought verification from the caretaker. He nodded, his hand opening lightly towards the trunk. Lydia kneeled down and took each item out of the trunk with the same silent efficiency with which she had taken her spoonfuls. Arthur waited for exclamations to explode into showers of laughing bubbles, but one by one each item, unremarked, was removed, handled as though they were as fragile and precious as unhatched eggs. There was assurance in the quietness, in the concentrated detachment, a procedure she knew, one observed by and shared with the caretaker who supervised without looking, apparently washing the pot, the bowls – it was only when she reached for the papers that the spell was broken: the caretaker hadn't taken his eyes off her.

'Please to leave – all times I say to leave papers.'

Lydia put them back in the trunk and, reluctant but obedient, closed it, sitting legs out in front of her, squeezing the clown's nose.

'One day you'll tell us,' she said to the nose while the caretaker dried the pot. 'Jack's got a story but he won't tell.'

Keith motioned a crooked finger, leaning Arthur towards him. 'I just want you to know,' he said, tone as low as he could manage, putting a hand on Arthur's shoulder, eyes again inclining where Arthur would really rather they didn't, 'that there was absolutely no exchange whatsoever of bodily fluids in your absence.'

'Oh shut up Keith,' Lydia said, throwing the clown's nose towards the table. The nose bounced off a leg.

'What? What did I say?' Keith was seeking the caretaker's defence, but the caretaker was confining his attention to the closed trunk.

'Keith,' Arthur said.

'Yes lad?'

'Please remove your hand from my shoulder.'

*

'So,' Keith begins, chest thwacked into compliance, 'this was when I was still with the wife and had all the purple on the monopoly, bit before our first came along, so right, how it goes is that I'm taking a breather in the gents from this do at the Dorchester and who should be organizing his flies but my man Shelley – honest to God I do a million double takes since truth be told I'm a bit bladdered but next thing I know he's saying he can tell I'm a poet and I say well truth be told I am – now alright, I know what you're thinking – hang on—'

Arthur was getting up, thanking the caretaker.

'You can't go,' Lydia said, throwing the clown's nose at Keith, 'not until Jack's told us.'

'And word of honour,' Keith said, placing the clown's nose on the table, 'my man Shelley asks me, a Poet, if I wouldn't mind glancing over—'

'Night all,' Arthur said.

'Oh wait just a little Arthur, go on, Jack promised.'

'I promise nothing,' the caretaker said.

'But you did – you're as bad as Arthur – come on, I'll help you start,' Lydia said, getting up to sit Jack and Arthur down. 'Once upon a time, long long ago, in a far, far away land,' she checked the caretaker, 'all the best stories start like that.'

'Long and far but not the best, so sad to say not.'

'I'll bet it is,' Lydia said, eyes on the trunk, 'I don't see why you have to get all gloomy about it, all those pages – that tiny writing – just tell us what it says.'

'Not for saying. Not for telling.'

'Well I can't see what the point of a story is if it's not for telling, even Arthur knows that.'

Arthur clenched – she wouldn't would she – but she already was –

'No, no,' the caretaker had his hand over his ears, 'only Arthur is for telling Arthur's story.'

'But it's mine too,' Lydia said, 'he gave it to me. It doesn't matter, I don't want it anymore – I'm bored with that one – he can have it back.'

But Lydia only had the words and she couldn't give back what couldn't be given away. The story of that other little Arthur that Arthur never was and never could have been, etched into Sylvie who had told and told it until it was etched into Arthur, and now no amount of telling or not telling could rub that other little Arthur out.

*

Since the case that never did go back was still inside the last door of Llanvanor the only evidence of number sixty-three was the unburied doll. Lydia tucked the doll in between her and Arthur – the doll missed her twin, Lydia could tell – he must promise to get her – when would they get her? Promise he must or he'd make the poor little one cry –

'When she's big enough and strong enough,' Arthur said, clenching a hand that was about to smack his forehead, sigh escaping him as he rolled over. Lydia got up and put on the light. The absence of lilacs showed Arthur Sylvie's empty hand open and her puckered palm ask who had stolen her last handful.

'Well when will that be?' Lydia asked.

Wasn't one doll sufficient? Arthur counselled himself to keep hold of his hand and his sigh.

'Please, Arthur,' Lydia said, rocking the doll, 'she won't sleep, at least tell her – tell her tell her and then she'll—'

The puckered palm, empty, opening, closing –

Lydia flounced over towards the cupboard – she had something for them – but he must shut his eyes and not peek –

Lydia –

No peeking!

Arthur slid back down the bed and granted himself a full sigh for his obedience. The wall hadn't given away the caretaker's rustle or shuffle for a good couple of hours but, instead of that godawful moan that would have been a lullaby in Maldon, the rustling and shuffling had begun again. The moan was late and if it had one redeeming feature it was its reliability. What the hell was he doing in there? Not that Arthur could care less, the caretaker could do what he liked, in any case it was the wall that was to blame – why didn't they just knock it through and be done with it? The pretence was enough to –

No peeking!

A small peek declared the wall's innocence: Lydia was sitting by the open cupboard twisting up sheets of paper.

'What are you doing?'

'I said no peeking!'

Arthur glared at the wall: the moaning had begun.

'Well since you've spoiled the surprise you might as well help me,' Lydia said, her voice breezing through imitated annoyance, breezing over that godawful moan – it was agony, she'd practically said as much herself and now she couldn't hear it. 'Come on,' she said, handing him a sheet of paper. It was covered in the caretaker's tiny hand, the letters packed in tight as though the space might run out.

'Lydia, you can't—'

'You're such a bore, Arthur! Don't be a bore – he obviously doesn't want all this and if he gets in such a state about it I'm only helping,' Lydia twisted up another sheet and took out a box of matches – the flame saw a puckered palm and tramped Arthur's feet over the scrunched pages before they had even been lit, the black gold and blue at Llanvanor blazing under the cool lamp in the Holloway Road. When Arthur was quite sure the flameless blaze had been tramped out he looked up to see Lydia rocking the doll, telling it not to worry and, beside her, the caretaker blinking away incredulity. Scrunched, stamped and torn, the caretaker kneeled down to survey the pages under and around Arthur's feet.

'You do not like my story,' the caretaker concluded.

'Oh no,' Arthur stepped over the evidence to the contrary, a page caught underfoot. 'I like, of course I like—'

'You like nothing,' the caretaker said, picking up the bits of paper, 'how you like? You cannot understand – you do speak no Polish.'

'Not a word!' Ignorance made Arthur's defence: he didn't understand or speak a single word – neither liking nor not liking were a possibility.

'I do not understand too – not a word,' the caretaker's mouth tried to smile.

'Don't be silly,' Lydia said, tucking the doll back in, 'you wrote it, of course you know what it says.'

'It is saying nothing,' the caretaker told a crumpled scrap.

'Well not after Arthur went and made a mess of it.'

'Lydia!' A *mess*? He was trying to stop her before she burned the place down was what he was doing – if there was anyone who – but the caretaker, nodding, didn't want either protest or explanation, 'You are very good for helping – and so now to sleep.'

Lydia was watching Arthur as the caretaker left. 'Here,' she said, bending to tap Arthur's leg so she could salvage what was left under his feet, 'now that wasn't a very sensible thing to do was it? I only thought you should have a little fire, one for telling stories by, something to keep you warm when I'm gone.'

Lydia tucked herself in beside the tucked-in doll and waited for Arthur – but the black gold and blue blazed in front of him, the empty hand closed, hiding the puckered palm, careful not to crush what wasn't there. A sickly cub pawed Arthur's chest – please would he tell, tell and they'd sleep.

*December 1968*

Coming, Arthur, I'm coming – legs wouldn't work, why wouldn't they – out – had to get – sshh they're sleeping, the boys are sleeping, Gerald is sleeping – coming, Arthur, I'm coming –

*You can't go to London, Sylvie dear, London eats girls like you alive –*

Please don't worry, Cynthia –

*Aunt Cynthia –*

You've been so kind since Mother – but I'll write, of course I will –

*But Sylvie dear –*

Yes?

*I don't want to be alone –*

Coming, Arthur, I'm coming –

*Miss... Sylvia –*

Sylvie –

*What experience do you have –*

I don't have specific experience, Mrs Karnovski, but I cared for my late mother and these references from the shop I was working in –

Coming, I'm –

*Mad! Absolutely mad!*

Legs – had to make them –

*Don't you always take the boys to the park on a Thursday?*

Had to get them –

*No, for God's sake woman, if you don't get up from that damn gas heater I swear to God I'll –*

Get them to take her – coming, Arthur, I'm coming – Mrs Cohen's cat sees still, she knows, eyes twinkling, be light soon – coming, Arthur, I'm –

*You will write won't you Sylvie –*

Sure this isn't the London they tell you about –

*Give me just one night and I'll change all that –*

coming, Arthur –

*We all have our little spells –*

Mrs Cohen's cat follows to the end of the road –

*Arthur... well I think that's a lovely name!*

coming I'm –

*not dirty am I Ma?*

up the hill and over the gates, back behind the bandstand – safe in the ground my little one, just a little longer, soon be big enough, strong enough –

*Wonder what they did with Mrs Cohen –*

Cold, so cold – reach out into that molten sky – better the war had taken –

*Should count y'self –*

Lucky, yes:

*Sweet Thames bleed soft till I*

*Speak*

*Not*

*

Arthur and Harry agreed to remember the knickerbocker glories they'd never had, to remember as Gerald remembered, rearranging the picture until it matched the one Gerald had composed: all four of them on a Thursday with the long spoons. Once assimilated, preparing themselves for a supposed re-enactment required minimal effort – but there was no way to dull the Sylvie Arthur saw projected onto the scene: wheeled in and propped up, ice cream dribbling down her chin, head flopped as Gerald brought the long spoon up to her again, 'Now where's my Sylvie's smile?' Second thoughts about the whole enterprise were nourishing Arthur's sympathy for Aunt Cynthia – it would be too much for her, both Harry and Arthur arriving out of nowhere, she could hardly hold herself together when they'd come on their own, she'd be spilling out of her skin. It was oddly disappointing, then, when her pared-back body hiccupped a step back from the door as she opened it, squirrel hands under her chin. Rapid, timorous eyes alternated between Harry and Arthur, keeping time with little gasping smiles.

'Oh my angels,' she said, already scurrying down the hall. Arthur looked at Harry – one of them should have called first. Harry shook his head and doubled a bright step after Aunt Cynthia – they had come for knickerbocker glories; they would have knickerbocker glories.

'Where's Dad?'

Aunt Cynthia was humming a determined hum, setting glasses down, pouring each of them a brandy, topping her generosity up and, still humming, perched on her chair.

'I don't normally start before lunch,' Harry said, raising his glass and taking a gulp, 'but cheers.'

It might have been the hour or the empty stomach but just watching Harry swallow while Aunt Cynthia hummed gave Arthur the queasy afterthought without the warmth. Something crept down Arthur's forehead and hung over his eyes.

'I'll just get your father,' Aunt Cynthia seemed to have said but they were being ushered up the stairs, Aunt Cynthia behind them until they were standing at the door to Sylvie's room. That same something that had crept down Arthur's forehead kept him from seeing through to Sylvie, though he could make out her shape, and Gerald's at the window, standing there, tugging at the curtains. Aunt Cynthia had stopped humming and all Arthur could hear was the scrape along the curtain rail. Harry's hand was on his back and Arthur turned to look at him. Another shape but, being right beside him, less clear – his outlines were blurring, blurring Arthur with him, again there was nothing to know himself against – just a stillness that was too still. Arthur tried to make out Aunt Cynthia, he wanted her to start that humming of hers, or for Gerald to tug at the curtains again, to hear the scrape along the rail.

'Just give me a few more moments, would you, boys?' Arthur heard Gerald a little too late. Harry and Aunt Cynthia had already gone down the stairs – he was meant to have gone down, but here he was still in the room, feeling the absence of Harry's hand on his back, watching Gerald stroke Sylvie's puckered palm without looking at her.

'Already gone though hadn't you, my love,' Gerald said, looking up a little as he stroked her cheek, 'miss my Sylvie's smile.'

It was a couple of hours before Gerald came down and Harry changed places with him. Arthur followed Gerald into the kitchen and meant to say something or go over to him but just stood there, both willing and not willing Harry's steps back down.

*

Already gone. No different then from the last time Arthur had tried to catch half-closed eyes that wouldn't be caught – eyes he'd spent so many years trying to avoid. No, it wasn't any different, no marker, nothing – gone as she already had – except the possibility of her ever coming back had been taken too. Left to take a last handful. Left and now always be leaving, always be going up the hill and over the gates, not watching the Sylvie who had never stopped going, never stopped digging, but as that Sylvie, not only on a Thursday but every day –

*Back back back* –

To where she planted him.

*I'll come with you, Ma* –

And there that someone else's little someone went, going as he saw again on the inside of his eye what Sylvie had seen and never stopped seeing on the inside of hers.

Arthur touched her hand, it wasn't cold –

*I just get so cold*, she'd told him that evening after she'd reached her hand into that blazing blue and black and gold –

So cold – not now, death had warmed her hand and melted the legs iced rigid. Half-closed eyes shut but her mouth had fallen open, the scream that had been frozen two decades released to stop her heart at nine o'clock that morning.

'So strange,' Aunt Cynthia said, 'because she was always such a quiet one.'

Aunt Cynthia was behind him – how long had she been there? Arthur hadn't heard her come in. She sat down next to him. Her head was on his shoulder but he couldn't feel it, only the warmth of Sylvie's puckered palm as he traced it – it seemed any moment she might lift it and trace that reading down his cheek. Arthur brought the palm towards his face but stopped before the reading made by a puckered palm could tell and tell. No more telling.

'Always wanted little ones,' Aunt Cynthia said, lifting her head from Arthur's shoulder. She smoothed her hands along her skirt and when they stopped and her voice faded out she was almost as still and quiet as Sylvie. It was that *almost* that got Arthur up.

'You'll go down and see your father, will you?'

See his father yes. See Harry. See himself in their faces. Couldn't go down then – only to go into the room he'd slept in last time he was here – where that total darkness and silence swallowed you whole – no objection now, all starting to dim out a bit, yes getting dim, dull, heavy too – heavy legs wading through space –

'Go on, Arthur dear, your father wants to put some words together, say something nice for your mother.'

*Something nice*. Couldn't he?

There was an unformed density between his feet and the steps down. Harry's voice was becoming clear and Gerald's pace – yes, he could hear his father pacing and Harry speaking –

'Well how am I supposed to know?' Harry's voice was rising as Arthur came into the kitchen. Gerald's pacing had stopped. He screwed the paper into a ball.

'Arthur!' Gerald slapped a smile on. 'Good. Sit down.' He handed Arthur a pen and ripped out a fresh sheet of paper. Arthur looked at Gerald, at Harry – Harry was mumbling, letting his head fall down towards the table.

'I don't see why it even bloody matters,' Harry said. 'It's only us and Aunt Cynthia.'

'You don't see—' Gerald's words were forced out through a constricted whisper as though he was trying to protect Sylvie from hearing them. He snatched the pen and paper from Arthur – surely this was the General on his way back and sudden, magnified voice and stature would loom together. Anticipation pulled Arthur's back straight but Gerald was slumping into his chair – there wasn't room for soldiers at this table, good, little or otherwise: the General wasn't coming. All three of them sighed Gerald's sigh.

'Now I think,' Aunt Cynthia's voice was emerging, 'we're all just a bit upset, that's all. It's been a very long day and everyone's just—' A redness was budding round Aunt Cynthia's throat. She clasped her hand around it, pushing her high collar down. Her hand looked unnaturally white against it. The redness was flowering up her neck and flushing her face, china hands trying to cool it.

'Tired is what we are,' Gerald said and nodded from Aunt Cynthia to the door. Harry's grip was tightening round the pen, another sheet of paper in front of him.

'Leave it,' Gerald said. 'We'll just say what we'll say.'

'Of course you will,' Aunt Cynthia said. 'Say what you'll say, we'll get it all organised in the morning.'

'Why don't you go to bed, Cynthia?' Gerald's omission of her title role unfastened a just-stilled cheek.

'No no,' she said, 'no I couldn't.'

Gerald's eyes closed. 'Well I could,' he said, getting up, appearing to move through the same dense space Arthur had on his way down before. Aunt Cynthia was watching him, hum stop-starting.

'Had the prettiest smile,' Aunt Cynthia said, pausing Gerald at the door. 'Her mother's smile.'

'Was it?' Caught by Aunt Cynthia, Aunt Cynthia was now caught by Gerald. He wanted her to go on.

'Oh yes, and her eyes too.'

Staring, speckled eyes – Arthur saw what had played on the inside of those eyes, what would now never stop playing out on the inside of his own – Sylvie up the hill and over the gates –

'What colour were they?' Gerald didn't ask as though he was testing her but as though he'd never seen them.

'Blue-grey.'

They weren't. They were grey-green. They were, weren't they? So long trying to avoid catching – maybe –

'Yes,' Gerald said, absorbing the memory for himself. 'Blue-grey.'

No. No they weren't – Arthur would ask Harry later, they'd find a picture – or when they got back to Llanvanor – when had they last taken pictures? It didn't matter – Aunt Cynthia was photographing imagined albums full for them now: Gerald's Sylvie's smile, Aunt Cynthia's Sylvie's blue-grey eyes – a final Sylvie for them all to share. Gerald mightn't have been testing Aunt Cynthia but she smiled as though she had passed, Gerald taking the chair opposite her as a certificate. If Aunt Cynthia had passed then Arthur must have failed – grey-green her eyes – he looked at Harry but Harry was waiting with Gerald for Aunt Cynthia. They would wait while she stop-started her hum, while she found the next picture and inserted a caption beneath.

'I'll never forget the day you got married,' she said, creating as she spoke, her steady voice keeping the secret that, other than Gerald and his mother, Sylvie hadn't known a single other person at the wedding – rather peculiar, Gerald's mother had said, no family. Did the girl just drop from thin air?

'Yes…' Gerald was blinking off the distance, blinking away whatever might betray Aunt Cynthia's camera. 'We… you remember?'

'Well of course! How could I forget? My dear little Sylvie in the dress I made for her mother – oh she was so worried what with the clothes rationing what she'd have to make do with – Don't you worry about that, Sylvie dear, I told her, I've got just the thing.'

Gerald began to shake his head, he couldn't see her – couldn't see his Sylvie –

'You will,' Aunt Cynthia promised. 'Now we'll all have a good night's sleep and feel much more ourselves in the morning.'

Gerald was rubbing his eyes, still trying to see, was he?

'Blue-grey, yes,' he said.

'And there's to be no worrying about anything. You and the boys will stay as long as you like, there'll be no need to rush back after it all. Important to be together at a time like this.'

Gerald managed to glance Harry and Arthur over but they just matched his vague double blink.

'You boys don't mind sharing the spare room, I'm sure, unless one of you stayed in – no –' Aunt Cynthia tried a hum.

'They'll share alright,' Gerald said, 'they're used to that.'

'Arthur did move out a while back, Dad,' Harry said, drawing Aunt Cynthia's gaze over to Arthur.

'Move out? What for?' Aunt Cynthia reached a sympathetic splay of fingers towards Arthur, 'well I suppose you were always a wee bit of an outsider, weren't you.'

'No he wasn't,' Gerald's eyes cleared and struck Aunt Cynthia. 'Never.'

Hum-diddy-hum went Aunt Cynthia as Gerald gave his goodnight nods.

Aunt Cynthia waited until they heard Gerald's door close before she spoke. 'Oh your poor father,' she said, picking the sides of a nail, 'I don't know how he'll ever—' She gave a little gasp and picked at another nail. 'But I don't want you boys to worry about a thing, I'll take the very best care of him – of you all – yes, you'll all stay –

of course you will, there's no need to go off back to London. Oh if only she'd never gone to London – Sylvie dear, I told her, Sylvie you mustn't go – London eats girls like you alive – and look!' Aunt Cynthia's eyes fluttered for respite until they came to rest on her picked nails. 'Well at least she's home now – it's only right she should be buried close to her mother's grave. We must all get back to where we came from in the end.'

Arthur waded towards the door, already it was beginning to play out again on the inside of his eye:

*Coming, my little Arthur –*

Seeing her dig and tunnel and go – back back back –

*Coming, Ma, yes, I'm coming –*

Aunt Cynthia was telling Arthur to take an extra blanket out the cupboard, asking Harry what should they do, what should she, oh her dear Sylvie –

*Coming, Ma, I'm –*

Arthur went into Sylvie's room but Gerald was already in there, standing at the window again. The curtain had been pulled off the rail and draped over Sylvie. Arthur didn't like it – she couldn't breathe – *Ma,* he wanted to say, *Ma, it's me – Arthur.*

'Dad?'

'Not now, chum.'

It took Gerald a few moments to turn around. 'Well,' he said, folded arms falling as his eyes skimmed Sylvie's draped body. 'I suppose that's it then.'

*

'Oh you clever thing!' Aunt Cynthia said to Harry as he finished putting the curtains back on the rail. Arthur had just spent the best part of an hour battling with the curtains – if Harry had just given him another minute he would have done it himself, it wasn't his fault the curtains kept slipping and the rail kept moving and –

Aunt Cynthia had to drop the bundle of sheets she'd stripped from Sylvie's bed to admire Harry's work.

'Where's Dad?' Harry lost his sudden easy grin as he stepped down off the chair, drifting out of the room before he was given an answer.

'Your father's just gone to organise one or two things – big day tomorrow!' Aunt Cynthia's alacrity was dismantled by a delayed realisation of Harry's absence; her hum, trying to follow, caught and morphed into what sounded to Arthur like a low train. She stood at the end of the bed and, as she closed her eyes, began wafting her hands, soft but insistent, clearing something away, her hands describing mist or smoke, troubling invisible veils. Arthur disappeared into them until they were clapped away, the hypnotist's jolt waking Arthur to see they hadn't just been preparing the spare room before the first Christmas guests arrived.

'Cynthia,' Arthur began, 'Aunt Cynthia,' his eyes collecting the bundle of sheets, the stripped bed, the curtains – he could hear Aunt Cynthia saying yes dear, what dear, are you alright dear and himself saying nothing, no, fine, yes, eyes giving back all they had gathered – what had he wanted to ask? It had felt so clear, so urgent – since last night – sure Harry was awake too, though neither of them checked, no darkness or silence so total this time, another body in the same room weakened it just when it have might have stopped Arthur from seeing Sylvie's body breathless under the curtain – as though before he had seen that he could have stroked the palm that would tell him, or confirm for him, the sense released by a scream, two decades frozen, melting to stop her heart. Just listened to Harry's breathing then, watching Sylvie, watching himself beside her, listening, watching, wondering where Sylvie's breath was now, then Lydia's – hearing one of her laughing bubbles pop – hadn't thought of Lydia until then but her face wouldn't hold, not over Sylvie's, open mouth, falling slack, stuffed before it could scream again.

'At nine o'clock on the dot we heard her. Terrible – and it was your father's turn to open the advent calendar,' Aunt Cynthia was calmed by the solidity of detail that needed no wafting or clapping of hands. Why was she saying that – Arthur hadn't spoken – had he said something?

'I should think the whole of Maldon must have heard. Oh,' the wafting hand flapped in front of Aunt Cynthia's face. She sat down on the bare mattress and patted a space for Arthur to sit, remedying Arthur's immobility with a beckoning hand that took his as he sat.

'Dad heard, then?'

'But of course he did, dear, you'd have to be deaf not to – like nothing else, the shock of it, I wonder my blood isn't still running cold –'

*I just get so cold –*

'Cold, yes, she was always so cold.'

'My blood, dear – never mind – I don't want you distressing yourself.' Aunt Cynthia shook her head. Arthur wanted to get up, talk to Gerald but Aunt Cynthia had gripped his hand and Arthur tried to lean away as her other hand came to touch his face. 'No, don't distress yourself, dear, you mustn't, for your mother's sake and it will only be a day or two now before I can put you in touch – so to speak.'

Cotton was accumulating in Arthur's larynx, he needed to swallow, he couldn't swallow.

'It can be a great comfort, dear, having a last word.'

No. No last words. She'd be in the ground. Gone. That was it. Arthur pulled his hand away but, as he did, there went Sylvie, playing out again on the inside of his eye what had played out on the inside of

Sylvie's: up the hill and over the gates, back to where she planted him. Not there Ma, he's not –

'Of course,' Aunt Cynthia said, 'such a comfort it would be to her too – helps them settle once they pass over, you see – and it was you she asked for every day – my little Arthur –'

Arthur wanted to say no, that Sylvie hadn't meant – not him – never was and never could be –

'Oh such a pity you couldn't have stayed – oh you poor dear, you mustn't blame yourself,' Aunt Cynthia was smiling, the back of her hand believing its coolness on Arthur's cheeks and forehead was containing the uncontainable – well it might have been containing Aunt Cynthia but Arthur did not need containing – not least because there was nothing inside him to contain – nothing – how was that? Had to find Harry, register this nothing against him.

'It's not my usual procedure,' Aunt Cynthia said, folding the pinkness of her palms in her lap. 'I normally tend to wait until they've made the crossing so to speak – but I could make an exception – under the circumstances – I did for Sylvie with her own mother after all.'

'No thank you, I'm not really into that sort of—' Arthur flexed his hands out, pointed his toes up in his shoes – what was this? This heaviness – this *nothing*?

'Well if you change your mind. Now then,' she said, picking her face and voice up before they drooped, 'why don't you go and have a walk, put some colour back in your cheeks?'

Arthur stood outside the cottage. He had left the door on the latch and could hear Aunt Cynthia's hum approach and recede and steps now – Harry's? – the door off the latch and close and open close an empty puckered palm and open close the coffin empty –

*Out! Had to get –*

*No, Ma, not now, it's late, it's cold –*

*Had to get – coming, Arthur, I'm –*

*Yes, coming, Ma, I'm –*

Not her little Arthur, but someone else's little –

*Coming, I'm –*

Up the hill and over the gates –

*No more digging, he's not –*

She's not –

Coming.

*I would have made her better*, Lydia reminded Arthur – standing on the mat outside the cottage and there a laughing bubble popped – 'Shut up! Christ, for once would you just—'

'Thanks a bunch, Arthur, I only asked if you wanted to come for a walk.' Harry was buttoning his coat up.

'What?'

'Aunt Cynthia said I should get some colour in my cheeks – before the big day and that – you'd think we were going to a wedding.' Harry projected what he could of a weak laugh.

'Colour, right, yes.'

*

Just say what they'd say, Gerald reminded them before they went to the cemetery, folding his lines into a pocket-sized square and tucking it into his coat. Harry would be next to say what he'd say, then Arthur. Only once the coffin had been lowered and later the evening prayers left unread and Arthur was promising Aunt Cynthia that yes he'd take care and be alright on the way back to London and call as soon as he arrived did saying what they'd say mean not saying anything at all: Gerald never did take his pocket-sized square out of his coat so Harry never went next so Arthur stood there watching the gravediggers in their bright woolly hats. Aunt Cynthia's mittened hands had clung onto each other before they made the same mistake of reaching towards Gerald's, his bulked out in his sheepskin and the brim of his hat almost over his eyes, not moving until the shovelfuls of earth had covered the coffin lid. Harry took Aunt Cynthia's arm and she smiled the moist smile of relief, eyes fluttering with overcome gratitude and Arthur, trying to look at Harry but the glare making him squint, feeling a jolt through him as each shovelful of earth thudded onto the wood like rubble falling, the sound of catastrophic apathy.

Arthur had gone into Sylvie's room just before he left. Aunt Cynthia had made the bed up and put flowers on the side table. Flowers. They weren't meant to do flowers. And the mirrors, no one had covered the mirrors –

*What's a jewish, Ma? Are you a jewish –*

No and besides, here, where she came from, where she belonged, they did do flowers and didn't cover mirrors, just as they did stockings and advent calendars – where Gerald did all these things too, where his Sylvie, whose nice smile had never been found, did all these things. Flowers, not just buds, but folds of crinkly yellows and orange, flaming round inky hearts.

'It isn't right,' Aunt Cynthia said, 'going off at a time like this. Still, at least your father will have Harry here.'

'Cheerio then,' Gerald said, a flaccid hand attempting the General's salute. Arthur came towards Gerald then but Gerald backed away, nodding, the labour to smile inducing a frown. Harry's drained face showed Arthur what the nothing he'd been carrying about looked like until that nothing was slit with a grin that lurched across Harry's face and, with it, Harry's arm, lunging to give Arthur's shoulder a bit of a shake, 'Be in touch soon, eh Arthur?'

*

'London.'

*Up the hill –*

'Not returning, no.'

*And over the gates –*

'Look where you're going, young man!'

*Back back back*

'Sorry…'

*To where she planted him –*

A hot sharp pain twanged up Arthur's shin –

'I say, do look where you're—'

Something or someone had collided and sent Arthur back from the platform's edge. He bent to rub his leg – what time was it? Wouldn't get back to the Holloway Road till eleven. Arthur assumed, without any particular interest, that the room would gape. He couldn't picture it, though, with or without Lydia; it wouldn't register, neither one seemed preferable to the other. The image of the canal drew itself for him: the head bobbing, the mix of limbs, too dull to convince, sinking below the surface, huge fingered leaves spreading their width over the water – but all his focus could catch was Sylvie going up the hill and over the gates, the swarming black dots in front of his eyes a static, confusing the banality of repetition. The lights on the train windows blotted the reflections of the carriage bright, and juddering small over and through them went Sylvie, juddering small, juddering out, just the park, colourless except –

'I must have a window seat – I always have a window seat – thank you – you see I get dreadfully sick if I—'

The train sway-stop-lurched Arthur down the carriage as Sylvie's hands and face spotted black dug beneath the inside of Arthur's eye –

*No more digging, Ma, no more –*

Arthur's head fell against the window. He put his hand in his pocket, letting Sylvie dig and tunnel till he lost her again and the only thing his eyes could make any sense of was the collection of sweet wrappers on the empty seat next to him.

*

Almost midnight and, little by little, Arthur's usurped territory accreted: Lydia in his grubby robe and slippers at a table newly dressed in imitation of the contents of the case that had been left at Llanvanor, a clean square of carpet that must have been cut from a leftover roll, indicating what Arthur's carpet might have been before he moved in, had been laid down, providing the rug to remind Arthur of the stains it concealed, Lydia's shoes on it, pointing neatly towards the door. Old Mother Hubbard's cupboard was open, displaying abundance, her hand inside the caretaker's hat, the other hand spinning it round until it blurred, the doll that was for telling propped up on a small crate, helped to sit straight with the ribbons that had tied its cut plaits, bound in glossy pink to the back of the chair –

'Well what else was I supposed to do? She kept on falling forward,' Lydia was justifying the composition before Arthur had quite worked out where his eyes had managed to move to, looking through the colourless winter of a park that would neither be quite seen nor quite cancelled out, trying to consolidate what was in front him – the doll, the ribbons, the chair, the hat spinning on Lydia's hand –

Lydia –

She was putting the hat on the empty plate in front of the doll – just so it doesn't go cold, she explained to it, kissing the doll's nose.

Lydia – here – quite sure she –

*Daddy's home, Daddy's home,* she was singing to the doll, checking the ribbons that held it upright were secure.

'My mother died,' Arthur said, eyes on the doll. He hadn't meant to say it. But he hadn't meant not to either. Spoken or unspoken the words had as much or as little significance as the blank that followed.

Lydia looked at Arthur looking at the doll. 'She missed you,' Lydia said.

'My mother died,' Arthur tried the words again but the repetition was too precise, trying to hear what he'd said in Lydia's face, but her limp smile was only a variation of that immovable nothing Arthur had felt and found mirrored in Harry's face. Lydia put on the hat and took the empty plate away from the doll, untying it to rock her as the ribbons fell to the floor, 'Nanna's dead,' she told it, 'nanna's dead, never get to meet your nanna now, never say hello, only wanted to say hello, didn't we.'

Soothing the doll, Lydia drained any reality that might have been offered to him when the earth thudded to cover the coffin. He wanted to hear himself say it again, that she was dead. Gone. In the ground –

*Up the hill and over the gates –*

'Liar!' Lydia announced, throwing the doll down. Needles had pricked her eyes and cheeks. It wasn't just that Arthur couldn't summon an objection, but that knowing it wasn't a lie wasn't enough to make it feel true. The doll was face down, a saucer of milk by its head.

'For Milly,' Lydia said, taking the hat off to scrape untwirled brown curls into a bun. 'In case she comes back.'

Arthur's nose made several adjustments. Milly. The cat. Yes, the cat.

'Except,' Lydia said, pulling her bun out, 'except – oh, aren't I silly? I forgot – you chucked her in the canal.'

'Oh not all that again Lydia, please,' Arthur sighed his own sigh, picked the saucer up and poured the milk down the sink.

'Well what did you do that for? It was good milk.'

*

Arthur waited for the sound of Lydia's sleep to trip the quiet before he got into bed. There had been nothing through the wall. No rustle, no shuffle, no moan and Lydia's sleep too settled to dent the emptiness opening up again. As he sat up and set blind eyes on the wall he felt the sickly cub's paw on his back, insistent kneading asking him to lie back down. The paw pressed over his chest, clawing into the hollow beneath it, burrowing, burrowing – *I would have made her better, why wouldn't you let me make her better? All I wanted was to say hello to her, Arthur, just hello, just* –

He pulled the claw out of his chest. He couldn't lie there. Not with that. With her. Lydia – not his – what was she doing here? He was meant to have come back to a room that would gape – yes, a gaping room, no more Lydia, no more telling and no more digging – but here she was, digging her sickly cub paws into his chest, digging for all the telling there was to be told – well there wouldn't be any telling – there wouldn't because she was going – yes, that was it, at last – he'd Worked It All Out without any need for his bench – yes yes goodbye goodbye and gone for good – and if she wouldn't go – no – no, he did not want to get rid of her, of course he didn't – he just couldn't stand her being there – not anymore, not now –

*I would have made her better, why wouldn't you let me make her* –

*Up the hill* –

*All I wanted was to say hello* –

*And over the gates* –

*Just hello, Arthur* –

*Back back back –*

*Just –*

*To where she planted him –*

Arthur put the light on and opened the door.

'Arthur!' Lydia scrabbled to the end of the bed. 'You can't be going out, it's the middle of the night – you're not even dressed.'

'I'm not going out.'

'Well then shut the door and turn the light out – and get back into bed.'

The stairs mapped out directions up the hill and over the gates. He left the door open, rinsed his face and hands at the sink and put his hands on Lydia's coat over the chair. She was sitting up, watching him as he dusted her coat off and held it out – no, he couldn't, she couldn't – shaking her head, crawling towards him, wrapping herself round his leg – she was right, she knew, she'd said he wanted to get rid of her –

'I do not want to get rid of you, Lydia. I want you to leave.'

'You can't – I can't,' she said, trying to pull the coat off him but Arthur was holding onto her coat, holding it out for her and he would stand there holding it out for her until she –

'Thank you, Lydia –'

got up –

'That's it –'

and slipped her arms in. He came round in front of her to button it and picked up her hat –

'That! – What would I want that for? It's not even mine.'

'Fine, then, if you don't want to take the hat—'

Arthur's eyes fell to Lydia's bare feet, waiting for them to move.

'You can't get rid of me, Arthur – you haven't got anything without me – I haven't got anything without—'

'Now put your shoes on, Lydia.'

'Please Arthur – where will I go? I don't have anywhere to—' Lydia couldn't bring his face towards her. Arthur just kept his eyes on her feet – her shoes, she needs to put on her shoes – but bare feet were stepping away without them –

*Up the hill –*

Arthur closing his door, standing against it –

*And over the gates –*

Lydia's shoes on the rug neatly pointing towards him, telling him to grab them and chase after her before she went –

*Back back back –*

*You can't, he's not there – no more other little –*

Her shoes, she needed her shoes – somewhere to go she was going –

Wait Lydia, your shoes –

Bare feet on the Holloway Road –

Arthur's empty stomach lurched upward, sent him to the sink and shot a mouthful of bile into it. He watched the water run and run and put his head under the tap. It was the middle of the night in the middle of December and he had let her go without taking her shoes and there her shoes were on the rug, pointing neatly towards the door he should be opening to go after her, to tell her it was the middle of the night in the middle of December and he, Arthur the gentleman,

Noble and Honourable, could never allow her bare feet cut and cold on the Holloway Road going all the way *back back back* –

Couldn't see Sylvie at all now, only Lydia – Lydia who'd taken herself and gone, had taken Sylvie with her –

*You haven't got anything without* –

No, only that nothing.

Arthur wiped his mouth, picked the doll up off the floor and sat it on the crate. It kept falling forward.

'Sit up!'

Well if it wouldn't sit up like he'd told it he'd have to make it. Arthur wrapped the ribbons round the doll's arms and neck and threaded it through the back of the chair, tying bows as Lydia had.

'That's better now, isn't it?'

*

'Better to have loved and lost,' Keith began, sucking hard on a cigarette and rubbing his chest, pulling air in before he took another drag.

'Careful,' Arthur said, 'you're getting ash on the rug.'

'Your Lydia—'

'She's not my—'

'Wanted something that would blend.'

'Well it doesn't. The carpet's filthy.'

Keith remedied the situation by dropping a little more ash on the rug.

'It's not even a rug anyway,' Arthur said, 'it's a bit of bloody carpet.'

'Your Lydia—'

'Shut up, Keith.'

'Biting the hand, alright, I'm going,' he said, putting a foot up on the opposite knee. 'Hey Arthur,' he said, pointing his cigarette at the doll still bound to the chair. 'I'm not being funny, but what's that all about?'

Arthur rolled his eyes and blew a bull's exhalation through flared nostrils. The doll was the doll was the doll and didn't need explaining; if Keith wanted an explanation he could search London for a shoeless Lydia and ask her. Keith stubbed his cigarette out and took his Landlord's Survey of the room, opening cupboards, peeking under the table, bending to inspect the bed. He folded his arms.

'Do you mind,' Arthur said, bringing his rolling eyes back to suggest Keith's exit with a look at the door.

'Not at all.'

Arthur was not hoping for a reply.

'Not. At. All.' Keith sat back down. 'Time heals all.' He rolled and lit another cigarette and gave his chest a good thwack in preparation before he took a drag. Eyes on the wall began to bring out the rustle and shuffle – it was the first time Arthur had heard it since he'd come back.

'I might just stick my head round,' Keith said, attempting sotto voce, 'he's been a bit of a recluse. I think he might be in mourning.'

'For what? I'm the one whose mother has just—'

'Death comes to us all. I'll just go and see how our prof is bearing up. All that fiddling about with bits of paper, it can't be good for a man.'

Arthur's head fell forward, eyes brushing over the ash on the rug.

Lydia-not-his-Lydia walking shoeless; Sylvie, dead, in the ground, gone –

See the coffin lower, hear the thud of earth fall – but there was no way to clasp this finality: Sylvie, more alive than before she was buried, taking her last handful –

*Up the hill and –*

But the doll wasn't having any of it. Alright, alright. Arthur moved the table and chairs off the rug, picked up Lydia's shoes –

*I would have made her better –*

Shook the rug out –

*Why wouldn't you let me –*

'Because Lydia!' Arthur caught himself but already Keith and the professor – caretaker! He's the bloody – had opened his door. 'What?' He shook the rug at them, backing them way, both narrowing their eyes at the doll.

'She is OK?' the caretaker asked. It wasn't a trick question. Keith squeezed his chin, laughed the laugh of the wise – until an unperformed coughing fit troubled its smooth undulations.

'She,' Arthur explained, 'is not a she. *It* is a doll and of course *it* is fine.'

As they left Arthur untied the doll and sat it on the floor next to him, yes, she – it! For the love of God, *it* – was fine.

*

'Gerald speaking.'

'Oh Dad, hello, it's—'

'Arthur. Everything—'

'Fine. I was just calling to see if everything was—'

'Fine.'

'Good.'

'Yes. Well if that's all—'

'I could come back up – to Maldon – if you—'

'What for?'

'I don't know. Just. Aunt Cynthia said—'

'What did she say?'

'Nothing.'

'Have you spoken to her?'

'No.'

'Arthur…'

'No.' He hadn't. Oh God, he should never have called. This was awful. Arthur put another coin in the slot. 'I haven't, Dad. Not since I left – should I come back? For Christmas—'

'We don't do Christmas, Arthur.'

No. No, of course they didn't do Christmas.

'Arthur…'

'Yes?'

'You are looking after yourself, chum?'

'Yes.'

'Not anything you need?'

'No.'

'Because if there's anything...' Gerald's voice was beginning to atrophy. 'And get some decent food down yourself, we were already starting to miss you if you turned sideways as it was. No one loses their appetite in this family – except my old man – so unless you want to end up—'

'I'm OK, really—'

'Why don't you come up to the cottage for Christmas?'

'But we don't do—'

'Up to you, old boy – hang on a sec – Arthur, are you still there?'

'Yes.'

'Good – hang on a – what's that?'

'What's what—'

'Not you, Arthur, I'm talking to your Aunt Cynthia – what? Alright I'll ask him, we were just on the subject – Arthur, you still—?'

'Yes, Dad.'

'Right. We're having a vote on the stuffing: sage and onion or chestnut.'

'What's the difference?'

'Chestnut then, good man.'

*

Already dark in the middle of the afternoon, having to stop to hitch up his trousers as he lugged the Christmas tree down Llanvanor, Arthur was beginning to feel chestnut stuffing in Maldon was a profoundly good idea – either that or he should have admitted defeat before he left the Holloway Road and let the caretaker put an extra hole in his belt. Arthur stopped again, dropped the tree, hitched up his trousers and wondered how long it would be before he made it with the tree inside the last door of Llanvanor – maybe he should just leave the damn thing in the middle of the street, cut his losses and get on the next train to Maldon – no, he was giving Llanvanor its first proper Christmas – what were those carols he'd sung with Sylvie and Harry outside the Tube those few years back then? – he must remember at least one of them – the tree was part of the same secret – no secret now – the General was gone and the Gerald in Maldon was probably humming along to Aunt Cynthia's hum, Harry too, all of them humming Silent Night or whatever – *Silent Night, Holy Night, All is* – all is what? What was it all? Bloody ridiculous is what it was – oh Lord, what was he doing? He was about to lose an arm along with his trousers, all for the sake of a tree – and what about all the paraphernalia that was meant to go with it? Arthur could get all that tomorrow, tinsel and an angel or something, some of those shiny balls – baubles – baubles? Who would come up with a word like that? Whoever came up with Christmas, that's who – still, Sylvie would have liked all that, she'd have made sure they'd had baubles and tinsel if they'd done Christmas properly.

Next door had been hidden under a fur hat but he had seen Arthur and marked his broken journey down to the bottom of Llanvanor – next door had to say, if Arthur didn't mind him saying –

Well actually –

That Arthur would have been better off asking his father to cut down that tree – he was going to have to do something about it, away on business or not – he couldn't still be away on business, could he? And Harry too, it must be months – next door didn't like to pry but was everything –

'Fine, thank you, yes.'

'Just you then – on your tod?'

'Yes.'

'Ah…' Next door was studying Arthur's face and the tree to work out the sum. A downward glance was more rewarding – were they new laces? Mind they were good and tight this time – next door bent to check and Arthur bent with him, losing his trousers as he tried to save his laces from unnecessary interference. Arthur rescued his trousers, leaving next door, smiling, to interfere without interference – that was better, next door approved, he was pleased to see the whole family hadn't deserted, first his mother, not seeing her, such a shame when every day he had seen her bringing the boys back from the park – could set your clock by it, my late wife used to say –

'No,' Arthur said. 'Only on a Thursday.'

'Every day – you remember my wife – Lucille – now look, I'm only next door so—'

'Thank you.' Next door, yes. Where next door belonged.

'If you want to pop your head round – maybe you could look into getting something done about that tree yourself unless you think your father might – time of year doesn't help – we're not getting any light at all – do you know today is the shortest day?'

No. No he didn't. All Arthur knew was that he was getting this Christmas tree inside and that tomorrow he was getting tinsel and baubles and that he was going to give Llanvanor its first proper Christmas.

*

The kitchen at Llanvanor was furnished just as it had been when Arthur first came back from Maldon – only that all too strange all too familiar Lydia was missing: Lydia dressed as Sylvie, making herself at home with a fresh bunch of dead lilacs – dried! – *dried* lilacs. At least there was no doll that wouldn't sit up straight, ribbon-bound to a chair. The case must be somewhere too – and the doll that was for planting out – he'd pack it all up tomorrow, take it all back to number sixty-three once and for all before it reprimanded him for letting his Lydia leave shoeless –

*The hat and the dress, the limbs and the head –*

Absurd! The hat and the dress couldn't possibly be floating up the canal – the dress was here – and the hat – well, that was still by the door to his room – his? What for? He didn't need to go back and deal with a ribbon-bound doll and frankly, one bunch of lilacs, dead or dried, was more than any man, gentle or not, Noble and Honourable or not, should have to contend with – Tear up the contract – contract? What contract? He was answerable to no one! – yes, cut his losses and run to one of the four corners of the earth – he might have let Keith know, or said something to the caretaker – what for? For a lot of questions he'd taken the room to avoid in the first place – they'd work it out for themselves and Arthur would, not before time, no longer be clocked or watched, questioned or unquestioned – not that he planned on staying at Llanvanor – he'd come back to give it its first decent Christmas and after that he was gone – all there was to it – certainly not up to Maldon – what the hell would he do with himself in Maldon besides eating chestnut stuffing till he no longer needed that extra hole in his belt with a Gerald that did Christmas and knickerbocker glories and Aunt Cynthia communing with the dead and being seasonally thankful that at least they were all together at a time like this – a time like what? – as though the tragedy had just suddenly befallen them, as though Sylvie hadn't been dead for months, years, and had never been more alive now that she'd been buried, as though she wasn't still going up the hill and over the gates – yes, there she went and there went Lydia-not-his-Lydia, in pieces, floating up the canal – how many sandwiches short was the Old Bear? – Perhaps fleeing the country altogether was the best bet – he might even change his name – but he was doing Christmas at Llanvanor first… Oh, why had he not just kept his eyes on course and taken the tree straight into the front room? If he had he wouldn't be being assaulted by the double bluff of the contents of the case that should have been back at number sixty-three months ago and a hatless, shoeless Lydia wouldn't be coming apart, floating, drifting, his-not-his-no-one's Lydia in pieces and the surface of the canal wouldn't be glittering glittering – but there Sylvie would be as she always had been, going up the hill and over –

*Not there, Ma, not –*

Arthur went upstairs into Gerald and Sylvie's room. Lydia had left the clothes she'd worn as Sylvie folded at the end of the bed. Arthur hadn't been in here since he'd come up with that tea for her before he'd moved out; Lydia was still just that woman with the twins then, just a voice calling out that it was time to go. He'd come up and Sylvie had smiled her broken-toothed smile, *not my Arthur*, she'd said. Didn't say anything about her last handful of buds though. Arthur wanted to open the cupboard, the drawers, find Sylvie in something – only her hairbrush on the side table – Lydia's hair in it – he pulled it out and meant to drop it into the wastepaper basket but it fell on the floor: she was everywhere Sylvie was meant to be – and he'd been everywhere that other little Arthur should have been – couldn't get rid of himself and couldn't get rid of Lydia. She had kept saying he wanted to get rid of her – why, when he had never – well he couldn't even if he had wanted to – even the pot by the front door had a last handful Lydia had left there in case Sylvie came back – he might not be able to get rid of Lydia but he could get rid of the buds – he'd take that last handful, for Sylvie, for that other little Arthur – dig him up to dig Sylvie up –

Too late to go now – didn't stop the Sylvie who had never and would never stop going – up the hill and over the gates then, the closed park to himself – just him, Sylvie and that other little Arthur.

The woman who had moved into Mrs Cohen's old house was coming out, the cat that was nothing like the tabby following her up to the gate. Was she staring at him or was he staring at her? She was going up the road now but Arthur already felt as though he'd been caught, holding the guilt of buds almost crushed. He turned inside and put the buds back in the pot. He'd take them tomorrow, pack up the case too, take it to number sixty-three – Mrs Simons or no Mrs Simons, leave it outside if he had to – yes, the buds and the case and then all that was left to get rid of was Christmas.

*

Arthur deposited himself in the front room with the cornered, undecorated tree until the morning of Christmas Eve when, flooded with the honour and nobility that could only be the result of sleepless dreams (and latterly an extra hole in his belt), he lunged for the case and its contents, thrust them at the nearest charity shop and, pop-eyed with insomniac goodwill, fled before the genderless Santa at the till discovered the inexplicable miscellany donated (the blouse and skirt Lydia had worn as Sylvie a last minute extra dash of Christmas spirit). What did number sixty-three need a Mr and Mrs Simons and one half of a set of twin dolls for? This was not – or was no longer – Arthur's concern. He positively *bounded* along the Finchley Road – there was no need to hitch his trousers up – not once! – He was even starting to feel a bit peckish – just get rid of the buds and Christmas and he might just have to pop back to Maldon to help them out with the stuffing –

Midday made Arthur a perfect innocent through the open gates to the park. Families and couples and clusters unfolded as he walked towards the bandstand. Every bench was taken – no matter – he wasn't here for his bench, he was here to get rid of –

'Arthur, hello, hello.'

Arthur caught himself just before he tripped, blinking at his feet before he could look up. His name was being called out again and a flapping hand was coming towards him, landing on his shoulder. Subaqueous half-moons appeared: the caretaker. No, no, this was not right, things were not in their place, they were not –

'Lydia say you always come here.'

'No I don't. Never.'

'We are missing you – here to sit.'

They were standing at Arthur's bench which had been regrettably vacated. Where was that unnecessary young man with a briefcase and crusts at his feet to fill it? Or this delightful couple – would they not benefit from –

The caretaker was smiling that benign smile of his, waiting for him to sit – but Arthur had left the Holloway Road never to return – surely he was exempt from this unbearable benevolence.

'Lydia tells me this,' the caretaker said, palm spread on the waiting spot of bench beside him. Tells? Tells him what? – Told!

'Told!'

'Ah yes, told,' the inevitably benign smile accompanied the inevitable retrieval of a paper-wrapped parcel. He set it on his lap and divided it, looking up to nod in the direction of the bandstand. 'And this too she tells – told – forgive – this she told.'

Had she now? Told, yes, just as he had told. A woman walking towards it, disappearing behind it, detailing a picture of two brave soon to be blue soldiers. Buds. Gone to scatter her last – Arthur's handful had been forgotten inside a pocketed fist. He drew the fist out, not opening it yet –

'What is here?' The caretaker was not referring to Arthur's fist, which shot behind his back, but to the inevitable half of a pickle sandwich.

'Nothing.' Arthur's fist uncurled behind his back, dropping the emptiness of a stolen handful.

'It is too good to see—'

Arthur brought his hand round, watching it open and curl tight again. He looked up, eyes searching until he felt the caretaker's hand on his arm, the caretaker's little nod catching on the periphery of his vision.

'Now look, Jack—'

'Jack?'

'Yes,' Arthur began but his eyes were searching again, pulled back towards the bandstand –

'You never call me Jack,' the caretaker said, a thoughtful mouthful bringing Arthur's eyes back –

'Well it's your name, isn't it? Professor, then, whatever you like—'

'I like Jack for so long as I am called – it is not my true name but I am if you say.'

Arthur looked at him for a moment, held by the caretaker's unfaltering eyes, clearer than Arthur had seen them before.

'And Arthur is your true name?'

'What? Well of course it—'

The woman came back from behind the bandstand and went towards the gates – but it wasn't a Thursday –

*Not there – he's not – her little Arthur not –*

'My true name, yes.'

'True Arthur.'

Arthur sat and began working on his half of the sandwich; voided of sensation it was a simple if mechanical endeavour. The caretaker was offering his benign smile to anyone who walked by. The final swallow was the only challenge. Several gulps trapped a balloon in Arthur's stomach. Must the caretaker smile that smile at *everybody*? It made him feel a little cheated.

'I am too glad to see you,' the caretaker said. 'Too glad – only I hope also to see Lydia.'

*The limbs and the head –*

Well the caretaker – Jack – wouldn't be seeing Lydia, no one would be seeing –

*Floating, drifting –*

Anyone. Gone with no more chance of coming back than Sylvie –

*Up the hill and over the gates –*

Sylvie who would always be coming back –

*Back back back –*

'You must miss her,' half-moons flickering as the caretaker gave up trying to set his gaze.

*Back to where she planted him.*

## *March 1969*

Three months since Christmas and Arthur was still finding bits of shattered baubles and pine needles in the front room. The armchairs had been disguised with quilts and the absence of the obligatory bowl of nuts concealed with old unread newspapers; little by little, Llanvanor was being buried. Arthur settled into one of the armchairs, no longer an imposter but a lodger in a stranger's house – only the walls seemed the same. He thought he'd have been out by the New Year – but this was hardly Llanvanor anymore and he couldn't leave what no longer appeared to be there. If he wanted to leave Llanvanor he'd have to dig it up – and digging was something Arthur was no longer prepared to do; graves have their purpose, even ones fashioned from a quilt and old papers. No chuckles, no half-closed eyes –

*Ma?*

Certain he'd never stop seeing her eyes, but they'd disappeared behind the bandstand along with her image that afternoon in the park. Surely they'd catch him up then, once he was out the gates or reached the corner of Llanvanor –

*Ma, I'm here, it's me, Arthur –*

He'd looked up from the bottom of the stairs to where those eyes might have been, catching his only as he turned. They'd pretended to light just then, drawing him back round to see them flicker out.

*Let me alone now, Arthur, let me be.*

When had he last seen her and held her eyes? Hers, not the ones in Maldon, staring, not the ones at the top of the stairs, half-closed, but grey-green, open, Sylvie's eyes. He'd wanted that ground she'd been laid in to keep those eyes away, for that earth to hold her down – until he felt that it had. Grey-green those eyes. He could see the colours apart but not speckled the way they were. Knew they were but couldn't see it. She'd begun to flit round the edges of his dreams though, just the last few nights, but there was no Sylvie by day. He could have stayed there in those dreams, where he could hold Sylvie's eyes and she his.

He hadn't been back into her room since before Christmas, but she'd opened the door in one of last night's dreams and called out for him. He couldn't get to her though, couldn't get up the stairs, his legs jointless now –

*Arthur, Arthur is that you?*

Just see her eyes in his mind, opening, grey-green, Sylvie's eyes, steadier than they had ever been when she was alive. Sure she'd be there when he got to the door –

*Yes Ma, it's me.*

But the door was closed, just as he had left it.

He closed his eyes to find hers again, waiting before he went and sat on her side of the bed, checking he hadn't lost her, the sense of her too fragile. He pushed his hands down into the mattress, anything to counter it, useless pressure to make a mark where she couldn't. It was only when he opened the cupboard and took out a box that he felt her eyes on him again. She watched him as he laid out her belongings with a collector's care: a bag of baby clothes, moth-eaten, two of the elves from Aunt Cynthia, notebooks with shopping lists and sums, the gaps between the dates growing, shopping lists replaced with the stops on all the different train lines, a time at each destination, the writing growing smaller, fainter, words breaking off, illegible, *no pills after Thursday, Friday last pills, Saturday — Gerald — Sun — ask Mrs — my little — tell but no — Tuesday last time — leave on — 426 pack all — buds…*

There were letters from Gerald too. He began to read one, stopped, folded it up and put it back. That was Gerald's Sylvie – how long before he and Harry had been born? Only saw it now, how far apart in the world he and Harry had begun, the sheer distance of it. Arthur picked up the letter from Gerald again. A Sylvie new to London – a Sylvie with grey-green eyes – Gerald had seen them, he'd seen those eyes –

*... Let me show you London. My London. The London...*

A flash then, pity lost under rage – Gerald had known a Sylvie that Arthur never could. He tried to hold Sylvie's eyes again in his mind but, closing again, they slipped. He looked over everything he'd found and felt Sylvie recede still further – was this what was left of her? Remnants that couldn't give her back. A hand fell on a notebook then – Harry's hand. Arthur wasn't sure it was there, it belonged in Maldon, part of a life he was irreparably dislocated from, the hand was just another object until it picked the notebook up.

'Happy birthday, old boy,' Harry said, inhaling a smile.

'When did you get here?'

'Few minutes ago. Here,' Harry said, taking a card from inside his jacket, 'from Aunt Cynthia. I got away just in time, she was threatening blancmange. Quarter of a century, Christ!'

Arthur dropped the card on the bed without opening it. 'You alright?'

'I don't know,' Harry said and then broke out into a short-lived laugh. 'Sorry, just that's all I've heard any of us say since you buggered off – *I don't know* – even Cynthia can't stretch beyond that. I came back just to see if I could string a sentence together.'

'You seem to be doing alright.'

'Thanks, chum.' Harry's eyes skated over the bed, 'You've made a start on Ma's things, then – thought I should get it all cleared out before Dad gets back.'

'Is he coming?'

'He hasn't said, just Aunt Cynthia reckoned I should.'

'Let's leave it for a bit, Harry.'

They started tidying it away without consulting each other, forensic eyes and fingers, detached, up-close, the weight of that same *nothing* falling.

'Harry?'

'Yes, chum.'

He'd had something to say but he'd caught Sylvie's eyes – or had she caught his? Couldn't speak yet, enough to hear Harry's voice, mumbling again that he didn't know, taking some of the weight of that *nothing*. He felt the stricture in his throat abate, tried again.

'Come up to the park for a bit?'

'Yeah alright, chum, alright.'

*

Next Door was outside, telling Harry what a fine young gentleman he'd become. And was he keeping himself busy? Next Door asked, because a gentleman must keep himself busy in times of trouble. That's what the doctor ordered. If the office was quiet he would happily take on an assistant for his new project, had Arthur told him about his new project –

'No, not yet,' Harry's old chuckle did its best, cut short as he elbowed Arthur.

'I'm getting Arthur on board, a fine archivist.'

'I'm sure,' Harry grinned admirably, tugging Arthur away, telling Next Door he didn't want for occupation.

'Dad's asked me to look into putting the house on the market,' Harry said once they'd passed the corner. 'Probably sell the business too.'

The house. The business. Shells. That was all. Take the people outside the place and it didn't seem to exist anymore, became something else. Arthur forgot for a moment that Llanvanor was no longer there, being outside filled it with chuckles and half-closed eyes again. Couldn't see another family in their rooms, inside their walls, someone else at the top of the stairs; it was either theirs or no one's. Arthur stepped out into the road and a pair of legs iced rigid tripped him as they slid under his eyes.

'You OK, chum?' Harry was pulling him up, his hand tight round Arthur's arm, all that was left of the heat that had just flushed through him as he caught his balance.

'Just don't go getting yourself run over, alright,' Harry said, 'I'm done with funerals for a bit.' No chuckle though, just the absence of Sylvie walking between them, then beside them, rushing ahead just before they reached the park gates. Harry and Arthur sped up but this Sylvie didn't want them to follow –

*Let me be, boys, let me be.*

'Her legs,' Arthur said, 'they wouldn't work. Why did they stop working?'

'They just stopped. Everything stopped,' Harry stopped then too, 'I want to go back to the house, Arthur.'

Arthur shook his head, Harry couldn't just leave him here – he felt suddenly small, small, dark and quiet.

'Please Harry, just for a bit and then I'll come back with you.'

'She wants to be left, Arthur, Christ, can't you just leave her alone? Oh look, I'm sorry, stick around here for bit if you want to.'

He didn't want to. He didn't want to follow or be followed. He just wanted to sit on the bench with Harry. Hardly soldiers, but brave enough. Harry gave Arthur's shoulder a shake, 'Pint later, eh chum?'

Arthur nodded.

'Hey, isn't that your girl?' Harry said.

Arthur looked across towards the bandstand, a woman bending, her brown curls falling. It couldn't have been Lydia.

*Leave her be, just leave her be.*

'It is Arthur, that's your girl, I'm telling you.'

The woman was standing up now – what was Harry saying? Harry? – she was coming over to him as Harry walked away. He could see the woman's shoes, the edge of her coat, a bag in one of her gloved hands, her mouth barely set in her face, eyes faint. He had to shut his for a moment, find Sylvie's first, let him hold those grey-green eyes first. He should have asked Harry – grey-green weren't they? Sylvie's eyes were closing, leaving him again. Arthur felt a gloved hand slip into his.

'She's not here, Lydia, she's gone.'

'I know, Arthur, I'm sorry.'

'Why did you come then?'

'To see you. Jack said he'd seen you here before Christmas so I came – not all the time, just every now and then. I wanted to see you, Arthur – I wanted to see you now that she'd gone. To see you without her.'

Arthur looked at the shoes on her feet, felt the hand in his. The hands inside those gloves, palms unscarred, Lydia's hands.

'You wanted to see me,' Arthur said, understanding less as he said the words aloud for himself.

'Yes,' Lydia said. 'And I wanted you to see me. Please look at me, Arthur.'

Grey-green eyes gone but Lydia's eyes there. See him. What did she see? He looked up at the face that had no smiles to spill, just open eyes, a parting mouth. He held the hand in his a bit tighter and felt his hand held a little tighter in return – it made more sense than what she'd said, what he might have said, just Lydia with unscarred palms inside gloved hands, there for now, there so long as he'd see.

A ball bounced in front of Arthur. He picked it up and saw a little boy in front of the bandstand, got up and threw it gently in his direction. The boy jumped to catch it and froze for an instant before he ran off.

'Hey,' the boy shouted, running back, 'thanks mister.'

# Acknowledgements

First and foremost, I would like to thank the generosity of all those who pledged for *A Small Dark Quiet* – without you this book would not have been possible. I also wish to acknowledge the curators of the *Fate Unknown* exhibition at The Weiner Library, which was an invaluable resource during the final stages of research for this novel.

Heartfelt thanks to Ally Gipps whose encouragement prompted me to unravel Arthur's story when it was little more than a sketch; to Sarah Jones and Trudy White for their thoughtful feedback on early drafts; to Kate Catchesides, Roz Dineen, Anisa Fakhro, Matt Gold, Flora Harragin, Kerstin Twatchmann and Vlad Vexler; to John Mitchinson and Unbound for giving this novel a home; to Elizabeth Cochrane whose insightful, sensitive analysis and suggestions made the editing a truly collaborative, creative process; to Xander Cansell and Josephine Salverda for guiding me through so patiently, and to Elodie Olson-Coons.